s

'A v … ng twists and a
satisf … doesn't get much
… *aph*

'A brainy page-turner … witty and engrossing' *Mail on Sunday*

'A dazzling romp' *Guardian*

'Binet . . . is an ambitious writer . . . he is also skilled at fast-paced narrative, which he can pull off even in a novel solely in letters . . . Funny and very gripping' *Financial Times*

'A racy and enjoyable detective story . . . as well as being a page-turning diversion, the novel is an interesting reflection of the position in which we now find ourselves' *The Times*

'Immensely enjoyable . . . compelling . . . Pontormo's murder is far from the only intrigue in the novel' *London Review of Books*

Praise for Laurent Binet

'One of the most successful French writers of his generation . . . a wild romp of a book that turns history on its head' *Guardian*

'Glorious, funny and profound' *Daily Telegraph*

'A bold and thrilling experiment in counter-factual history from a masterful storyteller' *Financial Times*

'Characteristically ambitious, brilliant . . . Combining all the pleasure of a period romp with vital questions about our shared origin stories . . . a triumph' *i*

'A hugely entertaining novel, taking delight in its own twists and turns' *Spectator*

'*HHhH* is a highly original piece of work, at once charming, moving and gripping' Martin Amis

'Lively, earthy, experimental, ambitious, clever and endlessly entertaining . . . Smart, witty, direct, cool' *TLS*

LAURENT BINET

Laurent Binet lives and works in France. His first novel, *HHhH*, was an international bestseller that won the prestigious Prix Goncourt du premier roman, among other prizes. *The 7th Function of Language* won the Prix du roman Fnac and the Prix Interallié. His most recent novel, *Civilisations*, was a bestseller that won the Grand Prix du roman de l'Académie française.

SAM TAYLOR

Sam Taylor is a novelist and literary translator. His five novels have reached an international audience, and his award-winning translations include works by Laurent Binet, Leïla Slimani and Marcel Proust. Born in England, Sam was a writer and editor at the *Observer* for eight years before spending a decade in France. He now lives in the United States with his family.

LAURENT BINET

Perspectives

TRANSLATED FROM THE FRENCH BY

Sam Taylor

VINTAGE

1 3 5 7 9 10 8 6 4 2

Vintage is part of the Penguin Random House group of companies

Vintage, Penguin Random House UK, One Embassy Gardens,
8 Viaduct Gardens, London SW11 7BW

penguin.co.uk/vintage
global.penguinrandomhouse.com

Penguin
Random House
UK

First published in Vintage in 2026
First published in hardback by Harvill Secker in 2025
First published in France with the title *Perspective(s)*
by Éditions Grasset in 2023

This book is published with the support of the Centre National Du Livre.

Printed and bound in Great Britain by Clays Ltd, Elcograf S.p.A.

The authorised representative in the EEA is Penguin Random House Ireland, Morrison Chambers, 32 Nassau Street, Dublin D02 YH68

A CIP catalogue record for this book is available from the British Library

ISBN 9781529926972

Penguin Random House is committed to a sustainable future for our business, our readers and our planet. This book is made from Forest Stewardship Council® certified paper.

MIX
Paper | Supporting responsible forestry
FSC® C018179
FSC www.fsc.org

'Try to discover who I am from my choice of words and colours.'

Orhan Pamuk, *My Name is Red*
Translated by Erdağ Göknar

'These are hard times for art.'

Michelangelo, in a letter to his father

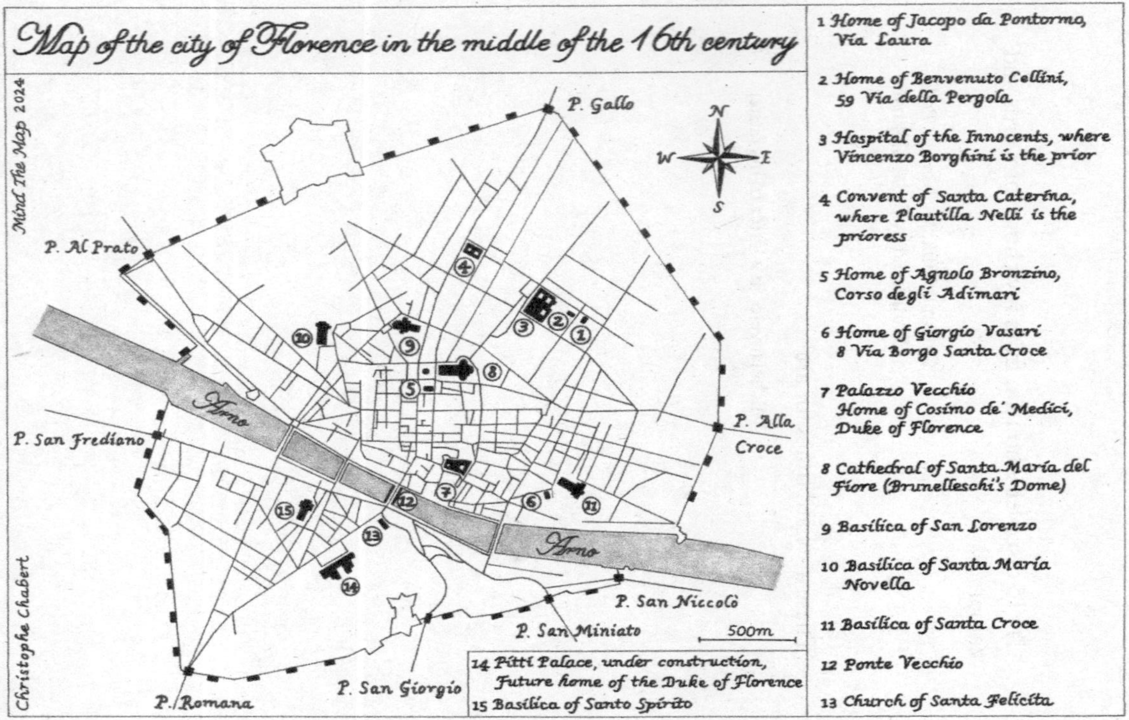
Map of the city of Florence in the middle of the 16th century
Mind The Map 2024
Christophe Chabert
P. Gallo
P. Al Prato
P. San Frediano
P. Romana
P. San Giorgio
P. San Miniato
P. San Niccolò
P. Alla Croce
Arno
Arno
N
S
E
W
500m
1 Home of Jacopo da Pontormo, Via Laura
2 Home of Benvenuto Cellini, 59 Via della Pergola
3 Hospital of the Innocents, where Vincenzo Borghini is the prior
4 Convent of Santa Caterina, where Plautilla Nelli is the prioress
5 Home of Agnolo Bronzino, Corso degli Adimari
6 Home of Giorgio Vasari 8 Via Borgo Santa Croce
7 Palazzo Vecchio Home of Cosimo de' Medici, Duke of Florence
8 Cathedral of Santa Maria del Fiore (Brunelleschi's Dome)
9 Basilica of San Lorenzo
10 Basilica of Santa Maria Novella
11 Basilica of Santa Croce
12 Ponte Vecchio
13 Church of Santa Felicita
14 Pitti Palace, under construction, Future home of the Duke of Florence
15 Basilica of Santo Spirito

Political situation in Italy at the time of the military campaign led by Francis, Duke of Guise, between 1556 and 1557

Preface

Let nobody say that I am incapable of repentance.

I once held very firm views about Florence and Florentines: in my mind, they were reasonable, well-mannered people, polite, even friendly, but devoid of passion, ill-suited for tragedy or madness. Unlike the people of Bologna, Rome or Naples. Why else (I thought) would Michelangelo have fled his homeland, never to return? He spent his whole life reviling Rome, yet it was the setting he required for his art. And the others? Dante, Petrarch, Leonardo, Galileo? Deserters and exiles all. Florence produced geniuses, then chased them away or at least failed to keep them; that was why the city's glory years ended with the Middle Ages. I was fascinated by the period of the Guelphs and the Ghibellines, but beyond – let's say – 1492 and the death of Il Magnifico, it seemed to me that Florence lost its lustre. When Savonarola ordered Botticelli to burn his paintings, it was not only beauty that he killed. By reducing idealism to his own blinkered fanaticism, he destroyed the very desire for the ideal.

After the departures of Leonardo and Michelangelo, what – or rather who – was left? I did not attach much importance to the Pontormos or Salviatis or Cigolis, and Bronzino struck me as too cold and dry, with his porcelain complexions and his stern style. In my opinion, none of those mannerists could bear comparison with any artists from the Bolognese School, and I never cared for Vasari, whose main achievement was as a salesman for other Florentine artists. Personally, my idol was Guido Reni – the Bolognese artist who, I believed, took beauty to its most elevated point in human history. Of course the Florentines knew how to draw, but to me they lacked expression. Everything they produced was too tame, too smooth. Give me a Dutch artist – any Dutch artist – over a Florentine any day!

Or so I thought. But I was wrong, I confess. And it took the events that I am about to recount to you to save me from my blindness. Because to see is to think. The viewer must deserve his painting. I was an idiot. And while I undoubtedly still am an idiot, at least I am now inclined to give Florence its due: in the middle of the sixteenth century, that city was not only a fertile breeding ground for genius but a crucible of boiling passions. And the latter, naturally, explains the former.

So here is what happened: a few years ago, I was visiting Tuscany, and while I was rummaging through the wares of an antique shop in Arezzo, in search of a souvenir I could take back for my friends in France, the one-armed shopkeeper, instead of suggesting some Etruscan statuette, offered to sell me a collection of old, yellowed letters. I sniffed suspiciously at the stack and asked if I could look through them, to verify their authenticity. The shopkeeper consented, and upon reading the third letter I took out my wallet and spent a small fortune to secure the entire bunch. I am familiar with sixteenth-century Italian history, and I believe that what these letters contain – as incredible as it may seem – is perfectly real. I returned to my hotel room and read, in a single sitting, the story that I am about to set before you.

Yes, these letters tell a story, and whoever was responsible for the monumental task of collecting and ordering them did a magnificent job: together, the missives form a tale so compelling that I stayed up all night devouring them, before catching some sleep at dawn and starting to read again the moment I woke. I quickly understood why these letters had been brought together. By the end, I also understood why they had been kept secret. Because what they reveal is so extraordinary that only historians will be able to truly judge its significance. I will say no more; the idea that each reader of this correspondence would experience the same emotions I did only intensified the open-mouthed stupefaction I felt when I finished reading them. There is, I think, no other reason behind the urgent need I felt to translate them from Tuscan.

I laboured over this translation for no less than three years of my life. I would like to think that my knowledge of Italian history and the Italian language has enabled me to render as accurately as possible the spirit, if not the style, of these letters. If, however, the reader finds infelicities in the prose, or if he is surprised by the coarseness of a particular expression, I hope he will be generous enough to acknowledge that the fault may not be mine, or that I may have rendered it that way deliberately, because my task was to make a sixteenth-century Tuscan correspondence accessible to the French reader from our own nineteenth century who is perhaps not familiar with this distant and – I would venture – somewhat overlooked period. For the sake of convenience, I have altered the years in favour of our Gregorian calendar: so, if a letter was dated January or February 1556, knowing that the Florentine new year did not start until 25 March, I corrected the year to 1557. On the other hand, I decided not to include footnotes, which have the benefit of highlighting their author's erudition but the drawback of bringing the reader back to the here and now. All you need to know is that the story takes place in Florence, at the time of the eleventh and final Italian war.

All the same, in a spirit of magnanimity, and despite the great temptation I felt to throw you in at the deep end, I have agreed to compile a list of correspondents – I almost said characters! – to aid you in the reading of a story that will, I hope, give you the sense of being inside a tapestry. Or, more pertinently perhaps, inside a fresco on the wall of an Italian church.

B.

List of Correspondents

Cosimo de' Medici: Duke of Florence, from the younger branch of the Medici family, who came into power fortuitously after Alessandro de' Medici was assassinated by his cousin Lorenzino, aka Lorenzàccio.

Eleanor of Toledo: Duchess of Florence; niece of Fernando Álvarez de Toledo, the Duke of Alba and viceroy of Naples, who is waging war against France and Rome on behalf of the Emperor Charles V and his son Philip II, the King of Spain.

Maria de' Medici: the duke and duchess's eldest daughter.

Catherine de' Medici: Queen of France; wife of King Henri II; the legitimate heir to the Duchy of Florence.

Piero Strozzi: Marshal of France; cousin of Catherine; son of the republican Filippo Strozzi the Younger (who was executed by Cosimo); leader of the *fuorusciti* (the name given to Florentine exiles); and the great enemy and rival of Cosimo in the struggle for control of Tuscany.

Giorgio Vasari: artist and architect; author of *The Lives of the Most Excellent Painters, Sculptors and Architects*; trusted adviser to Cosimo, who is constantly giving him work, including the immense renovation of the Palazzo della Signoria.

Vincenzo Borghini: historian and humanist; prior at the Hospital of the Innocents; close friend of Vasari, whom he assists in writing the second volume of his *Lives of the Painters*.

Michelangelo Buonarroti: sculptor, artist, architect and poet; responsible for building the great St Peter's Basilica in Rome.

Agnolo Bronzino: artist; former student and close friend of the artist Jacopo da Pontormo; official portrait painter of the Medici family.

Alessandro Allori: artist; Bronzino's student and assistant.

Giambattista Naldini: artist; Pontormo's student and assistant.

Sister Plautilla Nelli: prioress at the convent of St Catherine of Siena; artist; disciple of the Dominican friar Girolamo Savonarola (1452–98).

Sister Catherine de' Ricci: prioress at the convent of St Vincent in Prato; committed Savonarolist; friend and model of Sister Plautilla Nelli.

Benvenuto Cellini: goldsmith, sculptor and adventurer; creator of the bronze sculpture *Perseus*, featured beside Michelangelo's *David* in the Piazza della Signoria.

Malatesta de' Malatesti: page to the Duke of Florence.

Marco Moro: Pontormo's colour-grinder.

Ercole II d'Este: Duke of Ferrara; father of the notorious Alfonso II d'Este, who would inspire Robert Browning's famous poem 'My Last Duchess'.

Giovanni Battista Schizzi: regent of the Duchy of Milan.

Pope Paul IV : formerly head of the Roman Inquisition, he became pope in 1555; a member of the powerful Neapolitan family the Carafas, Paul IV was the sworn enemy of Protestants, Jews, artists and books (he created the *Index Librorum Prohibitorum*); allied with France against Spain; a brazen nepotist who helped the rise of his nephews, the Duke of Paliano and Carlo Carafa, two foul villains whose story I will perhaps tell another time.

Jacopo da Pontormo: artist.

I have been asked to draw up a list of those personages who, though they neither wrote nor received any of the letters in this volume, are mentioned in them. In my opinion, that would be an insult to the intelligence of my readers, who are not children and do not need to be spoon-fed. Did I have a list of the characters when I read these letters for the first time? No. But whatever . . . I suppose I can tell you that Bacchiacca was an old artist who specialised in painting furniture and interior decoration; that Pier Francesco Riccio was Cosimo's tutor, then his secretary and major-domo, before being removed from office and locked up on grounds of mental illness in 1553; that Benedetto Varchi was a former republican who became the regime's historian and led the famous *paragone* debate over the relative importance of different arts, making him Cosimo's version of what Angelo Poliziano had been to Lorenzo the Magnificent. But I think that will do. Let the curtain rise to reveal the stage, which is Florence in 1557 . . .

1. Maria de' Medici to Catherine de' Medici, Queen of France

Florence, 1 January 1557

My father would kill me if he knew that I was writing to you. But how could anyone refuse Your Highness such an innocent favour? He is my father, it is true, but you are my aunt. And what is it to me, all your quarrels, and your Strozzi, and your politics? In truth, your letter gave me such joy that you cannot imagine. The Queen of France asking me to tell her about her own home city, and offering me her friendship in exchange? What greater gift could the Lord God offer a lonely soul like that of poor Maria, surrounded only by children and servants? My younger brothers are too busy playing princes, while my younger sisters swear they will never marry anyone because nobody could ever be worthy of them – even the emperor's son! Meanwhile, within the cold walls of this old palace, I can sense that my mother is plotting with my father, without saying a word to me, leaving me sure of only one thing: that they are planning to marry me off. To whom? Apparently, nobody has thought it worth their time to inform me on that point. But look at me: here I am, already taking advantage of your friendship. Enough about me!

Because I have news . . . A dreadful tragedy has taken place in Florence. Perhaps you will remember the painter Pontormo? I am told that among all the artists in which our homeland is so abundant, he was generally considered – during the period before you left Italy for France, drawn there by your royal destiny – to be one of the best. Well, imagine: he was found dead in the main chapel of San Lorenzo, at the very spot where he had been working since time immemorial. Eleven years! It is said that he killed himself because he wasn't satisfied with the results of his labour. I met him a few times, at the home of his friend Bronzino, and I must admit he seemed like one of those ancient madmen who mumble into their beards. But it's still very sad, of course.

Thankfully, not all the news here is quite so dark, although I don't think you will find the rest too surprising. You know, I am sure, that the preparations for the Carnival start earlier and earlier each year, so that our public squares are already full of workers building rostrums while dressmakers toil in their homes. No doubt you will think me frivolous if I tell you that I like it when Florence is all dressed up in her festive finery, but what can I do? I love the excitement of Carnival season, particularly since I have no other distractions, apart from posing for one of the countless portraits that my father commissions Bronzino to make of every member of his family, alive or dead. Sitting still for hours on end . . . I will let Your Highness imagine just how much fun that is!

The son of the Duke of Ferrara – Alfonso d'Este, whom you perhaps met in France, since I am told he fought in Flanders alongside your husband King Henri – arrived this week to pay his respects to my father, who is determined to introduce me to him. I've heard he is a terrible bore – what a drag! Oh, but I can hear Mama calling me now. I kiss your hands, my new friend. I have burned your letter as you asked, and I will follow your instructions so that mine reaches you without arousing the slightest suspicion. It's such a shame that you and my father are at odds. But I am sure that your dispute won't last, and that you will soon come to visit your family and see your beloved Florence once again. Who knows – maybe Bronzino will paint your portrait too?

2. *Giorgio Vasari to Michelangelo Buonarroti*

Florence, 2 January 1557

This time, my dear Master, I am not writing to you on behalf of the duke to beg you to return to Florence. Alas, it is a very different subject that obliges me to disturb you in your Roman days, which are, I know, so filled by your admirable work and by the numerous vexations that confront your art on a daily basis, particularly since the election of your new Supreme Pontiff, who – unlike his predecessors – seems little inclined to appreciate beauty, whether ancient or modern.

Do you remember, fifteen years ago, when I used to consult you about everything? You were generous enough back then to give me your advice, and so it was that I began to study architecture in a more methodical and fruitful manner, which I probably would never have done without you. It is, once again, your methodical intelligence that I need today, albeit in a very different discipline. The duke has entrusted me with a mission that is both unusual and rather delicate.

Jacopo da Pontormo, whose talent you praised when he was still a young and promising student, is no longer with us. He was found dead in the chapel of San Lorenzo, at the foot of his famous frescoes, which he had until then kept hidden behind wooden screens. That news alone would have prompted me to write to you, since someone must inform you of this terrible misfortune. But the circumstances of his death have driven me to turn to you for advice yet again, dear Master.

For, having discovered his body with a chisel embedded in his heart, just below his sternum, it seems to us difficult to sustain the theory that this was an accident. That is why the duke has tasked me with investigating this sad story, all the more so since it contains several shady elements, which I will let you judge for yourself: not only was Jacopo's body penetrated by the chisel, it also bore traces of a violent blow to the head, delivered by a hammer which was found on the chapel floor among his other tools. Poor Jacopo was lying on his back, in front of his fresco of the Flood, which he appeared, from the traces of fresh paint we found upon it, to have repainted just before his death. You know as well as I how slow and painstaking Jacopo was in his work, how constantly he would correct his own errors, but I was greatly surprised by that alteration on a small part of the wall, which must inevitably leave a visible seam showing at a spot that cuts a figure in two. Knowing him as I did, I would have expected him to repaint the entire section of that wall if he was unsatisfied with even the smallest element of it.

However, the strange aspects of this affair do not end there. When the body was discovered, the duke sent men to the house where Jacopo lived, on Via Laura: a sort of attic which one must climb a ladder to reach. There, among the mass of drawings and sketches stored in his studio, was found a painting that you know only too well, because you drew the original sketch for it long ago: you will no doubt recall *Venus and Cupid*, which proved so successful that it inspired copies all over Europe – perhaps you know that I myself had the privilege of painting a few of these, not that they bore comparison with Pontormo's, though they were fortunate enough to find favour, no doubt because any work of art inspired by your drawings must inevitably bear some trace of your divine genius. That was back in the days before the return of the Inquisition, days which seem so remote to us now, when Cardinal Carafa had not yet become Pope Paul IV, and when nudes were not held in disgrace but highly sought after. Of course, nobody today would think of painting such a subject, but you know how eccentric our dear Jacopo could be. That, however, was not what drew our attention, because – putting aside the four years when Girolamo Savonarola stole the hearts of the simple folk – we other Florentines still understand and appreciate the beauty of the human body rather than considering it a diabolical obscenity. As it happens, the piece of fabric that Pontormo had previously added to cover the open thighs of the goddess had, on the copy that we found in his attic, been removed. But what startled us even more than that – and it is hard for me to find the right words to express this, since I have no desire to offend anyone, and particularly not His Excellency's family – was that, in place of Venus's face, Jacopo had substituted that of the duke's eldest daughter, Miss Maria de' Medici.

Now you can see just how unpleasant this story could become, and why the duke decided to entrust the resolution of the problem to someone in his inner circle, while simultaneously spreading the rumour that poor Jacopo committed suicide due to the state of extreme self-loathing into which he had fallen. The fact remains that this entire affair has plunged me into a thick fog of confusion, which is why – to help me unpick the tangled threads of this dark tapestry – I have taken the liberty of soliciting your great wisdom, which I know to be almost the equal of your talent and one of the most important elements of your genius.

3. Michelangelo Buonarroti to Giorgio Vasari

Rome, 5 January 1557

Master Giorgio, my dear friend, I cannot tell you how dejected I feel, to the point that I have not left my bed for what seems an eternity. In truth, I was already reeling under all the worries caused by the work on St Peter's, but Jacopo's death was the final nail in my coffin, so to speak, and I wept when I read your letter. Jacopo was a painter of great talent, and to my mind one of the best, not only of his generation (the one born between mine and yours, since I am at death's door while you are in the prime of life), but quite simply of his time. I do not know if I am truly the right person to help you find the author of this awful crime, inconceivable in the eyes of God and men; I fear that you are somewhat overestimating the extent of my wisdom, because here in Rome people have been saying for many years that I have grown senile and mad. Nevertheless, since I wish to be agreeable to you, just as I wish to honour Pontormo's memory, I am disposed to help you as far as my resources allow. Perhaps, from an oblique – that is to say, a non-Florentine – point of view, I may be useful to you in your investigation. If one wants to approach the problem with the rigour and logic of a Brunelleschi or an Alberti, one must, to find the culprit, first establish the opportunity, then the motive. Or first the motive, and then the opportunity. Who could have desired poor Jacopo's death? And who was with him that night to inflict the fatal blow? As I write these lines, my eyes blur with tears and I see him lying in a pool of his own blood, his heart pierced by one of those tools that, to us other artists, are the very stuff of life. Stabbed with his own chisel, struck by his own hammer . . . it is as if he were betrayed by his most faithful companions. But enough of these sterile effusions. My tears may be a tribute to the memory of our friend, but they will not help us identify his murderer. Finally, one last conclusion: the culprit is among you, in Florence.

I am afraid, my dear Giorgio, that I will not be able to help you any further, in the absence of additional evidence. After all, I am just a modest sculptor, and I cannot see all the way from Rome to San Lorenzo. Out of love for Jacopo, I beg you to be my eyes there and to keep me informed of the latest developments in your investigation.

But you did not tell me about his frescoes. What did you think of them? I have heard that the duke asked him to create something worthy of rivalling the Sistine. Give me your opinion, dear Giorgio; you know I have always put great faith in your judgement.

4. Giorgio Vasari to Michelangelo Buonarroti

Florence, 7 January 1557

Dear Master, let me reassure you: your Sistine will not be surpassed by Pontormo's chapel. I will do as you ask by describing all I saw there. First, in various compartments, in the upper part of the chapel, the Creation of Adam and Eve, their Disobedience, their Expulsion from Paradise, their labours upon the Earth, the Sacrifice of Abel, the Death of Cain, the blessing of Noah's children and the building of the Ark. Next, on one of the walls, fifteen fathoms deep and wide, the great Flood, where one sees a pile of corpses and Noah in conversation with God. It was at the foot of this Flood that poor Pontormo was found, and it is on this wall that he repainted a part of the whole, whereas the rest of it had dried long before. On the other wall he has depicted the Last Judgement, with as much turmoil and confusion as will reign on the supreme day. Opposite the altar are grouped, on each side, some nude figures leaving the Earth and ascending to Heaven. Above the windows, angels surround Christ who, in all his majesty, is resurrecting the dead before judging them. I confess I do not understand why Jacopo placed God the Father creating Adam and Eve below Jesus's feet. I am also surprised that he chose not to vary his heads nor his colours, and I would further reproach him for not taking perspective into account. In a word, the design, the colouring and the arrangement of his figures offer an aspect so pitiful that, despite my vocation as a painter, I must declare that I understand none of it. You would have to see it with your own eyes for me to explain it, but I doubt that your judgement would differ greatly. This composition includes a few torsos, a few limbs, a few joints that are beautifully detailed, because Jacopo took care to create extraordinarily accomplished clay models, but the overall effect is a failure. Most of the torsos are too big, while the arms and legs are too small. As for the heads, they are utterly lacking in that singular grace and beauty that one can observe in his other paintings. He seems here to have been focused so much on certain elements that he neglected the most important. In short, far from showing himself superior to the divine Michelangelo with this work, he fell short of his own standards, which proves that if we try to force nature, we end up depriving ourselves of qualities that we owe to her generosity. But doesn't Jacopo deserve our indulgence? Aren't artists allowed to make mistakes, just like other men? There remains the one question that will never be answered, because Jacopo took the answer with him to his grave: why did he decide, so soon before his death, to repaint a part of his Flood? Who can guess at the fathomless reveries of such a man?

In any case, the duke has, in his great wisdom, entrusted the completion of the frescoes to Bronzino.

5. *Michelangelo Buonarroti to Agnolo Bronzino*

Rome, 9 January 1557

Master Agnolo, I have learned from Vasari about the horrifying tragedy that has befallen Florence and all of us who love beauty and the arts, in the person of your master and friend, struck down at the scene of his greatest hopes, but also – and I know this all too well through my own dearly acquired experience – of his greatest torments. Indeed, what could be more agonising than painting a fresco? You spend the whole day with your neck twisted, your head upside down, ten or fifteen feet above the ground, wielding the paintbrush as best you can before the coat has dried, at which point you must start over from the beginning. In all honesty, had not Master Vasari described to me the circumstances of his death, which do not appear to allow much room for doubt, I would not have been surprised to learn that poor Pontormo had put an end to his life, because that is a thought that has assailed me on certain evenings of despair, when I felt like my neck and my back had been broken by the labour, and I had developed a goitre through the awkward positioning of my head, not to mention all the schemers and opportunists who are always so eager to spread lies and conspire against me. You know how my *Last Judgement* was attacked and decried almost twenty years ago, with that son of a bitch Aretino – may God have pity on his soul – even comparing it to a brothel located in the greatest chapel in Christendom. Not only have those critics not gone away, they have grown louder and more numerous. It has reached the point now where Pope

Paul IV, after first intending to have my work destroyed, has commissioned my good friend Master Daniele da Volterra to clothe my naked figures, so that poor Daniele, forced to carry out this unworthy task, is already known all over Rome as 'the breeches-maker'. So that is how things stand. The days when popes would send me lavish gifts are long gone. Even Paul III, to whom the world owes the return of the Roman Inquisition, once gave me a beautiful purebred Arabian which he claimed was the fastest steed in the East or the West. Back then, nothing was considered too costly if it meant they could obtain my services. And that poor beast languished in his stable, just as I languish in my lair.

I have no doubt that Jacopo suffered the same slights, because I remember certain jealous, malicious slanderers who inhabited Florence back when I left, and I see little reason to believe that such people no longer exist there. That is why I would like to hear in your own words how Pontormo's frescoes have been received, and above all what you think of them yourself, because while I have no reason to doubt Vasari's negative opinions, I will always value the verdicts of two people over just one, so long as those people are wise and honest.

6. Agnolo Bronzino to Michelangelo Buonarroti

Florence, 11 January 1557

It is true, is it not, dear Master, that you have not come back to Florence in the past twenty-three years, despite the repeated requests of His Excellency the Duke and the entreaties of your friends? Perhaps this new argument will overcome your resistance, and our poor Pontormo will succeed where all others have failed: I swear to you that his frescoes are of a splendour that has not been seen since your own Sistine. The great Michelangelo should look upon them with his own eyes, since no words could suffice to describe them.

Do not put your faith in Master Giorgio: although undoubtedly a man of great taste and integrity, he is also a courtier who bends his will to the demands of his master. You know all too well, as your letter confirms, how out of favour the nude body has become since the Roman Curia gave the papal tiara to the Inquisitor General, this Carafa with his insensitivity to the beauty of art, for whom any representation of the human body is an offence against God. Apparently, the extraordinary Flood created by Pontormo's peerless mind and hands was not appreciated by the duchess, whose Spanish taste is ill-suited to such a singular vision: piles of naked bodies, some of which seem to have swollen from prolonged exposure to water. There is so much truth in this painting that a rumour has spread through Florence that Jacopo visited the city's hospitals in search of drowned bodies that he could use as models. Of course, such tales are pure fantasy, but it is Pontormo's spectacular painting that has given rise to them: never have the drowned looked so alive as they do on these walls.

His Excellency Cosimo, although he does not share the duchess's prejudice against the representation of human flesh, being neither a Carafa, nor a woman, nor Spanish, has however long coveted the title of King of Tuscany, and since the pope is the only man capable of granting this wish, the duke is naturally wary of offending him. That is why he carefully avoided showing any mark of approbation when the screens covering the frescoes were removed and a few lucky courtiers were able to gaze upon Pontormo's paintings for the first time. I am sure, however, that the duke was delighted by the frescoes, and the proof of that lies in the fact that he has granted me the honour of finishing them, because he must know that as Pontormo's most faithful student I would never betray his legacy. And so, should God judge me worthy of this honour, when Jacopo da Pontormo's great work is finally completed by my hand, I will be able to proudly place my own name next to his. That will be his vengeance, and ours too, for nobody doubts that he was killed on account of his frescoes, due to the new spirit of the times, which is so ominous and inimical for people like us.

7. Sister Catherine de' Ricci to Sister Plautilla Nelli

Prato, convent of San Vincenzo, 5 January 1557

I cannot tell you, sister, how joyous the reaction here at the convent was to the news of the sodomite's death. In the refectory, the nuns were shouting and throwing their wimples in the air as they gave thanks to the Lord Jesus, abandoning all inhibitions. (And they had not yet learned the truth about the obscene frescoes at San Lorenzo.) As prioress I must remain dignified and restrained at all times, so naturally I refused to join in their wild celebrations, but I did not have the heart to reprimand them, even if one should never rejoice at a man's death. The previous night, I had been visited by a vision: a billy goat with a forked tail was struck down by a blond-haired angel, and its corpse, sliced clean in two, was thrown into the Arno. The angel's face was that of St Catherine of Siena, your patron saint and mine. God punishes the wicked and rewards His servants by making them the instruments of His retribution. Only by purifying herself of her vices will Florence be able to escape His divine wrath; if the city continues on her current path, then Friar Girolamo Savonarola's prophecies will be fulfilled and the French will return, or the Lutherans will overrun Germany, or Imperial forces will sack the city as they once did Rome, and the plague will return, and a thousand calamities will descend upon us, and this time Friar Girolamo – may his soul rest in peace – will no longer be here to save us. In my dream I saw an army advancing onto the plain, an army led by a prince with the head of a wolf. It is said that Pontormo was a Protestant. Had he not met his maker by the grace of a hand guided by God, the Holy Inquisition would eventually have thwarted him and burned him at the stake. While Rome may still be a den of iniquity, it is now led by a pope determined to wipe out heresy, and that at least is a good thing, even if in other matters this Paul IV is hardly any better than Paul III or any of those who preceded him in the past century (with the exception of Borgia, the vilest of them all). That is why killing a reformist and sodomite, whose punishment – in this life or the next – was inevitable, cannot be a crime. On the contrary, it is a holy act that will redound to the credit of its author at the Hour of Judgement. God simply could not tolerate these sins, and it was you he chose – as he chose me, as he chose Friar Girolamo before us – to save Florence.

We are expecting you at San Vincenzo, with your canvases and your paintbrushes, as we do every month. I will pose for you, and you will tell me everything in great detail. Until then, may God forgive me, I will conceal my impatience. Glory to Him, sister, and brava to you.

8. Sister Plautilla Nelli to Sister Catherine de' Ricci

Florence, convent of Santa Caterina, 6 January 1557

Sister, you know that my love for you is surpassed only by the love I dedicate to our Lord Jesus, whom you married at such a young age. But with all the respect and admiration I bear for you, I would ask you not to unburden yourself quite so fully in your letters, because, if they fell into the wrong hands, they could cause us great harm.

I, too, am eager for you to sit for me once again, and I hope to finish this new portrait before the start of spring. But as concerns the affair you mentioned, I would not want you to get any false ideas. Contrary to what you seem to imagine, I had nothing to do with the sodomite's death. I do not say that he did not deserve his punishment. Those frescoes are undoubtedly another impious manifestation of the corruption that reigns in Florence, but it was part of

God's plan that He should let me see them. I promise I will tell you everything once we are together again. Until then, I beg you to temper your enthusiasm. Unlike you, who bled as He did, I have not been chosen by Our Lord. I am merely a poor sinner who kisses your feet and His.

9. Giorgio Vasari to Vincenzo Borghini

Florence, 7 January 1557

I know in what high esteem you held Pontormo and I know that he was your friend, but I feel free to tell you that his frescoes are the most lamentable spectacle I have ever laid eyes upon, and it is a great pity that such an artist (because he does indeed deserve that title coined by Dante) should have wasted his immense talent on such scribblings. You know my religion on this question: the real culprit is Dürer. It is all the fault of the Germans. Pontormo is not to blame for having wanted to imitate that Teutonic style which seems to have infected the soul of all our brilliant artists, but he is to blame for having transposed the meanness of German mannerism into the facial expressions and attitudes of his figures. However, I do not wish to speak ill of the dead, and especially not of your friend, particularly after he has been savagely murdered, so I will say no more about that poor man. Jacopo was a tortured soul led astray by his love of innovation, but despite his errors he leaves behind evidence of his admirable talent. Even the great Homer fell asleep sometimes, after all. But you really must see these frescoes – I swear you will share my opinion: they are truly awful.

All the same, that would not be a motive sufficient to justify or explain his murder, unless a fellow painter or an art lover somehow sneaked behind the screens in the chapel and, disturbed to the point of madness by the horrifying sight of those frescoes, decided to wait until nightfall to attack his victim. While it is true that our compatriots are sometimes a little excessive and punctilious when it comes to art, I do not as yet give any credence to this particular theory.

Following the recommendations of Master Michelangelo, I have sought to match the opportunities and the motives of all those who might have desired your friend's death. For the moment, the results are reduced to his assistant, Battista Naldini, who has lived with him for several years, and his colour-grinder, Marco Moro, who was responsible for the screens. We know that the two of them argued with him in the days preceding his death, but people often argued with Jacopo, who was – as you well know – a difficult character. So, rather than wasting my time in idle speculation, I decided to reconstruct the night of the murder. Jacopo dined with Masters Bronzino and Varchi, according to whom he ate kidneys and drank a fiasco of wine. But he complained of stomach pains and left them before the end of the meal, saying that he was going to bed. If we are to believe Naldini, however, he never went home. From this, I deduce that he went directly to San Lorenzo to work on his Flood, for he had been seen many times before entering the chapel after nightfall to continue painting. But why did he repaint only one part of the section of wall that night, rather than all of it, thus leaving a visible seam? This is not at all like Pontormo, who was never satisfied and would constantly start again from scratch, seeking a perfection that probably existed only in his dreams. He must have known that, by repainting over paint that had already dried, the seam would be obvious to any educated eye, like a poultice on a wounded limb. The Pontormo we knew would never have accepted that.

To further muddy the waters of this case, another piece of evidence has just been added: one day last month, a woman visited Pontormo's lodging while he was absent. The ladder leading up to his attic room had not been removed, and the woman, notwithstanding the difficulties posed by the dress she was wearing, attempted to climb it. Finding herself face to face with young Naldini, she grew flustered and – after stammering an apology – quickly left. That at least is what Naldini told me, although he was incapable of describing the woman since she wore a hood like that of a nun and spoke in a whisper.

If you happen to pass through Arezzo on your way back from Venice, you should go to see Piero della Francesca's frescoes, because they are wonderful. I never tire of looking at them.

10. Maria de' Medici to Catherine de' Medici, Queen of France

Florence, 7 January 1557

Dear aunt, I am in despair and I hardly dare tell you about my shame, but who else can I confide in? Would you believe that when they were searching Pontormo's studio, they found a painting representing Venus (supposedly the goddess of love), naked, her thighs spread wide, with plump Cupid's leg sliding between them, and – I would rather die than have to write these lines – this Roman harlot had my face! Can you imagine a greater humiliation? Why did that cursed artist use me as the model for his obscene painting? I swear that I never did anything to harm or offend him. In fact, as I already told you, I barely knew him, having seen him no more than three or four times in my life, all at Bronzino's house.

I would still be ignorant of this infamy were it not for the friendship of one of my father's pages, who took pity on me and did not want me to be the last to learn of my shame. I am certain that the whole city is whispering behind my back, even if I didn't notice anything of the kind last Sunday at Mass. This young page, who is named Malatesta de' Malatesti, comforted me in my shock, and I do believe that, were it not for the marks of respect and affection he showed me, I would have sunk into a bottomless well of melancholy. You can tell a true friend by how they sympathise with you in your misfortunes, don't you think? All the same, I am so mortally afraid of scandal that I feel as if I might lose my composure at any moment; I become flustered when anyone speaks to me, I stammer, I almost faint. Oh, you would pity me if you could see how I tremble every time I must appear in public! I hardly managed to speak three words to the Duke of Ferrara's son when he was introduced to me, and even if he seemed to find that charming, his evident amusement and my father's irritation only added to my confusion. I was so preoccupied that I do not recall a single word we spoke to each other, although I know he asked me lots of questions, which was torture. I couldn't even tell you what he looks like, other than the fact that he struck me as rather self-satisfied. Good for him, I suppose. Not that I care. As soon as he had departed, I found that I was able to speak again and I begged my father to burn that horrible painting. And do you know what that awful man said? He chose to disregard the feelings of his eldest daughter and instead to keep the picture in his 'wardrobe' – an enormous room where hundreds of artisans come and go fifty times a day – on the pretext that this will help him clear up the mystery of the painter's death. The devil take him and his mystery! Why should I care who killed this Pontormo? I want that painting to vanish forever, and if it doesn't, I feel like I will die.

11. Catherine de' Medici, Queen of France, to Piero Strozzi, Marshal of France

Paris, 10 January 1557

Your bravery, my dear cousin, was once again lauded by the King of France, who is well aware that you are one of his most ardent servants, and the Louvre echoes with talk of your exploits. But did you know, my Lord Marshal, that it is possible to defeat one's enemies with means other than the sword? You and I want Florence, which is ours by right, and we have been thwarted in our desires for far too long by Cosimo il Popolano, who does not possess one-third of your courage nor one-quarter of my titles. As long as that obscure little Medici remains under the protection of Spain, it will be difficult for you – I would say impossible were it not for your famous bravery – to take the city through military action. But you know the Florentines: they will clamour for the Republic at the drop of a hat. But who will drop that hat? Certainly not your friends exiled in Rome and Venice. You and I both still remember their extraordinary uselessness when Lorenzino killed Alessandro, and their spectacular inability to seize an opportunity when it presents itself leaves me in no doubt: we can expect nothing from those people. So let them continue to meet in secret and hatch their plots all they like; such an opportunity will never arise again. But I know you to be cut from a very different cloth. You could take advantage of a much smaller opportunity to send Cosimo back to the nothingness from which he should never have emerged.

I have discovered a way of permanently weakening his authority. We will use the surest and most fatal of weapons: ridicule. There is, at this moment in Florence, a painting that represents the duke's eldest daughter stark naked in the most lascivious pose imaginable. Find a way to get your hands on this painting, send it to Venice, have copies printed, and distribute them all over Italy, all over Europe, even into Turkey. Show the painting to Aretino – the Scourge of Princes, as he is rightly called – and let him devise those clever libels at which he is so adept. The peace between France and Spain will not last forever. We will see then just how much a weakened Cosimo is worth to Philip when the Spanish king is busy on other fronts.

I do not say that this operation will be easy: the painting is in the possession of Cosimo himself; he keeps it in his wardrobe, at the palace. In this respect, the man you choose will be crucial: he must be well connected, audacious, and almost completely lacking in scruples. For my part, I left Florence too long ago. Would you by any chance know of someone who could perform this task?

12. Eleanor of Toledo, Duchess of Florence, to Cosimo de' Medici, Duke of Florence

Florence, 8 January 1557

Are you in such dread of my reproaches that you must run away like this? What reason could be more urgent than the enormous scandal threatening your eldest daughter to drag you onto the road at dawn, without even deigning to kiss your wife goodbye? Is Pisa under attack from the Turks? Is that why your presence there requires you to cancel all your appointments? I am telling you: that infamous painting risks turning Prince Alfonso away from our daughter and compromising the marriage. You, who pride yourself on your understanding of politics, must know the value of an alliance with Ferrara. But who will want to marry the creature represented as a lustful whore by one of the most famous painters in your court?

I beseech you: give the order for that painting to be destroyed, along with all the frescoes painted by that horrible artist. The truth is this: his death is a divine blessing. Cursed is he who closes his eyes to the signs of the Almighty! If those frescoes were merely obscene, I might forgive your indulgence, because you were not raised with the Spanish understanding of the need for chastity and propriety, but surely you cannot ignore the fact that those images stink of heresy? The fingerprints of Juan de Valdés – that is to say, the fingerprints of Luther – are all over those frescoes. Do you truly believe that Rome will grant the title of king, or even that of grand duke, to a sponsor of heresy? I beg you, my friend, to do what is necessary: destroy the painting and ask Bronzino to cover the walls of the chapel with limewash. Do this and you will make your wife happy, save your daughter's honour, and advance your own interests. I tell you again: the fact that your relationship with the pope is currently execrable does not mean it will always be that way. After all, he is an Inquisitor. Deep down, he has more in common with the Spanish than with the ungodly French from whom he thinks he can buy his safety. Charles V passed the Spanish throne to his son, and Philip is not his father: he will never allow another sack of Rome. And that is why you, the most politically astute man in the world – for you would not be where you are now if this were not true, nor would you have survived so long amidst lions and foxes – cannot ignore this truth: that we must not insult the future by giving up hope. May God watch over you. Come back to me quickly.

13. Cosimo de' Medici, Duke of Florence, to Eleanor of Toledo, Duchess of Florence

Pisa, 9 January 1557

Eleanor, my friend, affairs of state are not limited to our daughter's marriage, and the world outside our city walls does not cease to exist whenever we have a problem to solve. Tuscany cares no more about the prince of Ferrara than it does about some dusty Etruscan statue. Do you want another siege of Siena? Pisa must know who rules her. As for myself, I must verify the work of Master Luca Martini to assure myself that the drying of the marshes is progressing well; if not, the region will continue to be ravaged by malarial fever. Is that what you wish, my friend, you who love to come here on holiday with our children? Tomorrow I will travel to Livorno, and perhaps after that to Lucca, but I promise that I will be home within three days. In the meantime, I have entrusted our problem to Vasari. But listen carefully: if there is a murderer of artists at loose in the city, I must find him. Above all, I must get to the bottom of this affair. Those frescoes and that painting, which you hate so much, are concealing a secret – and I must make them talk, for there can be no secrets from the Duke of Florence. You may well rejoice at Pontormo's death, but for reasons of state it is imperative that we uncover the reasons he died. A prince in the dark is a prince in danger. Farewell, my friend. Do nothing, await my return, and – I ask you this especially – let Vasari do his work, and leave Bronzino in peace. You know that they are both worthy of my confidence. As for the pope, do not put too much faith in a commonality of temperament based purely on the fact that the pyres of the Holy Inquisition, to which he claims affiliation, were first rekindled in your homeland: after all, was not this Juan de Valdés – whom you revile as the equal of Luther himself and whose influence, according to you, is still such a stain on Italy's soul – was not he a pure-blooded Spaniard?

14. Cosimo de' Medici, Duke of Florence, to Giorgio Vasari

Pisa, 10 January 1557

My dear Giorgio, I beg you, solve this case as quickly as you can, for the duchess is harassing me, and you know what she is like. I have a daughter to marry off, a wife to appease, a country to administer and a city to rule. (Of those four, my wife is not the least difficult.) As a consequence of all this, I have little time to spare for mysteries. You mentioned a disagreement with the colour-grinder. Look into that. We know where the worst instincts of the plebs may lead.

15. Giorgio Vasari to Cosimo de' Medici, Duke of Florence

Florence, 13 January 1557

Following Your Excellency's excellent advice, I interrogated the colour-grinder Marco Moro about the altercation with Pontormo that, it was reported to me, took place in the days preceding his death, and this is what Moro told me in his defence. You know that Pontormo, in the eleven years since he first started working on the frescoes at San Lorenzo, had not permitted anyone, not even his friends, to enter the chapel or even look inside. Well, last year, a few young people, who were drawing in Michelangelo's sacristy next door, climbed up onto the roof and removed some tiles to create a hole, through which they could see (according to what Pontormo told Marco Moro) all his work. Jacopo spotted them and, although he was furious and apparently sought revenge, in the end he settled for fortifying his frescoes even more securely than before. But since he held Moro responsible for the roof and the wooden screens that were designed to protect the frescoes from prying eyes, he angrily reproached him for his negligence. At this, the colour-grinder reminded Pontormo that he still owed him unpaid wages (which was true at the time and is still true now, he claims), and that if the great artist wanted to erect a screen as high as the church's ceiling he could do it himself, unless he preferred Moro to build a second roof under the first one, as Brunelleschi did for the dome of Santa Maria del Fiore, but if he wanted that kind of work done he would have to pay him Brunelleschi's wages.

Since that altercation, Moro states that not a day passed without Jacopo trying to start a fight, since he was obsessed to the point of delirium with the idea that someone might knock over the screen or find a way to enter the chapel when he was absent. Sometimes he would upbraid the colour-grinder for his negligence and sometimes for his indulgence, persuaded as he was that, as soon as his back was turned, Moro was opening the doors of the chapel and welcoming crowds of visitors in exchange for a few silver coins. Their last dispute did not depart from these grievances, except that Pontormo said he had felt certain for some time that he had seen shadows prowling around the chapel and that he knew perfectly well what they were looking for, a complaint that Marco Moro dismissed as one of the artist's habitual delusions.

16. Piero Strozzi, Marshal of France, to Catherine de' Medici, Queen of France

Ostia, 14 January 1557

Your plan would be perfect, cousin, had Aretino not passed away three months ago. I am surprised that this news did not reach you from Venice. It is said that he died as he lived: from laughing too hard at one of his own obscene jokes. He was at a banquet at the time, and he fell backwards off the bench and cracked his skull. A fitting end for the Scourge of Princes, wouldn't you agree? I doubt anyone could ask for a better one. In any case, your beautiful plan is foiled, although that does not stop me wishing to compliment you on it: you have what I like to call a truly Florentine soul! May God keep it that way forever. But this is what happens when Fate allows a woman with a superior mind to become involved in politics: she proves herself so far above the rest of us, who are good for little more than churning up the mud of a battlefield, that we must bow down in tribute to such ingenious invention.

Who knows when we will see each other again, Catherine? War is a dreadful thing, but God chose me to wage it. In the meantime, I kiss Your Majesty's hands, and am, more than ever, the faithful servant of good King Henri, just as I was for his father, the great François.

17. Cosimo de' Medici, Duke of Florence, to Giorgio Vasari

San Gimignano, 15 January 1557

I trust, Master Giorgio, that you have not given up your investigation of this colour-grinder, who strikes me, from the evidence you reported to me, as someone steeped in vice and cupidity. Did he not admit of his own free will that he and Pontormo were locked in a dispute over money? I want you to dig deeper in this direction, and we will see where it leads us. Have you checked that no money was stolen from the artist's home? What did Naldini say?

The sooner this affair is behind us, the sooner we can return to our great plans. Talking of which, I had an idea while I was in Pisa that I must discuss with you. I wish to entrust you with some major renovation work on the Palazzo della Signoria, and to commission you to build a new church that will host an order of knights that I am determined to establish for the defence of Christianity. It is my intention that this order will bear the name San Stefano, in memory of the victory we claimed over the Strozzi two years ago in Marciano, on St Stephen's Day. Of course, we must convince the pope, and this will require so many embassies that the mere thought of it exhausts me in advance, but you know that nothing can stop me when it comes to labouring for the greatness of Florence, and I expect the same self-sacrifice from all those who work for me. Besides, even the Vicar of Christ is mortal, and this one is eighty years old.

As you can see, Master Giorgio, I do not intend to leave you idle in the coming weeks, months or years, so I would encourage you to make yourself available to me as early as possible by proving the guilt of our colour-grinder. Speak to Naldini and report to me upon my return, tomorrow or the day after, God willing.

18. Piero Strozzi, Marshal of France, to Catherine de' Medici, Queen of France

Ostia, 15 January 1557

I have been thinking about your ingenious plan, my dear little Machiavelli, and in the nocturnal silence of my camp, disturbed only by the hooting of owls and the muttering of the guards, I have had time to reconsider my conclusions. After all, it is possible that Aretino's death does not necessarily prevent the plan's execution. You asked me if I knew a man sufficiently audacious to steal something from the duke's own wardrobe. Well, what if this man also had sufficient verve to be a perfect replacement for the Scourge of Princes? Because I do know one such. And so, my queen, do you. If, as I hope is the case, I still retain a little influence and a few supporters in Florence, you will soon hear more about this man. I have written him a letter that I believe will convince him to take part in our little enterprise, and I am determined to have this missive delivered. Farewell until soon, cousin. My arm belongs to France and my heart to you: happily, since you and France are one and the same.

19. Agnolo Bronzino to Michelangelo Buonarroti

Florence, 15 January 1557

My dear and venerated Master, it is hard for me to write, weighed down as I still am by my grief for the loss of a man who was at once my father, my brother and my friend, who taught me everything I know about the art of painting and made me what I am, who saved me from the plague by welcoming me into his home when I was just a child, and who always showed me the greatest affection throughout his lifetime. But I cannot think of any better hands into which to place this little notebook than yours. It is a sort of journal that Jacopo kept, in which he wrote about his health, his meals, his work at San Lorenzo, and the minor events that filled his days. It was young Battista Naldini – his faithful apprentice, who was as devoted to him as a son – who found it in his room when he was going through his belongings. Since this notebook does not contain anything that might shed light on the cause of his death, I did not see any point in sending it to Master Vasari, who would have no use for it in his murder investigation. I hope that in this way you will keep a living image of the man who rightly considered you his master, and who was undoubtedly the best of us, your disciples.

20. Michelangelo Buonarroti to Giorgio Vasari

Rome, 18 January 1557

My dear friend, Master Giorgio, you have given life back to the dead with your admirable writings. It is a shame you cannot bring poor Pontormo back to life, but I hope that you will pay him the tribute he deserves if you ever decide to expand the list of your *Lives of the Most Excellent Painters, Sculptors and Architects*, and that he will find his rightful place in a future volume. I strongly fear I will no longer be here to read it, for I already had one foot in the grave, and now Jacopo's death – which has robbed me of sleep by awakening my gout – threatens to shove me bodily inside. In the meantime, I am enclosing with this letter a copy I have made of the journal that he kept during his last three years, and which Master Bronzino was kind enough to send to me. You will see that they are merely notes on the meals he ate and his state of health, on the progress of his work, with some little sketches in the margins, and on the visits he paid to his friends (among whom are some of your own, including Masters Varchi, Martini and Borghini). However – and this is probably just a small detail, but it gave me pause – I did notice this, which I cannot explain: on two occasions, the journal notes that the duke visited San Lorenzo, once on his own and once with the duchess. I recall, my dear Giorgio, that you assured me that nobody had seen Jacopo's frescoes prior to his brutal death. But I seriously doubt that he could have refused to show them to such princely guests. And the journal also states that a certain Marco Moro walled up the chancel to 'close San Lorenzo'. But if we include this Marco Moro, that makes at least three people, with the duke and the duchess, who had access to the chapel before the tragedy. This means it is not true that nobody was allowed to see the frescoes; on the contrary, several people had seen them. Therein lies the key to the mystery.

No doubt these reflections are merely the fancies of a mad old man, and I hope you will forgive me for them, but you did ask for my help. And, to the meagre extent permitted by my resources and abilities, and despite the remorseless demands of my work at St Peter's, I will not refuse you. I must be honest: my interest in this affair is not dictated solely by the friendship I feel towards you. It is also driven by the pity I feel for poor Pontormo. Not that I knew him especially well. I did not spend much time in his company, since I have been in Rome for so long, but I do feel a profound sympathy for him – now more than ever – because I sense that we shared the same solitary, tormented character, and that, like me, he devoted all his passion to his art, for the greater glory of God.

21. Giorgio Vasari to Vincenzo Borghini

Florence, 20 January 1557

Well, as if this affair were not already murky enough, I have just discovered that Pontormo kept a journal. Sadly, it is not exactly a monument to the glories of the Tuscan language, as I will allow you to judge for yourself:

monday, I wrote a letter to someone and my diarrhoea started. tuesday I painted a thigh, the diarrhoea got worse, with lots of white and blood-streaked bile, wednesday it was even worse, had to go 10 times more, needed the privy every hour so I had to stay at home and I sipped some broth.

friday evening I ate supper with Piero I think the diarrhoea is over, the pain too.

saturday morning, I managed two non-liquid turds they came out like strands of cotton, like strings of white fat, I ate a good supper at San Lorenzo a really nice beef stew and I finished the figure.

sunday morning I ate lunch at Bronzino's (*added in the margin: fish and mutton)* and in the evening I didn't eat supper, monday morning I had stomach pains; I got up but it was cold and windy so I went back to bed and stayed there until 18 hours,* I didn't feel good all day. In the evening, though, I ate some pig's cheek cooked with chard and butter and I still don't know what will happen to me, I don't think it's a good idea to go back to bed, although now at 4 hours† I think I'm better.

When Master Jacopo spares us these interminable intestinal updates, it is to provide us with a fascinating progress report on his work:

* Noon for us. Florentine timekeeping differed from ours: the 24-hour clock started at sunset (or, to be more precise, at the Ave Maria, around 6 p.m.).

† 2200 hours. For the sake of convenience, all other mentions of time in this book will be transposed directly into our modern system.

thursday I did an arm
friday the other arm.
wednesday I did that head under that figure, like this *(scrawls in the margin)*
thursday the thigh
friday the back.
on the 6th I did the whole torso.
on the 7th I finished the legs.

Have you ever read anything so profound and compelling? Ariosto has nothing on this guy! The rest of it is just more of the same: 'I ate lunch with Bronzino some chicken and veal', 'on Christmas Eve I ate supper at Bronzino's and I stayed the night there and I ate woodcock', 'I ate supper with Bronzino an ounce of bread', 'I ate lunch and supper with Bronzino some blood cake and liver dumplings', 'sunday I ate supper at Daniello's with Bronzino, there were dumplings', etc., ad infinitum. It's incredible how much time Bronzino spent with that old man!

But each to his own, and I would not have bothered telling you all this if not for the fact that Bronzino decided, somewhat strangely, to send this heap of inanities to Rome. I do not know what the Master was thinking, nor what Bronzino might have insinuated to put this idea in his head, but after reading this edifying prose, Master Buonarroti's barely concealed advice to me was that I should investigate the duchess, on the basis that she had seen the frescoes long before they were revealed to the rest of us following Pontormo's death. (And we know just how unacceptable those frescoes are to the Spanish taste, don't we? As if the gothicism that inspired them had never been practised by

Florentine artists! And as if, before Carafa became pope, the Council of Trent had not already condemned the depravity of painting nudes . . .)

Anyway, I have no idea what Michelangelo has in mind. Does he think I'm going to demand an audience with the duke so I can ask him where his wife was on the night of the crime?

Despite all this, the journal does also contain some information that might prove helpful to my investigation, and those are the leads I intend to follow. Pontormo spends a lot of time complaining about his apprentice Naldini, with whom he is constantly quarrelling, and whom he accuses of being heartless and ungrateful and of always keeping the best cuts for himself (because food – whether going in or coming out – appears to have been the old man's chief obsession) and even of being a thief. It is true that Pontormo wasn't easy, and the journal reports that Bronzino himself complains about this (look at this entry for 22 March 1556): 'Bronzino wanted me to come to lunch and he got angry and told me that anyone would think you were going to your enemy's house and he let me leave.' No doubt Bronzino thought he was being cunning by using Michelangelo to spread his accusations, but it is easy to see how this shitty document might blow up in his face. Has he not just been granted the most prestigious art commission in Florence apart from my own project to renovate the Palazzo della Signoria? After all, who has profited more from this crime than he?

If you go to Siena, you should see Ambrogio Lorenzetti's *Annunciation*. In my memory, that painting has something, though I don't know what, and I can find nothing about it in either my notes or yours. Please tell me if it merits a mention in the next edition.

22. *Eleanor of Toledo, Duchess of Florence, to His Holiness, Pope Paul IV*

Florence, 20 January 1557

Holy Father, you know as well as I that the agents of Luther are everywhere, that the practitioners of Sodom no longer bother to hide themselves, and that very often they are one and the same, proliferating and gaining ground, dressed up in the masks of art and virtue. Florence has not been spared, any more than Rome has, and in this regard at least – in spite of your differences concerning Siena and other matters – you are connected to His Lordship the Duke by a common interest in the righteous war that you and he are waging against this leprosy, as all good Christians must. My heart bleeds to see these two cities torn apart by disputes that do not even concern them, when, if they could only succeed in unifying, they might reign together and in harmony over all of Italy.

You must surely have heard about the scandal that has recently beset Florence within its most sacred walls, because even if the duke has done all he can to keep it a secret, rumour is a winged monster that cannot be stopped, and I have no doubt that it has already flown as far as the Holy See. I give my word to Your Holiness that neither the duke nor myself were aware of those obscene paintings, because the artist – who had lost his mind long ago – did not allow anyone to see them for several years.

Thankfully, God saw fit to intervene, and this old madman's providential death, while it may have come about in regrettable circumstances, prevented him from finishing his impious undertaking – and of course the duke cancelled the project as soon as he saw those heretical frescoes. Consequently, I have the honour of informing Your Holiness that there will be no second Sistine in Florence; not today, not tomorrow, nor ever.

23. Eleanor of Toledo, Duchess of Florence, to Agnolo Bronzino

Florence, 20 January 1557

My very dear Señor Bronzino, I rejoice at the duke's choice to entrust you with the completion of the San Lorenzo frescoes, because I know that you will understand better than anyone how you must perform the task that has been assigned to you, out of love for your homeland.

Naturally, I am depending on you, *querido maestro*, to cover up all those dreadful nudes which have no place in the house of God. I am aware of the affection that you felt for poor Pontormo, and it is out of love for him that I ask you to save his work by giving him back the dignity of which his old age clearly robbed him. The duke fully shares my feelings in this matter and expects you to bring these frescoes to order with all the grace, delicacy and modesty that you have always shown in the beautiful portraits you have painted of our family. God willing, we will continue to entrust you with that task for many years to come. For my part, I have no doubt that you will grant our wishes and, to prove to you the confidence that we are placing in you, I am sending you, via Master Bernadone of the Mint, the sum of three hundred florins.

24. Benvenuto Cellini to Catherine de' Medici, Queen of France

Florence, 21 January 1557

God must love you, madame, for he has placed me upon your path. You know how much affection the great King François, your father, showed me when he was alive and he called me his friend. Indeed, I can truly say that everything I am, every great feat I have accomplished, I owe to that magnificent king. So when it comes to serving his son Henri the Most Christian, by way of Your Majesty, I am not going to haggle. I have been called many things during the course of my rich existence: murderer, thief, infidel, sodomite, and also (in truth, these latter descriptions are perhaps justified) proud, insolent, bold beyond all reason and overly jealous of my freedom. But nobody has ever called me ungrateful. It is true that I was born in Florence, but my heart is in France. So I am your servant twice over.

That admirable soldier Marshal Strozzi, unique in this century for his courage, honoured me by recommending my services to you; he was right to do so. I am, after all, the very same man who fired the arquebus that killed the Constable of Bourbon. Master Strozzi explained the case to me a little: so I must steal a painting from the very heart of government power – from the duke's own personal wardrobe, in fact, where he spends several hours every day surrounded by a crowd of courtiers and guards – then remove the painting from the palace and secretly transport it through the city gates so that it can be sent to Venice? Perfect. The maddest missions are always the ones that I am most eager to carry out. As for the project of penning a pretty libel, with which you may do as you wish, you are without any doubt at all better off with me than you would have been with Aretino. Other than his puffed-up, convoluted manner of speaking, and his ingenious use of the truth (if somewhat fanciful and lacking in first-hand knowledge), and his eloquence, of course, such as it was, I do not see how this so-called Scourge of Princes was in any way superior to the common mass of authors of this century.

For my part, and I say this so that no suspicion of treachery might stain the fresh sheets of our working relationship, I feel no loyalty towards the duke, who has treated me so badly for so long, never rewarding my merits to their rightful value, and even less towards the duchess, that Spaniard – as miserable and arrogant as all of her race – who hates me even though I have never done her any harm. So I will carry out my mission for the joy of serving you and for the pleasure of tricking them. Your Majesty will hear from me soon.

25. Marco Moro to Giambattista Naldini

Florence, 21 January 1557

Times are hard, comrade, for poor wretches like us. Burn this letter and all the others and stop writing to me now. Above all, do not come to San Lorenzo and do not seek to see me or speak to me. For now the screens are still in place, on the duke's orders, and I am working for Bronzino, since he has taken the other's place. Nothing has changed here, in fact, except that the new one spends less time in the church and doesn't work in the evenings, or at least he hasn't so far. But we must keep a low profile. Anyway, I have no use for your services anymore. I will be back in touch if necessary. I am enclosing a stack of pamphlets that you can hand out to certain people in the studio – you know which ones I mean.

26. Marco Moro to the workers of the Arte dei Medici e Speziali

Florence, undated

Comrades, following the events that you all know about, we must suspend our meetings until further notice. We must also be discreet, which means not going anywhere near San Lorenzo. Pass the word on to the other trades and to all those who were present for previous meetings, or who showed a desire to attend. But be careful who you speak to. You know that the greatest enemies are always those traitors who pretend to champion a cause but who in reality are only looking after their own interests. Keep a low profile. Our time will come.

27. Vincenzo Borghini to Giorgio Vasari

Siena, 23 January 1557

Thank you, dear Giorgio, for encouraging me to make this detour via Arezzo. I had forgotten how extraordinary Piero della Francesca's frescoes are. I visited your wife while I was there and she asked me if you are planning to go home before the end of the month. You know how much Nicolosa loves you and how she pines for you, particularly since you leave her alone too often without any real company, which is why I always feel compelled to urge you to return to Arezzo more often, even if only to continue the work on your beautiful home. Or bring her to Florence, so she can look after your mother and help you by taking care of domestic chores. I am told you haven't even finished buying your furniture since you moved into the house on Via Larga almost a year ago. The three of you could live under the same roof, and you could return to Arezzo whenever you need rest and solitude. Believe me, every time I go back home to Poppiano, in the middle of the countryside, I feel like I am in Heaven.

As for what you tell me about your investigation into poor

Pontormo, since you honour me by calling me your friend and adviser, I feel duty-bound to remind you of a few home truths. First of all, you have not always considered Dürer to be Satan incarnate; there was even a time, in your youth, when you saw some beauty in his work. Do you remember? On the frescoes at San Lorenzo, which you lambast pitilessly as if they were some butcher's stall . . . well, I am not in a position to contradict you since I have not yet seen them, but from what you have told me, the *idea* bears some resemblance to the Sistine. Now, when it was Michelangelo piling up naked bodies – stop me if I'm wrong here, but I seem to recall you thinking it wonderful. I realise that times change, but you are not obliged to change with them.

I hope, too, that you will allow me to offer you some advice concerning the task you have been given: Be methodical. Be detached. Examine the facts coldly and weigh them with blind impartiality. Do not let yourself be swayed by rancour or self-interest. Remember the lessons of the wise Marsilio Ficino: it is truth that brings happiness. I do not doubt that you will take my modest recommendations to heart, because he who advises justly is naturally more persuasive. You should draw up a list of the various people, *without omitting anybody*, who had the desire or the ability (or, better still, both) to kill Jacopo. If I have followed you correctly, we have the colour-grinder Marco Moro, about whom I can say nothing since I do not know him; the apprentice Battista Naldini, whom I know from having once employed him as a drawing tutor at the Innocents, and who never gave me any trouble at all; our friend Bronzino (however unlikely this supposition seems, let us force ourselves to consider it); the duchess (do not protest – this is a mental exercise, nothing more); and the mysterious woman who went to Jacopo's house in his absence (according to Battista). Let us even add the duke, so that you cannot accuse me of being inconsistent! In truth, all those who were in Florence at the time could have committed this crime, couldn't they? But only one of them possessed a motive powerful enough to carry their plan to execution. What kind of motive? That is what we must discover. Was it an argument that turned ugly (in which case this heinous crime would have been caused by passion and anger)? A financial dispute (driven by greed)? A professional rivalry (dictated by pride or jealousy)? A political or religious motive (which would make this an even more delicate case)? You know as well as I that Pontormo was not insensible to the cause of clerical reform, and even if this name is now forbidden in Florence, it is true that the theories of Juan de Valdés were spread by Master Francesco Riccio, who was much more than the duke's majordomo and who (you are too intelligent not to know this) exercised a strong influence over all of us, before losing his mind. The duke, as I am sure you recall, had him locked up in Borgo San Lorenzo, where he has been for the last three years. Perhaps you could pay him a visit? I have a feeling he is not quite as mad as the duke wished us to believe. As for myself, I continue to roam Italy in preparation for our next, revised (and, above all, improved!) edition. Speaking of which, have you given any thought to what you will write about Pontormo? Knowing you as I do, I am sure you have already begun the chapter of the *Lives* dedicated to him, at least in your mind, if not on paper.

Do not forget what I said about Arezzo. Nicolosa hopes

to see you every day that God makes. Write to her, at least. That is surely the least that the famous author Vasari could do for his wife, don't you think?

28. Michelangelo Buonarroti to Giorgio Vasari

Rome, 23 January 1557

My very dear friend Master Giorgio, the more I think about it, the more I believe that the key to this mystery is to be found in that painting of *Venus and Cupid*. Why replace the face of the goddess with the duke's daughter? Despite the fact that I once drew the model for that painting, with no other intention than showing the beauty of Love but also its dangers and traps, I cannot deny that this substitution betrays a provocative and hostile intention regarding the ducal family, because I very much doubt that young Maria – who cannot have seen more than seventeen springtimes and whom her father is presumably intending to marry off – has anything in common, whether physically or morally, with my voluptuous, lascivious Venus. I also find it hard to imagine Pontormo suddenly developing a vicious lust for young virgins at over sixty years old. I believe that it is not the daughter but her father who is targeted in this painting. But why would Pontormo wish to attack his protector and benefactor, for whom he had been working tirelessly for almost twenty years? There is a mystery here that I cannot explain. You have examined the picture with your artist's eye – did you spot any clues? Assuming that Naldini was telling the truth about the hooded woman who visited Pontormo's house at night, what could she have wanted if not something connected to that painting? And who other than the duke or his family could have felt offended by such a piece? Do you know if Maria has any declared suitors? Is it possible one of them got wind of this insolence and was thrown into a murderous rage? Please, my dear Giorgio, keep me informed of the latest developments.

29. Giorgio Vasari to Michelangelo Buonarroti

Florence, 25 January 1557

My dear Master, the second-greatest creator after God, I cannot thank you enough for the ideas you so generously shared with me. There is indeed a declared suitor for young Maria's hand. It is the son of the Duke of Ferrara, the young Prince Alfonso, who does not, in all honesty, have the best of reputations, although that is often the case for young men and I would not like to jump to any hasty conclusions. Furthermore, I was able to observe the painting at my leisure and, as far as my eye could tell, I would swear that it truly was painted in its entirety by Pontormo, based on your drawing. Consequently, it is indeed possible that the woman in the hood came at night for this painting, hoping to steal it in the artist's absence, and that she was foiled in her attempt by the presence of Naldini.

I cannot imagine the duchess wandering the streets of Florence in the dark, like a thief. As for the possibility that young Maria herself could have gone to Pontormo's house . . . for that to be true, she would have had to know about the painting's existence, and there is nothing as yet to suggest that was the case. But, following your advice, which I know is motivated purely by the goodwill you bear me and your love of justice, I will question her about the matter.

30. Marco Moro to Giambattista Naldini

Florence, undated

Comrade, can you arrange for me to meet Bronzino's apprentice? A certain Sandro Allori. I'm told that he lived at his master's house too.

31. Agnolo Bronzino to Michelangelo Buonarroti

Florence, 25 January 1557

A plague upon the Spanish! The duchess wants me to repaint the frescoes so that they are more to her taste, but she can buy me with a few florins. I will finish my master's work as honourably as possible, the way he would have wanted it, as far as my meagre God-given talents allow. I swear this to you and to the memory of our beloved friend. *O tempora, o mores*: these people are forever quoting

Cicero, but they are far more guilty than we are. They consider themselves the defenders of every virtue, blind to the fact that – since they have abandoned the message of the Gospel – it is their own souls that have been led astray and corrupted.

32. Michelangelo Buonarroti to Agnolo Bronzino

Rome, 27 January 1557

I cannot tell you how relieved I was to read your promise, Master Agnolo, and yet my soul has been anything but tranquil since the death of our poor friend. Although I have not seen them, I feel certain that Pontormo's frescoes must be preserved at all costs because they defend an idea of art and divinity that I know we share. The idea, my dear Bronzino! You and I know there is nothing more elevated. That is why I have no doubts that you – better than anyone else could and just as well as I myself – will remain faithful to your master by completing his work in the spirit he intended. In doing so, you will be participating in the battle we are fighting against dark forces, exposing yourself to terrible dangers, because our enemies are crawling towards us like spiders. In Rome, I fear every day for my Sistine and I have even wondered if I should let poor Volterra veil my nudes, that solution appearing the lesser evil when compared with the possibility that the entire work will be destroyed. In truth, I often wish for my own death so that I do not have to see what becomes of my work, for I now have little hope that it will survive me for any great length of time. Besides, I can feel my end approaching: I am exhausted, and I do not know how I still manage to drag my aching body each day to St Peter's. Were it not for my conviction that I am serving the glory of God, and for the fear of abandoning my nephew Leonardo as well as the family of my dearly departed Urbino, who are in my charge, I think I would have already let myself die in my bed. These are cruel times, my friend, for the defenders of art and beauty.

33. Maria de' Medici to Catherine de' Medici, Queen of France

Florence, 1 February 1557

My dear aunt, I am enclosing a copy of a letter I received from that young gentleman, the page to my father the duke, which I cannot deny has greatly moved me, although I fear I should not have let it do so. Would it really be so wrong for me to answer him? He has seen the painting, which makes me want to die of shame. But he says so many kind things that I blush with pleasure. However, it is proving impossible for me to forget this humiliating affair: Master Vasari, one of my father's closest advisers, came to question me about the painter's death. And here is the most extraordinary thing: I felt guilty. But of what? I do not have the faintest idea.

34. Malatesta de' Malatesti to Maria de' Medici

Florence, 28 January 1557

I would blush at my own audacity, madame, were my blood not already pounding in my temples due to a feeling at once far nobler and more serious than my temerity. I am aware that the boldness driving me to write to you might seem like insolence to anyone without access to the contents of my heart, but I would like you to be the judge of that so I am not going to hide any of these emotions. Besides, my heart is beating so hard inside my chest that I feel I must let it out. I will not be able to sleep while this letter remains unwritten. If you are reading these lines, then that means I must also have found the courage to deliver it to you. In truth, though, I doubt any of this surprises you, if you have deigned to observe me even a little during the past few days. As the great Petrarch wrote, 'Often on the brow, we may read the heart', and your eyes turned towards mine must have fatally informed you of my tender feelings for you. I am well aware of my rank and of yours. But, though I am no prince, I am nonetheless a gentleman, and the education that my parents gave me has sufficiently prepared me to recognise grace and beauty when I see it. 'The greatest painters could not imagine a more perfect beauty.' Ariosto must have been thinking of you when he wrote that line, and if he wasn't, then he was wrong – unwittingly, of course, since he never had the pleasure of meeting you. But what am I saying? I do believe he knew you, and for proof I offer these other lines:

Her blonde hair floated in countless curls,
Softer and more sparkling than gold.

Or perhaps it is simply that I see you everywhere I look, even in books? You must be laughing at poor Malatesta, after making him lose his head like this.

I know, madame, that you are deeply upset by the defamatory painting found in the house of the dead artist. You should not be. The picture is well guarded, and hidden from sight inside a cupboard in the duke's wardrobe. For my part, I do not wish to conceal from you the fact that I was able to look upon it. True, it is not exactly the kind of tribute a young woman has a right to expect from a painter in her father's court. But, if I may, I would like to tell you that, despite the goddess's obscene pose, it is not without a certain beauty, since it contains a little of you. I swear upon my life that, absorbed as I was in contemplation of that image, my eyes never left your face. What does that body matter, since it is not yours, since it cannot be yours, because you clearly have nothing in common with that lascivious creature, you whose youthful paleness reflects your virginal innocence and whose stately bearing so resembles your royal mother's. Duchess, queen, princess, you are all of those for me, and many other things too, when I try to fall asleep at night by thinking of you.

I feel a great relief now, having confided my heart's desires to you, and my trembling hand can finally rest. I ask nothing of you in return, except a reply.

35. Giorgio Vasari to Vincenzo Borghini

Florence, 1 February 1557

The news from Florence, my dear Vincenzo, is that I have questioned young Maria, who not only knows nothing about Pontormo, having met him only twice in her life, but is not even aware that she has been promised in marriage to the Duke of Ferrara's son. Such candour does not make her a very convincing candidate for the crime. I seriously doubt that this young lady could ever do anything dishonest. Now we must turn our attention to her suitor, Alfonso d'Este. Have you heard the rumours about him? He is said to be taciturn and violent. Perhaps you could visit Ferrara on the pretext of seeing the frescoes by Tura and Cossa, so that you can glean more information? His father, the Duke Ercole, will give you a warm welcome, for he is a humanist, a patron of the arts, and I am sure he will not let you leave without first showing you his collection of Flemish tapestries, of which he is very proud.

36. Eleanor of Toledo, Duchess of Florence, to Cosimo de' Medici, her husband

Florence, 2 February 1557

My friend, I have been hearing extremely unfavourable reports of Prince Alfonso. It is said that he beats his servants and mistreats women. And do you know what else they say? That, following a horse-riding accident as a child, he is impotent. I beseech you to call this marriage off. Are you going to hand over our daughter to a brutish eunuch incapable of ensuring his and our lineage, good for nothing but abusing his wife? You are the Duke of Florence: every great family in Italy and in Europe would be proud to be related to you by marriage. Why not an Orsini, or a Farnese, or even a Habsburg? I have been told that the Emperor Ferdinand's youngest son, who is already archduke of Austria and count of Tyrol, is not yet betrothed. Do you think he would refuse the most beautiful region of Italy? Have pity on our daughter, my friend. For the love you bear me, write to the Duke of Ferrara. Tell him that our daughter is too young, that she suffers from melancholic moods . . . Tell him she has the French Disease if you must! Use your finest diplomatic phrases. Tell him that her mother is mad and cannot bear to be deprived of her child. Tell him my health is at risk. Find any excuse you like, but do not sell Maria to that man. The Medici blood is worth more than the Este family can offer you. Sell her if you must, but not so cheaply.

37. Cosimo de' Medici, Duke of Florence, to Ercole d'Este, Duke of Ferrara

Lucca, 2 February 1557

I write this note, duke, to confirm what your son must already have told you: the introductions with my daughter took place, and I have no hesitation in saying that the young prince made an excellent impression. There is nothing I would like more than to hear that her feelings are reciprocated. If so, we could agree a date in the spring. Naturally, the ceremony will be celebrated in Florence with all the honours due to your family and all the pomp and splendour for which our city is famed. Please do not imagine that, in fixing upon the spring as a wedding date, I am seeking to delay an event that is dearer to my heart than any other; it is simply, my dear duke, that Maria, although in her seventeenth year, is still a child, strongly attached to her parents and her home, and the duchess and I will have only a few months to prepare her for the great joy of marrying your son.

38. Catherine de' Medici, Queen of France, to Piero Strozzi, Marshal of France

Fontainebleau, 3 February 1557

Cousin, I would like to ask you two questions that have recently occurred to me. Why have I not had any news of your man or of his mission in Florence? It feels like a century ago that he promised me he would accomplish the most prodigious feats imaginable, and yet nothing seems to have happened. Which brings me to my second question: have you considered the possibility that this man is, in fact, nothing but a useless idler? It is true that King François was very impressed by his art, but the man I recall was essentially a ruffian with a big mouth who spent most of his time demanding money for work that he never finished. So I think perhaps you should consider someone else, because in my opinion we are running short of time to recover the painting, which will surely be destroyed once the truth about the artist's death has been discovered.

39. Benvenuto Cellini to Catherine de' Medici, Queen of France

Florence, 7 February 1557

Madame, you may doubt whatever you like, but not this: anything that a man dares, I dare. You entrusted me with an impossible mission. And to achieve the impossible, I need time. It is not simply a case of entering a fortress guarded by a thousand men and then stealing a wooden panel measuring six feet by four in broad daylight. First, I must locate the object, which is no mere detail. You told me it was in the duke's wardrobe: excellent, but that room is a dreadful mess that cannot be described to anyone who has never seen it, and the duke has not thought fit to hang the painting on the wall for the enjoyment of the duchess, who lives in the adjoining apartment – another complicating factor. I suppose that the painting is hidden inside one of the countless cupboards in the wardrobe, but the frequent visits of the duke, the duchess and their children, added to the ceaseless flow of painters, goldsmiths and artisans, make it more than a little difficult to ransack the place. At this very moment, you must imagine old Bacchiacca working there all day carving decorative wooden sculptures on a bed destined for the duke, and his presence alone is enough to hamper my search. It is not for want of audacity that I have not yet carried out the plan you were shrewd enough to entrust to me, but simply want of time. If I knew precisely where the painting is kept, I would have little trouble finding the right moment to seize it, because that is an act I could accomplish in the blink of an eye.

40. Benvenuto Cellini to Piero Strozzi, Marshal of France

Florence, 7 February 1557

I will do what I said I would do. But neither the Queen of France nor you yourself, Master Piero, can imagine the insurmountable difficulties that your servant must first overcome. The Florence that the two of you once knew and that, God willing, it will one day become again, is currently a hive in which bees seem to swarm in all directions before converging on the single point of the duke's damned wardrobe. From dawn until dusk, the entire city files through there, and at night it is guarded by a thousand men. I could claim this is due to the excited preparations for the Carnival, but I am not going to lie: the palace has been in a state of constant renovation for the past fifteen years and there is no reason to believe that the work will ever stop. We owe this eternal building site to Vasari, the duke's whore, who is adept at giving the appearance of working quickly while actually dragging out his commissions to keep the ducats raining down onto his little rat's face.

Add to this the fact that one must first cross the duchess's apartments to reach the wardrobe. Now, since a murky affair involving a necklace that I see no point in describing to you in detail, that woman has nurtured such an aversion towards me that she flies into a rage whenever she lays eyes upon me. Consequently, every time I arrive at the palace, I must mope around for hours while I wait because the duchess spends hours doing her business in the very antechambers through which I must pass. And since she is always unwell, I am – like her shit – never able to pass through without bothering her. Sometimes, entering silently and unexpectedly into those private chambers, I have even found the duchess in the midst of her ablutions. So, you see, even the most ambitious enterprises may hang by the rotting guts of a sour-faced Spanish woman.

Even after navigating that first obstacle, I must then suffer another ordeal, because finding this painting is more difficult than spotting one particular sail amid the Ottoman fleet, or Atahualpa's gold in the mountains of Peru. One thing the duke's wardrobe does not lack, you see, is paintings. The ones hung on the walls are portraits of Medicis, to which the duke has whimsically added the face of that old slut Aretino, painted by Titian himself. The portrait of young Maria is missing, as you might have guessed. The shelves, on the other hand, are sagging under the weight of the duke's beloved Etruscan statuettes. His bed takes up a good sixth of the room, if you include Bacchiacca, who works on it all day long. There are also lots of bizarre curiosities: a mirror that sends back thirteen reflections of your face; a dried chameleon; glass vials filled with poisoned oil; fragments of rock with fish prints in them; a strip of canvas with seven stones attached to it, each accorded a certain virtue . . . I'll spare you the rest, which is of dubious interest. If you have managed to get past all this clutter without bumping into old Bacchiacca or getting bitten by little Giorgio, the duke's vicious little mutt who never stops nosing around, you now have nothing to do but open the thirty-odd cupboards one by one: in those you will find loads of other paintings, plus silverware, porcelain figurines, tapestries, and all kinds of fabrics. When you have finally found what you are looking for, you must simply make your way back through the rooms where the duchess is still busy shitting for Spain, then escape from the palace with the loot under your arm, saluting the Bargello guards on your way out. I think you will agree that it is no simple task.

41. Maria de' Medici to Catherine de' Medici, Queen of France

Florence, 7 February 1557

Rescue me, dear aunt, for I am dead. My father delivered his verdict, and I fear that it is final, as all his decisions are. I must marry the son of the Duke of Ferrara, that Alfonso d'Este who struck me as rather scary and who, rumour has it, is one of the wickedest men in Italy. I can expect no help from my mother, who is fully in agreement with her husband's plans, as always. Those two really are a perfect match – I have never seen them disagree about anything. So I have nowhere to turn but to you. I have heard, I think, that you spent time with Alfonso d'Este at the court in France: please tell me that this prince is a gentleman, friendlier than he appears, and that this marriage is not the prison it presently seems to me. Tell me, above all, that I will be able to continue seeing my Malatesta.

Yes, since you didn't expressly forbid it, I must confess that I replied to his letter, which had quite the effect on him: he looked so sad before, and then suddenly so happy. It is quite astounding what a few words written on paper can do to a person. His revived cheerfulness appears to have sharpened his audacity: since receiving my reply, he has not missed an opportunity to come and see me, and we chat like brother and sister, or like two old friends. What will you say when I tell you that he took advantage of a moment when everyone else was away, to lure me into my mother's chapel, where he sought to steal a kiss from me? I swear I tried to resist him, but my lips refused to obey. It was a divine sensation, and I felt transported straight to Heaven. I don't understand why that has to be a sin.

But now, while I am bathed in the most glorious happiness, I see dark misfortune on the horizon. Is life always like this? Or am I alone doomed to such bad luck? Why would God be so cruel as to take away the delights he has only just offered me? I want to believe that there is some grand design behind all this, but amid the desolation and confusion that afflicts me, I cannot guess what it might be.

42. Catherine de' Medici, Queen of France, to Piero Strozzi, Marshal of France

Paris, 9 February 1557

God is on our side, dear cousin! Look at this letter from Il Popolano's daughter and at my reply, which I have had copied for you. Warn your man that the page will help him by supplying him with the information he is missing, and then he will have no excuse to keep delaying the act.

I must admit that I am growing increasingly fond of this young girl: beneath the exterior of a perfect idiot, which is simply the character that is expected of her and the model to which she strives to conform, there lies a shrewd intuition that being born a woman is a curse, coupled with a determination to escape it, which will prove extremely useful to us if events turn in our favour. And so, thanks to his daughter, we will be able to lead Cosimo down the path of our choosing: to weaken him to such a degree that, with only a little push, he will be utterly ruined.

43. Catherine de' Medici, Queen of France, to Maria de' Medici

Paris, 9 February 1557

Allow me to speak to you, my dear child, as if you were my own daughter.

I once dreamed of love too. But the heavy burden of being born a Medici, added to the misfortune of being a woman, quickly made me understand that it was not in Our Lord's plans that I should be granted more than the most fleeting glimpse of carefree happiness. I was born an orphan, looked after by my aunt who was soon taken from me by God, hidden in a convent during the troubles of 1527, sequestered in another convent where my head was shaved and I was forced to eat rotten donkey meat, promised to a brothel at ten years old by rebellious republicans, rescued by my uncle Pope Clement, raised by your grandmother alongside your father, who was not yet in the position he occupies today and who showed no signs of ever elevating himself to such heights, fell in love with my cousin Ippolito who was poisoned by his cousin Alessandro, then sent to France like a piece of merchandise to marry the second son of good King François. By this point I had been hardened by my experiences – my temperament darkened by misfortune, my spirit steeled by many vexations, my heart embittered by those who had persecuted me – and I arrived at the court having not yet reached my twenty-fifth year, torn between grief at this exile and the hope of finding a new home. But as you will soon learn, or as perhaps you have already guessed, no court will ever provide the kind of refuge that a young girl might dream of. I received the honours owed to my rank, but I also had to contend with traps and conspiracies more deadly than those I had known in Italy. Accused of having murdered the dauphin because his death promised me the crown, I was saved from the executioner's axe only by the generosity and genuine affection that the king felt for me. For ten years, my enemies called me a barren-bellied bitch because I did not manage to give the new dauphin an heir, and I lived each second in the permanent terror of being repudiated. I finally became a mother, and then the queen, but I was not freed from their insults. The only Italians that the French like are our painters and inventors, so they have never ceased treating me as a foreigner, while they consider Henri's favourite – my cousin the Duchess Diane – to be the true queen. And, not wishing to hide anything from you, my child, I must confess that, more often than not, the king neglects me for that slattern. And yet it was I who assumed the regency when Henri went off to wage war in Flanders, I and I alone who bore the burden of ruling and who ensured the provision of supplies to the French army, without which Imperial troops would have marched on Paris. Yes, this little Florentine orphan saved the great Kingdom of France.

As for love, you will remark that it has claimed a rather small place in my life. Is my marriage happy? I will let you be the judge of that, but I fear one should not look at things in such terms. If you marry the young prince of Ferrara, it will be for one reason only: so that your father can make allies of the powerful Este family. We women are mere pieces on the chessboard of empires, and while we are not without a certain value, we are assuredly not free in our movements. Your duty as the duke's daughter is to obey your father; your duty as the duke's wife will be to serve your husband as he wishes by giving him healthy heirs. I wish you the strength that enabled me to have ten, seven of whom – thanks be to God – are still alive, and not the fragility of my mother, who did not survive my birth. You will suffer in silence the whims of your master, his rages and his infidelities, and – if God wills it – he will treat you well, although from what I have heard about the character of this young prince, I would not be particularly optimistic on that count.

Nevertheless, I can see that you are enamoured of this young page, whom you describe with every sign of true passion, just as I can see that he is enamoured of you, so I would be neglecting my duties as your confidante and your aunt if I did not warn you against the kind of ideas that will inevitably cross the mind of a girl your age. Naturally, you will be welcomed in France with open arms if you and this young man commit the mad act of eloping together, leaving behind your homeland and your family. Your father will forgive you in the end, of course, because fathers always do. But think of the scandal: you will, in a sense, be proving that awful artist right to have depicted you the way he did in that obscene painting. As long as that painting remains in Florence, so must you. But if the time ever comes when, despite my firm orders to the contrary, you opt for the perils of elopement and a life of adventure with the man you love and who loves you, then the painting must disappear.

Without wishing to prejudge a decision that will define the happiness of your entire life, I would like to say that, when it comes to this particular enterprise, I might be in a position to help. Tell your friend to inform Master Cellini of where the painting is hidden. That gentleman will take care of the rest.

Farewell, my niece. I beg you not to commit this folly, and never forget that nothing is more important for a woman than her honour and her duty.

44. Marco Moro to the workers of the Arte dei Medici e Speziali

Florence, 9 February 1557

Comrades, the events at San Lorenzo cannot and must not compromise what we have begun. It is a blow, but it is not the end. Because our cause is just, our victory is assured in time. Now we must lie low because the duke's men are sniffing around like dogs. Who killed the painter? That is a question of no interest to us. It is none of our business. What concerns us, comrades, is poverty and hunger. When Pontormo's murderer is found, will our fate be improved? The duke's dogs will tire of this eventually, and a week or a month from now we will start to meet again, at San Lorenzo or elsewhere.

I know some among us were afraid of banding together, even if they were doing it for the cause of the common people, because they thought others might consider them presumptuous or accuse them of harbouring ambitions. But after observing that many Florentines meet every day, without any precautions, in private spaces or diverse assemblies, not for the good of all but to serve their own personal ambitions, we came to the conclusion that those of us who meet for the good of the greatest number should have nothing to fear, since those who do it for the enrichment of their peers or for pointless ends are not persecuted. And what happened? At each of our meetings, workers from the other guilds joined us, swelling our ranks, because what we want for ourselves they also want for themselves. Because what concerns us concerns them in the same way. Because our condition is theirs and their condition is ours. Because, in a word, we are brothers. So it is logical and legitimate that we should come together in a brotherhood that breaks down barriers between trades and erases distinctions between the arts.

The duke put an end to the wars between the nobles by driving them out of Florence, confiscating their belongings or having them killed. But what did he do when he discovered that men of letters were secretly gathering to philosophise? Did he punish them? No, he brought them together in an academy created especially for them. The duke kept the guilds of the arts and the old institutions of the Republic. And while it is true that he governs Florence with an iron fist, he is not hostile to the principle of assemblies nor of their representatives, as we are reminded every day by the existence of those consuls of the arts whom we see strutting around in their beautiful, expensively tailored robes. Soon the duke will have no choice but to accede to our demands, because they are justified and because our numbers grow with every passing day. And what are our demands? Simply this: we who are nothing aspire to be something.

45. Vincenzo Borghini to Giorgio Vasari

Florence, 9 February 1557

I am cross with you, Master Giorgio, because you must have known that for me to visit Ferrara, as you asked me to do,

I would pass through Florence. And what do I find? The city in uproar – more jugglers, musicians, jousters, dancers and academicians than I could count, and Varchi running around in all directions, and a wooden statue of Boccaccio perched on a float, and the duke himself back home for the Carnival. But of Vasari, not a sign. Did you really have to choose this week to go to Arezzo? Oh well, at least give your wife my regards. I am consoled by the thought that she will have the pleasure of your company in my stead, and that she will kiss you just as tenderly as I would have done.

As far as our investigation is concerned, I went to visit Master Francesco Riccio in his cell, since you decided not to take my advice by visiting him yourself. And I am glad I did so, my friend, because I was correct in believing that he might be a useful source of information. First of all, you should know that our man is entirely sane and every bit as lucid as he was back in the days when he wielded such influence over the duke. No doubt you will remember that the duke could never decide on any artistic commission without first consulting his trusted major-domo, a state of affairs that prompted much moaning and resentment among the artists of Florence, including, perhaps, you yourself. It was Riccio, too, who – in concert with Varchi – first brought up the subject of the frescoes at San Lorenzo, and so it is he, just as much if not more than Pontormo, whom you should blame for the perplexity into which those painted walls have plunged you. But I will come back to this.

So, what truly happened? Allow me to report exactly what Francesco told me: in fact, even if his onerous workload had driven him to the edge of exhaustion, his health was never the cause of his fall from grace. The duke claims he removed Francesco from power to protect him because, with what was happening at the Council of Trent, he felt he could no longer guarantee his safety, since his Valdesian beliefs were now considered heretical. But really, the duke, however indulgent he was towards Francesco's ideas, ultimately cared only about his own interests (these are Francesco's words). And so, in his quest for the title of King of Tuscany, His Excellency Cosimo sacrificed his most faithful servant. Master Francesco, though, is fully aware of the imperatives dictated by reasons of state and, while not going quite so far as to be grateful for his master's decision to dismiss him and lock him up, he does not blame him either. Everybody knows that rulers are also servants in a sense, and those of us from the birthplace of Machiavelli understand this better than most.

It has proved impossible for me to verify Francesco's account completely. Perhaps he is right, and perhaps not, when he attributes his fall from grace to the duke's ambitions. But of one thing we can be sure: Francesco Riccio is alive and he is not mad. With those two pieces of information in our possession, we can now deduce with certainty the following conclusion: while someone in the duke's entourage may have had Pontormo killed, the duke himself would not have done so. A man capable of sparing the life of Riccio, despite the difficulties that his philosophical and artistic views might have caused, would never have ordered the death of Pontormo who, whatever you may think of him, remained one of Cosimo's favourite artists. (Moreover, the duke spared Varchi, who is still part of his inner circle, and more powerful than ever, despite – so Riccio assured me – sharing the same forbidden sympathies and having played a similarly important part in organising the frescoes.) So we are in the happy position of being able to rule out a scandalous theory that, I need hardly remind you, was not promulgated by either me or you.

One further word: I went to see Bronzino at San Lorenzo. You know how rarely I disagree with your judgements, which I consider to be the most assured of anyone I know, and how similar our tastes and opinions are in almost all matters. But I saw the frescoes, and they are not what you described. Those piled-up bodies are the most terrible thing I have ever seen, but therein lies their whole value. I see no meanness in Pontormo's images, but the spectacle of humanity in all its grandeur and its misery. If Bronzino carries out his task correctly, as I believe he is capable of doing, then the chancel of San Lorenzo will rival the Sistine. You know as well as I that it is not men who change their tastes, but politics that change men. What shocks people today in those paintings, other than the nudity (which is no longer viewed as acceptable), is the absence of saints (with the exception of St Lawrence, of course), angels, popes and bishops, designed to reaffirm Jesus's pre-eminence over all of them – the very reason that the artist was so bold as to represent him above his own father, because Riccio and Pontormo wanted to promote the idea of a direct relationship between men and their Saviour, without any superfluous intermediaries. And as you also know, now that Rome sees Protestants behind every door, it does not take much to reek of heresy.

I hardly need ask you, my friend, to make sure that this

letter – parts of which might be misunderstood – does not fall into the wrong hands.

46. Giorgio Vasari to Vincenzo Borghini

Arezzo, 10 February 1557

Master Vincenzo, please be assured that I am in despair at not having been able to welcome you on your return, but I very much hope you will wait for me before going to Ferrara, and that we will celebrate our reunion together. This was an unplanned trip that could not have come at a worse time, in the middle of the Carnival, when the shows are never ready until the last minute and everyone is begging me to solve a host of problems, whether painting a theatre set, or supplying straw for the horses, or changing the wheel of a float, or mending a torn costume, or fishing a drunken musician from the Arno . . . Of course, I did not return to Arezzo for personal reasons, but because I was summoned here by the city's Council of Priors, of which I am a member and who elected me their gonfalonier some time ago, with the duke's approval. The Council requested my aid in that capacity for a particularly complicated affair: the hospital in Arezzo has been occupied for months now by some nuns who took refuge there after they were forced to leave their convent by the war in Siena. The Council has not been able to drive them out, and the hospital can no longer heal patients because all the beds are taken by the sisters, whose attitude appears to be that they would rather die than give up their new lodgings. And I am the one tasked with resolving this *casus belli*.

I don't wish to bore you any longer with this farcical tale, however, so let us return to the subject at hand. I am very glad that you went to see the frescoes because I would like your opinion on the part of the Flood that was repainted, with that crude seam that I have still not been able to explain. You knew Pontormo: never would he have tolerated leaving such a flaw; he would have repainted the entire section, or at least Noah's body and the sheep on the right and the giraffe's feet, until he reached the corner of the wall. I was thinking about this, and I had an idea: what if it wasn't Pontormo who repainted that part of the wall? What if someone else retouched Noah, the sheep and the giraffe? Why? I do not have the faintest idea. But, as fanciful as my theory might seem, it is no less implausible than that of Pontormo being sloppy with his seams. I also examined that section as closely as I could, and what I found only intensified my confusion: the draughtsmanship is so faithful to the rest that there seems no doubt that it must be the work of the same artist. But there is something in the colour, insofar as I can judge now that it has almost dried, that strikes me as slightly different; in truth, something that clashes, as if Pontormo had tried too hard to create those acidic tones he was always so fond of: the pink of Noah's loincloth, the bluish glimmers on the sheep's back, the pale yellow of the giraffe . . . as if he had repainted that section in haste, without anticipating how the colour would change when it dried.

But you probably shouldn't give too much credence to the ravings of a madman, Master Vincenzo, for that is what I have become after obsessing over this affair for so long. I do not even know myself why I am about to raise this issue with you, because I am sure it is nonsense, but – amid the confusion caused by what I thought I'd seen in the frescoes – I went back to examine the painting of *Venus and Cupid*, which the duke keeps in his wardrobe. I don't know what I was looking for, or rather I know all too well, because I didn't find it; that painting is a copy, of course, based on Michelangelo's drawing, but I am almost certain that this copy was painted by Pontormo and that nobody else could have inserted the face of the duke's daughter. In any case, I did not spot anything that suggested such a possibility. However, my friend, now that you have seen the frescoes, could you also go to the palace to take a look at Maria's face and give me your opinion? In your wisdom, you may notice something that I missed.

In the meantime, I hope I can find the solution to evict my nuns so that I may return to Florence as soon as possible and hold you in my arms. Then we can go for a fiasco of Trebbiano at Gaddi's because, God willing, I will be back in no time.

47. Sister Catherine de' Ricci to Sister Plautilla Nelli

Prato, 10 February 1557

Forgive them, my God, for they know not what they do! Your portrait is so wonderfully done, Plautilla, that it has made some of the other nuns jealous. Thankfully, the finger that

God pointed at my cradle protected me from the attacks that my status as one of the chosen always provokes, and has since I was a young girl, when I would leave my peers to their children's games so I could act out the mysteries of the Passion in front of the crucifix at the monastery where my parents had placed me. I remember all those who, later, would doubt my ecstasies when our Saviour came to speak to me, and who even suspected me of inflicting the stigmata of the Passion on myself. But while everyone, including Pope Paul III, finally admitted the authenticity of my visions, the message that Christ spoke through my mouth during the twelve years when he visited me every Thursday was not sufficient to wipe from the Earth the sin of envy, which seems to me, and more so every day, the deadliest of all. How deaf people are to the teachings of the Creator!

We must thank God for placing Plautillas on our path while also accepting that life must be filled with the trials He sends us and which it is up to us to overcome. Long ago, it was Sister Marie-Gabrielle Mascalzoni who accused me of imposture. After your departure, when we were all admiring the divine grace of your painting, it was Sister Marie-Séraphine, supported by Sister Marie-Perpétue and Sister Marie-Modeste (may God forgive them) who claimed that I was guilty of pride and hypocrisy in offering my face to your portrait of St Catherine of Siena. A plague upon those slanderous bitches! Thankfully my Lord, who has never abandoned me, came to my rescue once again, striking me with an extraordinary ecstasy, during which Brother Jerome appeared to me in person, half-burned in his habit, a halo shining above his head, and reassured me, since we have no way of knowing what St Catherine of

Siena looked like, that it was wholly just and appropriate for me to offer myself as a model and for you to paint my features as if they were hers, given that I have been walking in her footsteps since the day when I changed my name from Alessandra to Catherine, and given all the indubitable signs God has sent me to encourage me along that path. He added that your painting was so beautiful that it should be seen by everyone, and that is why, with the agreement of the subprioress and the Father Confessor, I have hung it in the refectory so that all the sisters may contemplate it while they eat, at least four times every day (and five times for the more gluttonous among them, for you know that at San Vincenzo not everyone is exempt from that sin. May God help them to find in your painting the inspiration they need to rediscover a temperance more suited to our order).

48. Sister Plautilla Nelli to Sister Catherine de' Ricci

Florence, 11 February 1557

You must know that, deep in my heart, St Catherine of Siena and you are a single being, and I could not have painted her with any other face since I believe that your holiness is already the equal of hers, and I have no doubts concerning your future beatification. In any case, I rejoice at knowing that my portrait pleases you, and even if it is not worthy, I am sensible of the honour you have paid me by hanging it in the refectory at San Vincenzo. Should anyone fall prey to the sin of gluttony in that place, may your image lead our sisters away from their error with the example that you set them – you who, as I have been told and as I have observed for myself, abstain from meat and eggs and eat only vegetables and herbs.

But I do not believe that the sisters of San Vincenzo who are in your care are really such terrible sinners, and if you wish to see a place of perdition then I invite you to come and visit me in Florence, which is, at the moment, not exactly an exemplar of sobriety. As happens every year during the Carnival, the city is soiled by debauchery and drunkenness, so much so that my sisters and I prefer to remain cloistered rather than go out into the streets, which stink so vilely of urine that I imagine you must be able to smell them even in Prato. Such matters are immaterial to me now, however, because I am devoting almost all my time to a painting: a *Deposition* in a new style that I hope you will like at least as much, if not more, than my previous pictures.

49. Marco Moro to Giambattista Naldini

Florence, undated

Allori refuses to cooperate by informing me of his master's comings and goings. If we want to start meeting again, though, we must be certain that Bronzino will not walk in on us unexpectedly. For now, I am not aware of him going back to work on the frescoes in the evenings, but the risk is too great and if he did find us there, we could not be sure that he would keep silent about it. In fact, from what I am told of the situation at court, it seems more likely he would denounce us to the duke. That old madman Pontormo was unpredictable. Bronzino seems less so, which brings certain advantages but also makes him more dangerous, because if he did report anything about our activities, they would listen to him and believe what he said.

I don't need to remind you what is at stake, nor how it concerns you. I am counting on you to convince young Allori, who must, like you, help our cause, even if, like you, he does it for the money.

50. Sandro Allori to Giambattista Naldini

Florence, 11 February 1557

Battista, who the hell is this Marco Moro? The rogue came and gave a long speech and I didn't understand a word of it. By the way, why is it that we painters are affiliated to the Guild of Doctors and Pharmacists?

51. Giorgio Vasari to Vincenzo Borghini

Arezzo, 11 February 1557

You would not believe, Master Vincenzo, how stubbornly those damned Dominican nuns are defending the territory they occupy. Promises, threats . . . nothing does any good: they absolutely refuse to leave, and the Council of Priors has almost been reduced to laying siege to the hospital where they are entrenched. When I went to them, in my position as gonfalonier of Arezzo, they barely even deigned to receive me, saying only that they had no intention of surrendering until we found another building large enough to house all of them.

It is true that I cannot simply send them out into the streets. I wrote to Siena to ask if they could return to their former convent but, with the Sienese government being under Spanish influence, I fear our Imperial allies will not care too much about a few nuns, given how busy they are hunting down the republicans who have taken refuge in Montalcino.

In the meantime, the sick are being treated at the Duomo San Donato, but that is no more than a temporary solution because the parish priest is already complaining about how awkward it is to hold Mass there. That is why the Council of Priors has begged me to stay until we have cleared up this mess, meaning that I must delay my return to Florence by a few days. In all honesty, I do not know how I can resolve this situation and I thought perhaps your Hospital of the Innocents, which is much larger than the one here in Arezzo, might be able to host a few dozen nuns – only temporarily, of course, just while we find them somewhere else to live. What do you say? You would be doing me a huge favour! In any case, I will be in Florence within two days, even if it means launching an assault against the sisters.

52. Vincenzo Borghini to Giorgio Vasari

Florence, 12 February 1557

I fear, Master Giorgio, that we have bigger things to worry about than your nuns, and I would be greatly surprised if, once he has read this letter, the gonfalonier of Arezzo does not jump onto the first charger he can find and ride it at a gallop back to Florence, where more urgent and important duties await him. And yes, since the matter is so close to your heart, I will – for the love I bear you – welcome half a dozen of your nuns (but no more!) to the Innocents. But now, please, forget about that, and forgive me if I cannot bring myself to care very much about these silly little disputes. You can be sure that the hospital in Arezzo is now the least of your concerns. My friend, if I was not at the source of the incredible news that this letter brings you, I wouldn't believe it myself.

Following your instructions, I went to the duke's wardrobe to examine the shameful painting. I was led there by one of the duke's pages, who took me through the labyrinth of messiness that you know all too well, to the cupboard where the picture had been hidden. As God is my witness, Giorgio, I am not the sort of man to tell you tales: the painting was not there. I ordered all the cupboards opened; we spent the whole morning searching every nook and cranny. No sign of the painting anywhere. Alerted by the noise we were making, the duchess – whom I had thought absent, since I hadn't seen her when we passed through her apartments – came to ask what the matter was. I need hardly describe her fury when the reason for our agitation was explained. I thought that she was going to condemn us to the same fate as the Pazzi, and even as I write these lines I am afraid that she still intends to have the page and me hanged, along with everyone else who was present: old Bacchiacca, who was working on the duke's bed; young Buontalenti, who was drawing maps; Cellini, who was cleaning some Etruscan statuettes; not to mention all the guards and valets on the first floor. I am even more fearful, however, that her rage will be as nothing compared to that of the duke, who, thankfully, was away at the time, busy surveying his Kingdom of Tuscany. All the same, I have no doubt that the duchess has alerted him, and we expect his return at any moment. I beg you to hurry, Master Giorgio, if you don't wish to see your friend's body hanging from the windows of the palace, because nobody but you has the duke's ear these days, and you are the only one capable of appeasing his wrath.

53. Giorgio Vasari to the Duke of Florence, Cosimo I

Florence, 13 February 1557

To provide His Illustrious Excellency with the complete and methodically detailed account he demands of the circumstances surrounding the unexplained disappearance of the painting, as noticed on 11 February by Master Borghini, here is the report written at Your Lordship's request by his humble servant Giorgio Vasari, artist, architect, historiographer, and member of His Excellency's Secret Council.

At sext on 11 February, the prefect of the Hospital of the Innocents, Don Vincenzo Borghini, went at Vasari's request to visit Your Excellency's wardrobe so that he could examine said painting in search of any clues that might have escaped our inquisition, and it was on this occasion that the painting was discovered to be missing. Thinking at first that it was simply a mistake, Master Borghini had all the other cupboards opened, without success. Thence it emerged, after noting down the statements on the subject graciously dispensed by Her Excellency the Duchess, that, since the painting had not been moved on the orders of Her Excellency or Your Lordship, it must – however illogical this may appear – have been stolen.

Based on my initial conclusions, drawn up with the cooperation of Your Excellency, the painting must have vanished sometime between 6 February, when Your Greatness saw it inside the cupboard for the last time, and the day before yesterday. During those five days, the following persons were noted to have passed through the wardrobe: Masters Varchi, Borghini, Bacchiacca, Ammannati, Bandinelli, Bronzino, Cellini, Bernadone, the carpenter Girolamo, the stonemason Mariano di Simone, the sand supplier Domenico di Pasquino, Your Excellency's pages, guards, manservants, and a large number of labourers and servants sent there to perform various tasks, the sheer number of which – added to the fact that we do not know the exact day or the exact time when the theft might have taken place – makes it difficult, if not impossible, to suspect one rather than another among such a crowd, for want of a reason that would direct our suspicions in one particular direction, especially since, firstly, nobody saw anything, and, secondly, no painting the shape or size of the stolen one was marked in the register of outgoing objects. Since this image was painted on wood rather than on one of those canvases that painters use increasingly often these days, it would have been impossible to roll it up or hide it in any way, in consequence of which its disappearance seems a mystery verging on the miraculous.

The thief must, though, have found some ingenious method of removing the painting from the palace, whether by fooling the guards or through some other stratagem, because despite our extensive searches it has still not been discovered. Whatever the solution to this mystery, all Your Excellency's informers are busy tracking it down at this very moment, and the Bargello guards are searching the homes of all those who set foot in the palace during those five days. Nevertheless, since His Excellency would prefer to keep this matter quiet, we must act discreetly, which is why the guards are unable to search every house in every quarter of the city.

That being said, since all of this is connected to Pontormo's murder, we are following several other leads, which are, I may assure Your Excellency, at an advanced stage and which promise to bear fruit very soon, namely the search for the woman spotted at the painter's house, and that strange anomaly observed on one of the panels of the frescoes at San Lorenzo. I went back to look at the panel again and remarked that the colours of the retouched part were, as they dried over a period of days, becoming noticeably different from the rest of the painting, to the point that the repainted part was clearly visible, which can signify only one thing: it was painted by a highly skilled artist, but not by Pontormo.

There can be little doubt that solving the mystery of the painter's death will enable us to understand that of the painting and its disappearance. That is why I ask once again for Your Excellency to show the same trust in me that he has so generously shown over the past two years, since I returned to Florence to put myself entirely at his service: with the help of God and the assistance of Prefect Borghini, I promise Your Excellency that I will solve this case and find the painting.

54. Giorgio Vasari to Vincenzo Borghini

Florence, 13 February 1557

Vincenzo, I am entrusting this note to a sergeant of the militia with the hope that it will reach you at the Innocents. I handed my report to the duke, describing the advances of our investigation in the most favourable light possible, but in truth I possess very little to appease his impatience. Those imbeciles at the Bargello are scouring the city to arrest as many prostitutes as they can find: is that how they hope to find our nocturnal visitor? And I, who am no better than they, go with them to give the impression of action, and because I've had enough of standing around at San Lorenzo, ruining my eyes by trying to penetrate the secret of Pontormo's Flood while Bronzino works on the panel of the Resurrection of Souls. Bronzino is not as grumpy as

Pontormo was, but like all artists he hates it when people watch him work, so I decided to leave him in peace. I spent so long examining the fresco that I feel like I am starting to swell up like one of those hideous drowned men, the victims of God's wrath. I admit that there is something impressive about those walls, in the sacred terror they inspire, a feeling that seems only to deepen with prolonged contemplation. In the end I felt like I was suffocating, and now that I am sitting at a table in a brothel in Santo Spirito, writing this letter while all around me the Bargello guards try to grab hold of the honest, half-naked whores who struggle and squeal in protest . . . well, I can breathe again. This happy chaos helps me clear my mind. Obviously, I am not going to find Pontormo's nocturnal female visitor in this place. But since – knowing as we do his tastes in that regard – we can dispense with the theory that he had a romantic rendezvous with a woman, perhaps we must pursue this avenue of thought: the woman did not go to Pontormo's house to find the painter; she went because she knew he wouldn't be there. If I am right about this, then what was she looking for? Presuming that Naldini wasn't lying to us and that this woman truly exists, let us imagine that she came for the painting: in that case, I must admit that we cannot rule out the duchess or her daughter, the only people to our knowledge who have an equally strong motive for getting their hands on the painting, which greatly offended their honour, and for taking revenge on the author of that offence. It is also possible that Naldini did lie to us, and in that case our suspicions must return to him. But there is a third theory that we should take into consideration: Naldini didn't lie; a woman really did enter Pontormo's house by night, but she wasn't there for the painting. But in that case, why was she there? Other than paintings, drawings and sketches, there was nothing to steal. Most of what he kept in his studio was preparatory work for San Lorenzo. There must be a connection between the chancel at San Lorenzo and Pontormo's studio, and that connection concerns the frescoes. But I still don't understand where all this is leading! Please, my friend, I need you to help me clear the thick mist that seems to have descended upon this case. Meet me tonight at Daniello's. We can drink a fiasco of good white wine, and dine on capretto, and if we happen to see Varchi we can ask him for his thoughts on the matter. But not a word about the duchess or her daughter, of course.

55. Giorgio Vasari to Michelangelo Buonarroti

Florence, 14 February 1557

If only you were in Florence, unique and magnificent Master, to see the fresco with your own eyes, because it is your eye and your unparalleled perspicacity that we need. I am now almost certain that the repainting I noticed on the panel of the Flood was not by Pontormo. How do I know? Because, after several weeks of drying, there is a marked difference in the colours. For me, that leads to only one possible explanation: whoever did this did not know the recipes Pontormo used to mix his colours and, failing to anticipate how they would alter as they dried, simply did his best to match them. But if I am right, then the forger did a spectacularly good job of imitating Pontormo's style. This could only be the feat of an extraordinarily skilful and gifted painter. (A supposition that doubly acquits the colour-grinder, since he does know those recipes but has no skill at painting.) Of course, there is no lack of talented painters in Florence, and that means we must suspect them all, with the exception of Master Salviati, who has been in France for the past year, where he is decorating the Cardinal of Lorraine's chateau. But suspect them of what? Of repainting part of a wall? I still cannot make the connection between this painting and Pontormo's death, and yet the two must be inextricably linked. Is it possible Pontormo found someone repainting his Flood? He hated the idea of anyone even seeing his work, so how would he have reacted to such a violation? Did he grow angry? Was there an argument? Could it have escalated into a brawl, during which the intruder hit him over the head with a hammer before killing him with a chisel? If the scene I have just imagined bears any resemblance, even a distant one, to what really happened near the altar at San Lorenzo, then we must assume that the motive for the killing was some form of rivalry. If we add to that the unbelievable skill with which our intruder counterfeited Pontormo's style, then everything converges on one man. I do not believe young Naldini capable, at this point in his apprenticeship, of imitating his master so perfectly. In truth, of all the students who passed through Pontormo's studio, there is only one who can claim sufficient mastery. Tell me, divine Master, what you think of these flights of fancy, which are boiling my brains and costing me sleep, but which I must first disprove before I can dismiss them entirely.

56. Agnolo Bronzino to Michelangelo Buonarroti

Florence, 15 February 1557

It is a unique task that I have been assigned by the unfathomable workings of Fate: first it brought me great sorrow by taking Jacopo from me, and then great honour by ordering me to complete his work. May God grant that I am worthy of it, but if it turns out that I am not up to the task, it will not be due to a lack of passion or self-sacrifice.

I am not going to teach the divine Michelangelo what it means to devote oneself, body and soul, to one's art. Nevertheless, I wanted to share with you a feeling that you have perhaps forgotten because I doubt whether you have ever devoted your genius to the service of another, at least not since the time when you were a young apprentice with Ghirlandaio. So you will perhaps not believe the state – a mixture of exaltation and anguish – into which my work at San Lorenzo has plunged me. Heavy is the burden of finishing Jacopo's frescoes. But great is my joy at walking in his footsteps! Day after day, I enter the spectacle of these walls – his Flood, his Christ, his Moses, his drowned men, his bestiary – and I live among lions, giraffes and sheep, I tremble before God's wrath, I get drunk with Noah, I die with the dead, am resurrected with the chosen, I climb aboard the Ark then ascend to Heaven with the other souls, and while I exhaust myself forever searching for the right tone, my hands bleed like those of Adam and Eve as they bend to their labours . . . Am I in Heaven or in Hell? I could not say. I am like Eurydice walking behind Orpheus; I plant my feet in Jacopo's footprints; I am his shadow, and yet I remain at the mercy of his genius. When I paint after him, when I press my brush to the wall, I barely even notice the presence all around me of those irritating people who come to see my work and his. I am alone with Jacopo. I must feel like him, see like him, paint like him, think like him. I must adopt his language. My voice must become as one with his. I must sink into his soul. Of course, nobody knew him better than I, and I remember the time when people would get our work confused, so strongly had his teaching forged in me a comparable style. But you know, divine Master, that style is nothing without spirit, or rather style and spirit are one and the same. The more I work on his frescoes, the more I feel as if I am penetrating his secret. But even you, peerless Master, whose genius is more divine than earthly, must have felt sometimes how fragile are the sources of inspiration: at any moment, the spell can be broken. At any moment, Jacopo's ghost might return, point an accusing finger at me and, without needing to utter a word, dismiss me as an impostor. I must advance, calm and resolute, through the dark forest of his soul, recognising each tree, each branch, each clump of earth, the texture of moss on a root, knowing when to add a singing bird, a fox emerging from its den, mushrooms growing in shade, a sow suckling her little ones, a trickle of sap on a tree trunk. I must be at home in his work. I must live inside Jacopo.

And at the same time, I cannot cease being myself. I am like an interpreter, translating the speech of a foreigner, reproducing what he hears as faithfully as possible while choosing his own words. In short, I must become Pontormo while remaining Bronzino. I must not merely imitate him. I must become him. I cannot cease being myself, but nobody else must know this. Except, perhaps, for someone who knows me and my art as well as I know Jacopo and his.

For technical questions, I am, thankfully, able to depend on his colour-grinder, who teaches me about his preparation and his mixes, and who helps me keep the same tones he chose when he was still living. I wish more than anything that you could give me your opinion of my work. I am almost certain that the duke, Vasari and all the other Florentines will not be able to tell what is mine and what Jacopo's, and I take no particular pride in that. But it is to your eye, the supreme test, that I would like to expose our work – Jacopo's and mine.

By now you will have guessed my intentions, Master Michelangelo, the single great glory of arts and letters: I dream, as we all do here, of seeing you return to your homeland. And in my case, I dream it not only for the radiance that your genius would spread over all of us, but for the honour you would do me of coming to visit me at San Lorenzo. By the time that blessed day arrives, I do not know whether Vasari will have allowed me to correct the very slight alteration of colours in Noah's head, which happens to be the last part of the wall that Jacopo painted – the very reason why Vasari will not let me touch it. Not that it matters too much, since, other than the slight excess of acidity in the colours, the subtlety of the line and the beauty of the rendering shine through just as brightly as all the rest.

57. Michelangelo Buonarroti to Giorgio Vasari

Rome, 16 February 1557

Master Giorgio, my dear friend, as God is my witness, it was very much against my will and with the greatest repugnance that I obeyed the pope's order, ten years ago, to oversee the construction of St Peter's in Rome. Moreover, if we had continued working upon it as we did back then, that building would by now have reached a stage that would enable me to go to Florence as I wish. But the lack of funding slowed everything, just when we were about to tackle the most important and most difficult parts of the project. If I were to abandon St Peter's now, I would bring shame upon myself; and it would be a sin to forfeit the reward for all the troubles I've endured over the past decade for the love of God.

To return to the subject that concerns us now, it is true that I would have to see this repainted section of wall myself, since you seem to be focusing your investigation so strongly in that direction. But are you sure that only Bronzino could have repainted Noah with his giraffe and his sheep? Have you seen Naldini's most recent work? Perhaps the boy has progressed more quickly than you could imagine. Bronzino himself has a young assistant, Sandro Allori, whose qualities he is always praising – and rightly so, to judge by what I saw him produce during his stay in Rome. And what about you yourself? Couldn't you, too, have repainted that part of the wall? You see, if you really think about it, Florence does not lack for possible suspects. Moreover, it is not absolutely certain that the person who repainted Noah is also the murderer; nor can the possibility be ruled out, despite your brilliant deductions, that Pontormo himself repainted his work. Your suspicions are based on the notion that this would contradict both the rules of fresco painting and what you know of Pontormo – an offence to your love of logic. But haven't you yourself suggested to me on several occasions that Master Pontormo was a little eccentric, to say the least, and possibly even half-mad? I am not trying to lead this investigation in your stead, I simply wish to caution you. To my mind, it would be premature to accuse Bronzino because, quite simply, you have no proof. It is not enough to profit from a crime to be guilty of it. The Duke Cosimo is the living proof of that, given that he became the ruler of Florence at seventeen years old following a murder that he did not plan or commit.

58. Michelangelo Buonarroti to Agnolo Bronzino

Rome, 17 February 1557

Master Agnolo, as God is my witness, it was very much against my will and with the greatest repugnance that I obeyed the pope's order, ten years ago, to oversee the construction of St Peter's in Rome. Moreover, if we had continued working upon it as we did back then, that building would by now have reached a stage that would enable me to go to Florence as I wish. But the lack of funding slowed everything, just when we were about to tackle the most important and most difficult parts of the project. If I were to abandon St Peter's now, I would bring shame upon myself; and it would be a sin to forfeit the reward for all the troubles I've endured over the past decade for the love of God.

I wish it were otherwise, believe me, because your letter has excited my curiosity, giving me, if that were possible, an even more urgent desire to see this fresco – an ambition that I still one day hope to fulfil before God calls me to Him – once you have completed it, for I consider you a most excellent painter who does not suffer in comparison with your late, lamented master. Regarding the strangeness of the colouring that you mention, if you think that this section of the painting impairs the whole, you should paint over it entirely. If, on the other hand, you believe that the incongruity is so slight as to be hardly noticeable, then perhaps you may leave it as it is.

As for your supposition that I have never found myself in your position – taking over and completing another artist's work – you flatter me, my dear Agnolo, but you are thinking about it only in terms of painting. What do you imagine I have been doing in Rome all these years? Nobody can deny that Bramante was, in architectural terms, the greatest of them all since ancient times. He it was who drew up the plans for St Peter's so that the building would not be full of darkness but rather clear and precise, its surroundings bright and secluded so as not to interfere with any other line of the palace. Just as you are protecting Pontormo's work from the duchess, who urges its destruction, it is Bramante's legacy that I wish to defend and to safeguard against that stupid Sangallo (may God have pity on his soul) and all the enemies of art who are spreading through Rome now, as they are through all of Italy.

59. Marco Moro to Giambattista Naldini

Florence, 17 February 1557

Do you believe, Battista, that your situation in life is closer to mine or to your master's? Now that he is dead, have you taken his place? Strange, isn't it, that it's Bronzino who I see at San Lorenzo every day, not you? It's Bronzino who is visited by the duke and invited to the palace. It's Bronzino who wears those handsome courtier's clothes, while you are dressed in grease-stained rags. It's Bronzino who rubs shoulders with the nobility, and paints their portraits, and is treated as an equal by Varchi, Vasari, Borghini *et al.* But who cares about you? How long do you think they'll let you stay in your master's house? It's Bronzino who will inherit it and who will tell you to leave. Bronzino or some long-lost cousin – just you wait and see.

Pontormo didn't treat you as his student, but as his manservant. I ground his colours and you did his shopping. He was never satisfied and spent all his time yelling at us both. The difference is that I would leave him when my day's work was over, while you slept in his house. You apprentices are always boasting about your skill at drawing. However, I don't see what good those abilities have done you. How much knowledge of painting, sculpture, drawing or music does anyone need in order to go to the market and buy groceries for dinner?

Have you forgotten, Battista, how you constantly cursed your master? Were you satisfied with your situation back then? And, since his death, has it improved? You will tell me that Bronzino used to be in your place, and that one day your time may come. But listen to me, comrade, when I tell you this: not everybody can be Michelangelo. I have dug up some information on this Sandro Allori: he is the son of a prosperous blacksmith who made his money selling swords. He is also the grandson, on his mother's side, of a bourgeois Pisan. His father is an old friend of Bronzino's, and the artist would go to his house every day to eat lunch. So now I understand why he refuses to help us. But who are you? Son of a sailor, brought up at the Innocents, bought rather than adopted by an irritable old painter who treated you like a slave. They are the *popolo grasso* who made a pact with the nobility after vainly dreaming of taking their place, just as the Medici once took the place of the Albizzi and the Strozzi. But you are the *popolo minuto*, and if you don't watch out you'll soon be dragged back into the plebeian mass you thought you'd escaped.

Don't wait for that moment, Battista! Join us now! If the class of artisans, shopkeepers and apprentices allies its strength with labourers, servants and sales assistants, we will all benefit, because we will carry enough weight to demand the creation of new guilds, not vertical in structure but interdisciplinary, which will earn us new rights. The major and minor arts have always been divided into specialist domains, lined up like ancient pillars: cloth, banking, wool, silk . . . Their representatives are always wealthy merchants, irrespective of what they sell, and never the people who work for them. But doesn't a wool carder have more in common with a silk weaver than with the merchant who employs him? Just as a messenger is closer in status to a sales assistant than to a moneychanger. And what about you, Battista? What do you think is the surest way of improving your lot? Waiting for the nobles to deign to notice your work and honour you with a commission? But why would they do that, when they could give the work to a Bronzino or a Vasari or a Salviati or a Bandinelli? You may as well buy a lottery ticket, because I doubt whether all those men will be so obliging as to get themselves murdered. And when Bronzino finally does pass away, who will they think of to succeed him – you or Allori? You must see how hazardous that path is. I am offering you another way. It is not without its obstacles, but it would rescue you from solitude by giving you the brothers you have never had, because I would bet you anything that Allori will never be a brother to you. I am really not asking anything very onerous of you: the next time you see him, find out which night Bronzino is inviting someone to supper – and let me know as quickly as you can.

60. Malatesta de' Malatesti to Maria de' Medici

Florence, 17 February 1557

Be of good cheer, madame, because the object of your displeasure has disappeared, thanks to an enchantment that leaves me with a sense of pride in having helped in its success and an even greater feeling of joy at knowing that you have been freed from the torment that was keeping you awake at night. I want your dreams to be shaped by love, not anguish, for that is what you deserve as the princess you are, and that is why I respectfully propose myself as the substance of those dreams, since, according to what you were generous enough to intimate to me, my person does not leave you indifferent. And so I flatter myself, with an audacity that continues to stupefy me, that I can be the one to sweeten your nightly visions.

Nevertheless, while the peril that threatened your reputation has been removed, the one that threatens to consume your entire life is still hiding just behind the door, ready to burst into your bedroom and slither between your sheets. Tell me, I beg you, if you have changed your mind. Can you now imagine yourself without dread as the Duke of Ferrara's wife? Is the goddess who gave me her lips really prepared to give the rest of herself to another man? One word from you and I would, regretfully, disappear; I would leave your father's service and you would never hear from me again.

But if your feelings remain unchanged (as I would like to believe, because I can hardly doubt that constancy is one of your many qualities), then rejoice: you are free, or very nearly so. France awaits. Bring only what is necessary. Do you have a maid or a confidante who would be prepared to come with us? I will take care of finding the carriage and horses. You need only choose the day of our departure. I entreat you to hurry, though. Remember the nature of the man to whom you are betrothed, and that every passing day takes you closer to that horrific marriage.

61. Piero Strozzi, Marshal of France, to Benvenuto Cellini

Rome, 17 February 1557

So, my friend, what is the story? All of Florence is abuzz at your exploits, and yet you remain silent. You did not accustom us to such modesty when you were at King François's court. The queen is burning to know how the devil you accomplished it, particularly since Her Majesty – I can confess this to you now – did not have absolute confidence in you, at least as concerned the success of this enterprise. Above all, let me know how you plan to smuggle the object out of the city; if by any chance you need my help, I will see what resources I can place at your disposal. There are, thank God, still men in Florence who would be ready to aid you, out of love for my family and for the Republic. Tell me what you need, my friend, and in the meantime I am sending you the queen's warmest congratulations, in addition to my own. What you achieved is a stroke of genius. There are few men in this world who could live up to such a reputation as yours. Now all you need do is put the finishing touches to your work by coming to Rome, where you will be welcomed with all the fanfare you have merited. There is no lack of work here for an artist of your abilities, and even if the pope is no great friend of the arts, we – the Strozzi – are, as are the other exiled republicans. And if that is not enough for you, I will introduce you to the great Roman families the Orsini and the Colonna (for I think you already know the Farnese). As soon as you are here, I will organise a great banquet in your honour, and I will invite Michelangelo too, if that would please you, for he has been a good friend of mine these past twenty-two years, since I took him in and cared for him after the siege of Florence. But if you prefer to return to France – where I will no doubt be myself, as soon as the Duke of Guise, who wants to march on Naples with my men, has abandoned that insane idea – then the welcome there will be no less agreeable, and Queen Catherine will personally ensure that you do not lack for commissions. So hurry, Benvenuto, because wherever you go – to France or to Rome – you will be greeted like the hero that you are.

62. Maria de' Medici to Malatesta de' Malatesti

Florence, 18 February 1557

How eager you seem, my dear friend, to tear me away from the love of my parents! I must admit that your letter alarmed me. Do you really think I could just pack up and flee like a Bohemian? And besides, who says that my reputation has been saved? I know that the cursed painting is no longer in my father's wardrobe, but how can I be sure it has been destroyed? Did you burn it? Would you bring me those ashes? For all I know – and this is the impression I have from the reactions of my mother, whose wails echo around the palace, and my father, who has been plunged into a state of permanent wrath – the horrible object has not yet been discovered . . . and therefore it remains possible that it will, at any instant, reappear. At least when the painting was in my father's possession, he could make sure that nobody saw it. Whereas now, if it falls into the wrong hands, who knows what will be done with it, and in that case what will become of poor Maria?

63. Malatesta de' Malatesti to Maria de' Medici

Florence, 19 February 1557

I throw myself at your feet, madame, to beg your forgiveness. You are right to reproach me for my unparalleled brusqueness. What a brute I was, to order a young girl to leave her house, her family, her homeland, to set off on a wild adventure like some vagabond, without even a backward glance! I may as well have told you to jump out of the window in the middle of a stormy night.

However, I implore you to consider this: no matter what happens, you will not live at the palace for much longer. I know you do not wish to leave your beautiful Florence, but since that must occur anyway, let it be for Paris and not Ferrara! In France, you will find not a Duke of Este who is a stranger to you, but an aunt who is queen and who has proved her love for you, by ordering an extremely delicate operation from hundreds of miles away. Above all, you will have me alongside you to watch over you and to cherish you tenderly until death.

As for the painting, have no fear: it is in the hands of one of our men, for whom I would answer with my life.

64. Benvenuto Cellini to Piero Strozzi (copied to Catherine de' Medici, Queen of France)

Florence, 19 February 1557

The superhuman task with which you entrusted me, my Lord Marshal, is on the way to being accomplished even if it is not quite yet done. Allow me to recount the extraordinary circumstances of the current situation as it pertains to our affair, and to explain to you why I have not yet deposited the object at your feet.

Perseus killed Medusa with the sword of his courage and the shield of his cunning, and I have never used any weapon other than those two while surviving the plague, the sack of Rome, the siege of Florence or the dungeons of the Vatican.

So, while I was prowling around the duke's wardrobe, pretending to work on a small golden vase engraved in bas-relief with figures and other beautiful decorations, a young whippersnapper approached me with a face that signalled conspiracy at a hundred leagues. I would have kicked him out of the room had I not soon gleaned from the gibberish that he whispered to me that you had sent me this snot-nosed little brat to show me where the painting was hidden, which he then did by pointing at the cupboard in question. The most difficult part of the enterprise was thus taken care of, for now I had only to carry the painting under my arm in plain sight of the entire court, the palace guards, and the duke and duchess themselves. Yes, alas, the duke spends a great deal of time in his wardrobe, since he takes so much pleasure in watching me work. Thankfully, affairs of state drew him far from Florence, so that obstacle was at least momentarily removed. But it meant that I absolutely had to act before he returned.

The problem was that, with or without the duke, I still had to contend with that crowd of unwelcome guests, starting with old Bacchiacca, who was building the duke's bed as slowly as if he were working on a Venetian galleass. There were also some young goldsmiths who were constantly asking me questions because they wanted to find out the secrets of my art; Varchi, who was forever walking around with some Turkish ambassador or Roman cardinal or German upholsterer or Imperial emissary; those cockroaches Bandinelli and Ammannati; and that chamber pot Vasari. But when Vasari, too, was forced to leave Florence on a mission whose purpose I never discovered, I understood that God was offering me the opportunity I had been awaiting.

Outside, the Carnival festivities were still going on. At nightfall, when the first explosions of fireworks were heard, the young goldsmiths, guided by their desire to enjoy the spectacle, went running to the palace windows. Soon, alerted by their shouts of enthusiasm, everyone in the wardrobe went to join them, save for Bacchiacca. With the master of the wardrobe busy working on his registers, I was thus left alone with the old man. Great Caesar was quick in thought and deed, and so am I. I ran to the cupboard, removed the painting, then slid it under the bedframe so that nobody could see it unless they lay on the floor. As I listened to the fireworks crackling in crescendo and the admiring cries of my colleagues, I nailed the painting in place with the aid of some planks, forming a sort of coffer under the bed that rendered it perfectly invisible. Poor Bacchiacca watched in amazement as I accomplished all this in the blink of an eye. Before the others came back, I told him to keep his mouth shut or I would kill him. And since he knows me, because he's an old friend, he will obey. At first, nobody noticed that the painting had been moved, but to allay suspicions I kept going back to the palace every day until its disappearance was discovered – by that idiot Borghini.

Now they are searching the whole city for the painting, which remains where I left it. I am not unhappy with this master stroke, but you see, Lord Strozzi, that the Queen of France will have to wait a little longer before she has her Pontormo.

65. Malatesta de' Malatesti to Maria de' Medici

Florence, 20 February 1557

I recently remembered a story of long ago, and I am going to tell it to you, madame, for your benefit and, perhaps, for mine. There was once a young man who fled a civil war in England, where he had been a moneychanger, and returned to Florence to see his uncles. As he was passing through Bruges, he met a young Englishwoman who was also fleeing her homeland, for reasons that she kept secret – along with her identity, for she was disguised as a priest. The two young people became friends and decided to travel towards

Italy together. They stopped at an inn that was full, so they had to share the last vacant bed. When the young man discovered that, rather than a priest, the person sharing his bed was a woman with plump, firm, delicate breasts, and when she told him about the love she had felt for him since they had begun their journey together, he was delighted and, without knowing anything else about her, agreed to marry her. And so, sitting on the bed in front of a painting of Our Lord and placing a ring in his hand, she became his wife. And then they spent the rest of the night in each other's arms, romping on the bed to their mutual pleasure.

The virgin turned out to be no lesser personage than the daughter of the King of England; her father wanted to marry the very old King of Scotland, and that was why she had fled, disguised as a man, taking some of the crown jewels with her – to Rome, where she intended to throw herself at the mercy of the pope. When she did finally reach the Vatican and was presented to His Holiness, she asked him to openly bless the marriage she had entered into with the young Florentine in the sole presence of God. And the pope, realising that no backward step was possible, granted her request. Then, after solemnly blessing the union, he told the newlyweds they were free to go. The princess and the young moneychanger decided to go to Florence, and then to Paris, where they were received with great honour by the King of France. From there, two knights who had been escorting the lady returned to England, where they spoke so eloquently to the king that he forgave her, and she and her husband were welcomed to the English royal palace. A little later, the young Florentine was knighted, and the King of England gave him the county of Cornwall.

The young man showed such merit as a lord that he succeeded in reconciling the son with the father and bringing an end to the war, leading to a period of peace and prosperity on that island and earning the lord of Cornwall the favour and love of all the country's inhabitants.

I hope, madame, that you enjoyed this true story as much as I did, and that it will inspire you in your future conduct and choices.

66. Maria de' Medici to Catherine de' Medici, Queen of France

Florence, 22 February 1557

Aunt, forgive me for turning to you once again, but I must talk to someone I can trust. You have been so generous to me! And I so desperately need your advice. The young knight Malatesta is urging me to leave Florence with him, like a thief in the night. He claims that the painting is in a safe place. What should I do? I am the duke's daughter, not a thief. How could I run away, like a vagabond? It would be a betrayal of my father, and as for my mother, I fear she would die of grief. I feel certain she would not survive the loss of a single one of her children. In fact, I don't care about that painting. Come what may, I am a Medici. I belong to my family, to my clan, to Florence and to God.

But I must confess something. As my father's page, Malatesta has the right to move around the palace as he wishes, and one night he sneaked into my bedroom to have a talk with me about the preparations for our secret departure. He wanted us to leave that very night, and to convince me, he held me by the waist and whispered into my ear so as not to wake my lady's companion, who was sleeping in the room next door. The knight was so insistent and his hands held me so tightly. I swear to you that I wanted to resist, but it was as if my body refused to obey me, and it – not me, for I was saying 'No! No!' – surrendered to his caresses. I couldn't call for help because the servants would have found him in my room, and my father, I am certain, would have had him hanged. I had no dagger to act like Lucretia and I was not myself, in any case, for my heart was consumed by a burning fire. I thought I was going to faint. I was terribly frightened that someone would catch us in the act, but thankfully nobody heard anything and Malatesta left me in the middle of the night without being seen, after swearing eternal oaths to me. He says that we are married before God, and by way of proof he says that at some point – I do not know when, or about what – I said 'yes'. But I do not believe that my father would share his point of view. He is not in Florence at the moment, thank God, because I would not be able to look him in the eye.

I spent the rest of the night in such a state of stupor and agitation that I could not fall asleep, and since this morning I have not been able to stop crying, so much so that my mother, unaware of the true reason, is worried that I am ill. Oh, how wretched I am! There was a moment that night when I no longer knew what I was doing, and I thought I was going to die. It probably would have been better if I had. For the love of God, tell me what I should do. Or am I lost? Now I think about it, why didn't he simply destroy the painting, if it's in his possession? Oh, I feel like I'm going mad! You are the only one who can help me, and you are so far away. I am entrusting this letter to my faithful chambermaid, who knows how to have it delivered to the French court without raising suspicion.

67. Catherine de' Medici, Queen of France, to Maria de' Medici

Fontainebleau, 25 February 1557

My dear child, do not torture yourself more than necessary, and allow me to pass on to you a few lessons that life has taught me. The most important point of your story is that you managed not to cry out. That is a very good thing, because for us women it is public shame that is most to be feared, and whatever your confessor might say – if you are silly enough to tell him about your nocturnal adventure – it is not a sin to sin in silence. I remember something an older woman told me when I was younger than you are now: honour is nothing more than the opinion of the world, and that is why a woman must use all her talent to ensure that people do not tell tales about her. Honour, essentially, consists not in what you do or do not do, but in the idea of yourself – positive or negative – that you give the world. Sin if you must, but guard your reputation. In your situation, the surest way of ensuring that outcome is to secretly marry your page. What I mean by this is not that you should merely exchange oaths before God in the solitude of your bedroom, but that you should repeat them in front of a priest; in this way, you can correct what will become merely a momentary lapse that you will bury deep in your heart and that you alone will remember. Once you are reconciled with God, there is no reason why you cannot appear before your parents in the arms of your husband. They will be angry, of course, but they will have no choice but to accept the situation once they witness the touching scene of their daughter married to an honest knight who has fulfilled all his duties: the very proof that, once again, despite everything, God's will has been done.

68. Catherine de' Medici, Queen of France, to Piero Strozzi, Marshal of France

Fontainebleau, 25 February 1557

Now, this is success, cousin! What does it matter that the painting has been moved, if it has not left the palace, and if your man still isn't in a position to bring it to us?

Young Maria, who has more common sense than you and Cellini put together, has grasped the situation perfectly: she will not move until she receives proof that the object is in our hands or has been destroyed. Not that it really matters. In fact it is better this way. If she were to come to Henri's court to marry her lover, and France were to welcome her with open arms, it would inevitably be seen for what it is: not merely an act of provocation, but a declaration of war against the duke, who would undoubtedly discern my hand behind this venture. Our relations may be frosty, but I would prefer to avoid, as much as possible, any unnecessary diplomatic complications. We do not need to add another crisis to the perils and disturbances that already trouble Christendom. But a crisis in Florence? Yes, absolutely. As long as France is not directly implicated. In politics as in all things, the first rule is always: do not get caught. And the second: strike quickly, and by surprise. If ever the poor child did decide to elope with her page, the best thing would be to send her to Venice or Navarre or some other remote province.

69. Piero Strozzi, Marshal of France, to Catherine de' Medici, Queen of France

Rome, 1 March 1557

You are decidedly harsh, cousin, on a man whom, for my part, I consider extremely resourceful and who has described to me his latest feat, of which I am a little jealous, in truth, since it is so perfectly conceived and executed that I wish, I confess, that I had carried it out myself. You asked for audacity, and he offers you something even nobler and rarer: imagination. Now that everybody thinks the painting stolen, it will be far easier to steal it. While the Bargello guards are busy searching the city, nobody will think to watch the wardrobe. They are searching everywhere except in the very place where the painting is hidden: therein lies the genius! True, we are only halfway there, but I think I can say that the hardest part is behind us. With all eyes turned away from the palace, the guards' vigilance regarding what is taken out of there will undoubtedly be diminished.

Patience, cousin: your plan is working perfectly. As for the possibility of young Maria eloping with her page, I can only encourage you to fan the flames. Nothing could thrill me more than the success of a plot that will humiliate both the Duke of Florence and the Duke of Este, whom everybody agrees is a prize ass.

70. A manifesto from Marco Moro to the workers of the Arte dei Medici e Speziali

Florence, 1 March 1557

A spectre haunts Italy – the spectre of the Ciompi Revolt! All the princes and nobles of this land, from Naples to Venice, who have been tearing each other to pieces for years, ravaging our cities and our fields, would reconcile within the hour, from the pope to the emperor, and join forces to prevent this spectre from rising again: the alliance of the common people and the plebs.

When the guilds were created, many trades carried out by the common people and the plebs were not represented by a guild. So they were affiliated with various arts, the ones that were closest to their professions. As a result, when they were not paid enough for their work or when they were oppressed by their masters, their sole recourse was to the head of the guild with which they were affiliated, and they never obtained justice.

That was the age when the Guelphs and the Ghibellines were fighting a never-ending war whose causes nobody could remember. When the Guelphs finally triumphed and expelled every Ghibelline out of Florence, the victors split into two new factions, Whites and Blacks, so they could continue their meaningless war. Who won, White Guelphs or Black Guelphs? Why should we care? You may as well ask the lamb which colour it favours for the fur of the wolf that eats it. In the sad world where we live, nine hundred out of a thousand live like sheep, heads bent to the ground, weighed down by dark thoughts, while a handful buy their way to Heaven by profiting from the work of others. If you observe human conduct, you will see that all of the wealthiest and most powerful men have succeeded purely through fraud or through force; you will see that they hide the turpitude of their conquests under the name of profit, legitimising what they have usurped through trickery or violence. Those who do not follow these methods, due to a lack of prudence or excessive stupidity, end up sinking into bondage or penury. Faithful servants remain servants, and good men remain poor.

I hear some who call for the Republic. But what is the point of the Republic if power remains in the hands of the few, to the detriment of the many? Do you really want another farcical situation where lots are drawn from purses and the same names keep coming up? Do you believe that, if the Strozzi returned, they would care about you? Why should it matter to us whether we are governed by one man or several? What we want is not the Republic but justice, or in other words a Republic for all.

Some people, among them the most fatalistic, aspire to the Kingdom of God, placing their hopes in a celestial afterlife to console them for their earthly suffering. But what we seek is not a paradise after we are dead. We seek the Kingdom of God on Earth, here and now, in Florence, in the year of Our Lord 1557.

When the Ciompi stormed the palace, this is what they demanded, and this is what they got: to form three new guilds, the first for carders and dyers, the second for barbers, doublet makers, tailors and other manual arts of the same order, the third for the common people; to always have three members of the government from these three new guilds; to grant these new guilds places where they might assemble; to spare their members from the requirement, in the next two years, to repay a debt of less than fifty ducats; to demand that the public treasury cease charging interest on debts and claim only the capital. But because they were not organised and were betrayed by their leaders, the rich soon took back from the Ciompi what they had gained through their audacity.

One hundred and seventy years later, we do not ask for more than the people asked for back then, but to secure it we will act with prudence and not impetuosity, with patience and without chaos, and when we are sufficiently powerful and organised, we will obtain all that the Ciompi obtained. But, unlike our brothers of yore, we will not let anyone take it back from us.

71. Sister Catherine de' Ricci to Sister Plautilla Nelli

Prato, 1 March 1557

The devil, sister, is decidedly not lacking in weaponry in his war against our poor, persecuted Holy Church.

I received your painting. Thankfully, nobody else has seen it. How could I possibly show it to anyone? I am afraid, my poor Plautilla, that seeing Pontormo's obscene paintings must have made you lose your reason. Why would you choose to pay tribute to our Lord Jesus Christ by imitating the style of that cursed sodomite? Must I remind you that he is burning in Hell at this very moment, by the grace of God? No, of course not.

All that flesh! The body appears – may God forgive me – both rotten and sensual, exciting ignoble instincts among those who surround the subject and who ought to be weeping at such a spectacle rather than looking ecstatic. 'It is the Spirit who gives life; the flesh profits nothing.' Have you forgotten those words from John? The art of painting, which was merely a simple servant, has – like a prostitute – seduced many sons of the Church, dragging it down into the desire for flesh. Housewives sometimes mix poison with flour and carelessly hide it somewhere to kill vermin. But their children find the flour and eat it, unaware of the poison within, and the flour kills them.

The painter's ambition is to lead men to some virtuous ideal by means of a suitable representation, just as food may seem disgusting if it is represented in an abominable light, or appetising if represented in a more beautiful and admirable light. Why, my dear sister, did you turn away from your former style, so pure, so true, so innocent? I beg you, for the love of God, pull yourself together before Satan insinuates himself all the way inside you. Wake up, Plautilla! I await your next visit. We will begin a new portrait together. Nothing has changed, isn't that so? Everything will return to the way it was.

72. Giorgio Vasari to Vincenzo Borghini

Florence, 2 March 1557

Vincenzo, my friend, please drop everything and go to the convent of Santa Caterina. A letter of the greatest interest has been found by our agents who searched a messenger coming from Prato. I will leave the palace with a guard of six men and meet you there. We will wait for you outside San Marco.

73. Sister Petronilla Nelli to Sister Catherine de' Ricci

Florence, 2 March 1557

Sister, please forgive my hand for the trembling that prevents it from correctly forming these words, which I scrawl in haste. This morning, something unprecedented occurred. The prioress of our convent, to whom I am linked by blood, for she is also my younger sister, was arrested by the duke's men. Eight guards came to lead her away. They barely even gave her time to put on a cloak. While they were searching her room, I ran to her, alerted by the unusual agitation, and she was able to whisper to me that I must warn you. That is what I am doing now, in the hope that you will be able to help rescue me from the confusion into which this inconceivable event has plunged me. What is going on? What do they want with her? What will happen to her? None of the men would answer my questions. Please enlighten me, for the love of God, because the only thing I was able to understand was this: they were looking for a painting.

74. Vincenzo Borghini to Giorgio Vasari

Prato, 3 March 1557

Master Giorgio, this may interest you. We arrived at the convent of San Vincenzo just before supper and we summoned Sister Catherine de' Ricci. We showed her the letter. She did not appear overly troubled by it, but she was not able to offer any satisfactory explanation of what she had meant by 'Pontormo's obscene paintings'. On the other hand, we found several books by the Dominican friar Girolamo Savonarola in her room, and in the hearth we discovered the burnt remains of what might well have been a painting whose size and shape correspond quite closely with the one we are looking for, although obviously the state of the object – practically reduced as it was to ashes – makes it impossible to affirm that with any certainty. We also confiscated her correspondence.

I plan to return to Florence this evening, where I will take Sister Catherine to the palace so that you can interrogate her yourself at first light tomorrow.

75. Giorgio Vasari to the Duke of Florence, Cosimo I

Florence, 5 March 1557

To immediately inform His Most Illustrious Excellency of the new evidence relating to the death of Pontormo and the disappearance of the painting, this memorandum is composed by your devoted servant, based on the words of two Dominican nuns: Sister Plautilla Nelli, prioress at the convent of Santa Caterina on Piazza San Marco, née Pulisena Margherita, daughter of Piero di Luca, merchant; and Sister Catherine de' Ricci, prioress of the convent of San Vincenzo in Prato, née Alessandra Lucrezia Romola, daughter of Pier Francesco, banker; the two women having been questioned separately and continually at the palace from daybreak on Sunday 3 March until nones today.

These two nuns, belonging to the order of St Dominic and – as is often the case with Dominicans – influenced by the memory and the writings of the late friar Girolamo

Savonarola, felt compelled to hunt down the impiety that reigns (according to them) in the society of Florentine artists in the service of Your Excellency, and particularly that of the painters, whom they describe (each separately, with only slight variations in the phrasing) as 'degenerate sodomites with bestial morals, whose souls will rot in Hell'.

Having heard rumours about the frescoes at San Lorenzo, and wishing to verify for themselves the evil that those walls were supposed to harbour, presumably in order to loudly denounce them afterwards, they decided that at least one of their number ought to try to see them, so that they could establish incontrovertibly the blasphemous character of said paintings. And so they chose Sister Plautilla, since she lived in Florence, not far from the chapel, while the other lived in Prato.

It has now been established that Sister Plautilla entered – on several occasions, always at night – the chapel of San Lorenzo, with the complicity of the verger, who let her in (he says) due to her status as a religious leader, in contravention of the strict orders he had been given; and she it was, too, who went to Pontormo's lodging, a visit confirmed by Naldini, who recognised and identified her. In any case, she does not deny any of this.

On the other hand, she strongly denies being responsible in any way whatsoever for the death of the painter. However, the letter intercepted by His Lordship's services leaves little doubt over the fact that she was in possession of the painting of *Venus* found at Pontormo's house, which she sent to Sister Catherine in Prato, who destroyed it before our arrival, apparently believing it to be the work of Sister Plautilla. (The incredible circumstances in which the painting was stolen remain as yet unexplained.) Sister Plautilla continues to swear by all the saints that the painting mentioned in the letter was in fact a *Deposition* that she herself painted and sent to Sister Catherine, but there is nothing to support her claims and everything would suggest that this is merely an invention designed to exonerate her.

The most probable theory, therefore, is a conspiracy of two women against the work, which they considered perverted, of a painter whose morals and style they condemned. Did Pontormo find Sister Plautilla in the chapel, leading her to attack him so that she could escape without being caught, or was the murder premeditated? That detail is still obscure. For her part, Sister Catherine seems convinced of her friend's guilt and claims that Sister Plautilla would have carried out the act for the greater glory of God.

In any case, it is true that Sister Plautilla is a painter too, and not without talent. There is a *Last Supper* that she painted herself on the wall of the refectory at the convent of Santa Caterina on San Marco, along with several portraits of Sister Catherine de' Ricci at the convent of San Vincenzo in Prato. Consequently, even though she has not yet formally confessed her crime, it is almost certain that Sister Plautilla possessed a motive, an opportunity and possibly (although I do have certain reservations regarding this last point, which I will mention later) the necessary means to carry out her heinous crime in the circumstances we have outlined: namely, the ability to kill the painter, who was old and weak, and also to paint over the damaged part of the wall. Indeed, if we continue to believe, as I do, that the part of the wall that was repainted and that shows Noah surrounded by animals was not the work of Pontormo himself but of his murderer or of someone present at the moment he was killed, then Sister Plautilla's mastery of the art of painting only increases the probability of her involvement on the night of the murder (even if we do not yet know why she would have bothered repainting that section of wall, given that she thought the subject matter so shameful). Nor can we dismiss the theory that the *Venus* found at Pontormo's house was painted, or at least retouched, by her, as Sister Catherine seems to believe. This crime of *lèse-majesté* would undoubtedly have been motivated by a desire to offend Your Excellency, whom she judged responsible for the supposed obscenities in the frescoes of San Lorenzo. But, given that the painting was found in Pontormo's studio, that would imply that Sister Plautilla had paid previous visits to the artist, and perhaps even met him, which seems highly improbable.

A second objection is the perfection with which Pontormo's style was imitated. It would be easy to prove with dozens of examples that women have shone in all the sciences and all the arts at which they have tried their hand. And it is true that Sister Plautilla has distinguished herself in artistic terms with her copies. Moreover, her *Nativity of Christ*, copied from Bronzino's, shows the heights she might have reached had she, like all professional painters, been able to paint from nature. But her own works demonstrate that her heads of women, which she had ample opportunity to study at her leisure, are far superior to her heads of men, which she was obliged to imagine. Often in her pictures she reproduces the features of various ladies with such perfection that they could not be improved. One cannot say the same about the men in her paintings, who resemble lifeless puppets. The question that remains, then, is this: while we can confidently state that she had the ability to add Maria's face to Venus's body, did Sister Plautilla have the capacity to paint the head and body of Noah in the same style as Pontormo, to the point that the forgery is almost impossible to discern?

I will keep Your Lordship informed as soon as I am able to offer new conclusions.

76. Cosimo de' Medici, Duke of Florence, to Giorgio Vasari

Florence, 5 March 1557

Please accept my congratulations, Master Giorgio. Once again you have justified the confidence I place in you with an efficiency that has never failed in the four years you have been in my service. I can see that there are still a few points to clear up in this case, but nothing, I imagine, that the strappado cannot bring to light. For the rest, I have neither the time nor the inclination to closely examine the details of a plot involving women inspired by Savonarola. Send me the nun's detailed confession once you have it, then we will hang her from the palace windows alongside her accomplice, as in the old days. While I do not wish to make more of this affair than it deserves – hence why there is no need to go into detail regarding the reasons for the punishment – it is never good to allow a climate of too much leniency. That is why our will is that the bodies of the two conspirators should be left out for the crows until the end of the Carnival.

As for you, Master Giorgio, come and see me tomorrow at terce, and I will tell you about our plans for the Palazzo Pitti and its gardens.

77. Vincenzo Borghini to Giorgio Vasari

Florence, 5 March 1557

Giorgio, Varchi is inviting us to supper to celebrate the arrest of the troublemaker. Join us at Daniello's later. Until tonight, Grand Inquisitor . . .

78. Vincenzo Borghini to Giorgio Vasari

Florence, Hospital of the Innocents, 6 March 1557

I don't know how you feel about him, Master Giorgio, but I consider the god Bacchus an ingrate because we paid him a magnificent tribute last night and all he gave me in return is a terrible humming between my ears and a bodily feebleness that renders me incapable of any task, notably that of leaving the house. Indeed, it has taken all my strength to drag myself to the table and write you this letter, after bringing up a considerable amount of the excellent Trebbiano that, to my misfortune, like the idiot I am, I drank in such reckless quantities last night. That is why you will not see me at the palace this morning, and I beg you to forgive my absence. But this is what happens when I dispense with moderation, forgetting that I am in the autumn of my life; I am no longer the young man I was, capable of swallowing a barrel of wine at night and going off to war the next morning, fresh as a daisy, or almost. Nevertheless, and since I would not wish for anything in the world to betray the trust you place in me as your friend, I will attempt to gather my few remaining wits so that I can carry out the service you asked of me yesterday: namely, to examine the letters from Sister Plautilla that I seized from Sister Catherine's bedroom. Be assured that I will send you a faithful report on what I find, and that I will inform you immediately if I come across any clues that might help you sweep away the final shadows from this mysterious affair.

79. Giorgio Vasari to Vincenzo Borghini

Florence, Palazzo della Signoria, 6 March 1557

Gather your wits, my dear Vincenzo, and take as much rest as you require, because I need you to concentrate on this task as only you know how. It is true that we indulged to excess last night, and I imagine Varchi is in a similar state to you this morning. He has not yet turned up at the palace, anyway. As for me, it took a great effort of will to drag myself out of bed, and my head feels as though it is being squeezed in a vice. But never mind, it was still an enjoyable evening! I'm sure it would be good to do as Alberti did, recording our table talk for posterity, but you know as well as I do that the duke's patience is thinning, and the executioner is already braiding the rope that he will use to hang the two nuns. We are running out of time to discover the truth. However, the night has only intensified the scepticism I feel, and now I am going to explain why.

As you know, while we were celebrating, the two poor nuns were being interrogated, and that interrogation went on until late at night. This morning, the man responsible for questioning them made his report to me. As always happens, the responses he was given do not tally. Sister Plautilla says she knows absolutely nothing about a painting showing Princess Maria as Venus, and stubbornly continues to talk about a *Deposition* that she sent to Prato. Sister Catherine de' Ricci, for her part, denies ever having received this *Deposition*, and refuses to say what painting she burned or why she did it. The former proclaims her innocence; the latter seems convinced of her friend's guilt. Sister Plautilla wrote a confession that I have copied for you, but as you will see, it does not really offer us any new information. How can we know who is telling the truth? I have reread the letter from Sister Catherine that led us to Sister Plautilla, and it gave me pause to think. I will now share those reflections with you.

What if the 'rotten and sensual body' of which she writes was not that of Venus, but of the dead Christ? Because why should those contemplating the body 'be weeping at such a spectacle' if the spectacle in question was the lustful Venus inspired by Michelangelo's sketch, the aim of which, after all, was to represent 'the triumph of love'? You will perhaps say that Sister Catherine was outraged by this breach of modesty, just as her beloved Savonarola once was, and that, for her, anyone contemplating such obscenity ought to weep with shame. I can see the merit in this interpretation, but it does seem to me a little forced because, clearly, she is not talking about those viewing the painting but the figures inside the frame: 'those who surround the subject'. For that matter, who are these people whom she claims are 'looking ecstatic'? In both the Michelangelo sketch and the Pontormo painting, the only elements other than Venus and Cupid are the grimacing masks that represent allegories for the dangers of love. On the other hand, if we accept the idea that what Catherine de' Ricci is describing in that letter is a *Deposition*, then all these incongruities disappear: the ecstatic expressions are worn by the mother of the dead Christ and by those who usually attend such a scene – Mary Magdalene, Joseph, Nicodemus, maybe an angel or two . . . In this hypothesis, it is not the obscenity of Venus's parted thighs that scandalises the nun, but the beatific expressions of Mary and the others who seem, from what she writes, to be rejoicing in the death of the Son of God. Assuming she is telling the truth, this could be defended from a theological point of view since it is Jesus's sacrifice that washes away man's sin, but then such a painting would be no less shocking to many, particularly the more devout religious types, as would anything that goes against tradition.

By the way, you have seen Pontormo's *Venus*: would you describe her body as 'rotten'? It is true that Ricci's mention of 'all that flesh' fits perfectly with the image, but isn't hatred of the flesh a characteristic of certain godly people? Isn't it, in fact, the central obsession of Savonarola and his followers? There is a Bronzino painting of the crucified Christ in which His body, emaciated as it is, would no doubt make a nun blush with shame.

Finally, if the letter really was referring to Pontormo's *Venus*, why would Sister Catherine believe or pretend to believe that the painting was the work of Plautilla? Is this a sort of code? Is Ricci simply ignorant when it comes to painting? Anyway, if I am right, and the painting that was burned in Catherine's fireplace was a *Deposition* by Plautilla, then the people we are about to hang are innocent.

80. Sister Plautilla Nelli to the Duke of Florence, Cosimo I

Florence, 6 March 1557

I am guilty, Your Excellency, since I must confess.

Guilty of having encountered God and Sister Catherine when I was still a child.

Guilty of having learned to read scripture and of having tried to understand its message, and even of using it as the basis for my conduct in life.

Guilty of having dreamed of a world purified by the teachings of Friar Girolamo Savonarola. Guilty, like him, of having worked for the greatness of Our Lord and against the corruption of men. Guilty of having fought against pride and making a vow of humility. Guilty of having wanted to help my fellow humans and to take care of the poor and to bring lost souls back to the path of holiness.

Guilty of having learned to draw and paint when I was young, guilty of not having thrown to the bottom of a well the paintbrush that my father gave me. Guilty of having persevered in this art and of having enjoyed some success. Guilty of having wanted to paint like a man.

It is true that I wished Pontormo dead. When I discovered the frescoes at San Lorenzo, my first impulse was to grab a torch and burn it all, but God held my arm because it would have been sacrilege to desecrate His house. I held the torch close to the walls and, little by little, I saw something else appear in those forms that I had at first believed to be the work of a demon. When I looked more closely, the horror I had originally felt gave way to admiration. However impure his morals, this man had not been inspired by Satan. In that pile of tortured bodies, in those features deformed by the fear of death and judgement, was the whole story of humanity – its damnation, its redemption and its salvation – told in a way that made it seem more real and terrifying than any of my dreams. It was like inhabiting one of Friar Girolamo's sermons. Suddenly, seeing those walls, I felt the ecstasies of Sister Catherine. And I – who have never been to Rome, and who know so little of the wonders of Florence – discovered in the bodies and the faces that Pontormo painted a force and a power that I had never even guessed at before.

From that instant, I wanted to learn – and of that, too, I am guilty. I came back, night after night, waiting until Pontormo left before slipping silently behind the screens inside the chapel, and there I remained, in the light from torches that burned my fingers, contemplating those forms that expressed everything about the fate and tragedy of mankind. But it was dark, and I feared that someone would discover me. I wanted to penetrate more deeply into the secrets of his art. With my recklessness fuelled by the need to understand his style, I went to his home, hoping to steal some sketch that I could use as a model for my own art. But God did not want me to succeed in this undertaking: every time, I was foiled. Either he was at home or his assistant was, and on the night his assistant saw me there, I had firmly believed that this time the house was empty and that I would finally be able to enter his studio, where I imagined a thousand wonders, and I had already placed my foot on the ladder when young Naldini looked down, giving me such a fright that I never dared go back there again.

But I couldn't just abandon my quest, because those forms I had seen painted on the walls of San Lorenzo haunted me, they kept me awake at night, and so I returned to the chapel. The night Pontormo died, I saw that the interior of the chapel was lit up, and that he was not alone, so I went back to the convent. That was not the first time I had been unable to enter the chapel; on other occasions, I would sometimes hear voices, and that was always enough to dissuade me from venturing inside.

I must stop writing now, because I am also guilty of having my shoulder dislocated by your guards, who tied my arms behind my back, then hung me by them and dropped me, several times, into the void below. It was God's will that I should endure that torture, and I thank Him for it, because what I learned from Pontormo's frescoes is as precious to me as if Michelangelo himself had been my master.

81. Vincenzo Borghini to Giorgio Vasari

Florence, 6 March 1557

I am writing to you once again, Master Giorgio, from my bed, for my guts and my skull are not in the best condition. That said, the little lucidity that I am starting to recover urges me to share with you a thought I had while reading your letter: I must disagree with you when you say that Plautilla's confession does not really offer us any new information. For it tells us one thing we didn't know: through her repeated visits to San Lorenzo, she had a great deal of time to study Jacopo's art. Didn't you yourself say that she has a gift for imitation, mentioning in particular a splendid *Nativity* copied from a Bronzino? In that case, why should she not have been able to copy Pontormo's *Venus*? Or, even more simply, repaint Venus's face to resemble Princess Maria? Because if Naldini saw her one night, preventing her from entering Jacopo's studio, there is nothing to say that she did not succeed in her attempt on another night.

As for the frescoes at San Lorenzo, and the repainted section which you have always considered to be the key to this mystery, everything suggests that her prolonged study of the painter's style could have supplied her with the one thing she lacked, possessing as she already did the motive (for the murder, at least, if not what drove her to repaint that part of the wall) and the opportunity: the ability to paint a man's body.

I do not say that this necessarily means she is Jacopo's murderer, simply that she cannot be eliminated from the shortlist of painters capable of so perfectly imitating his style. In my current sorry state, thinking about our investigation to forget my own sufferings, I decided to draw up a list of those painters, which I would like to submit for your enlightened judgement.

First of all, we must set aside all those who could paint as well as Pontormo but who do not live in Florence or were absent from the city at the time of the murder: Michelangelo, Daniele da Volterra in Rome, Titian and Tintoretto in Venice, Salviati in France . . . In truth, our city is so rich in talent that there remain plenty of names to fill up the rest of my page: Bronzino, Allori, Naldini, Bandinelli. And to that list we must now add Plautilla Nelli . . . and you yourself, Master Giorgio, for it would be a grave offence not to add your name to these others, who do not outstrip you in terms of either talent or reputation! I hesitate to write Cellini's name since that rascal is a goldsmith and not a painter, but he wasn't a sculptor either before casting his *Perseus*, which – it must be acknowledged – is admired by all and considered by some to be the equal of Michelangelo's *David*.

82. Giorgio Vasari to Vincenzo Borghini

Florence, 6 March 1557

Thank you, my dear Vincenzo, for your precious advice, even on this day when you seem on the verge of giving up the ghost.

I do indeed have a few remarks to make about your list. I agree that the latest evidence makes it impossible to eliminate Plautilla Nelli. If we pursue your brilliant reasoning for the others, it is true that we do not know what progress Naldini has made recently, and the same is at least equally true for Allori, whose early works revealed a genuinely promising talent. On the other hand, I have my doubts whether Bandinelli, an accomplished artist who long ago reached maturity, could suddenly improve to the point where he was Pontormo's equal.

For I must concede, Vincenzo, that as strange as they are and as corrupted by the Germanic style that gnawed at Pontormo's mind to the extent of quite possibly driving him mad, those entangled bodies are beyond the abilities of most. And while my vanity suffers to confess it, I must admit that I myself would not be capable of painting those frescoes.

That leaves Cellini, who is, it's true, a somewhat peculiar case. I am not sure what to say about him. I suppose we cannot strike him from the list. Perhaps it would be a good idea to ask him: 'Master Benvenuto, would you be capable of painting a perfect copy of the frescoes at San Lorenzo?' If he replied no, then – knowing his proverbial vanity – we would have to conclude that he truly was the murderer.

But enough of such speculation for now. The longer I spend looking at your list, the more one name seems to shine out like a flash of gold leaf on a Giotto painting. Even if it pains me to say this, the only one who immediately brings together the conditions that we know to be essential, the only one who even comes close to the brilliance of a Michelangelo, is Pontormo's greatest student, capable of copying his master's work to such a level of perfection that we have long struggled to tell them apart. It is Bronzino, and none other.

83. Agnolo Bronzino to Michelangelo Buonarroti

Florence, 7 March 1557

The rumour has now spread through the entire city: I am Jacopo's murderer. And it is Vasari who has spread it. Who else other than I could have repainted that part of the fresco, imitating the style of my late master so perfectly? And am I not the principal beneficiary of his death, since the duke has commissioned me to complete this prestigious project? As for his *Venus*, based on your sketch, how easy would it have been for me to replace the goddess's face with Princess Maria's, given that she has been posing for me for months?

But I, too, am capable of inventing theories. True, Vasari is a mediocre painter, whose main quality is the speed at which he works; some might say he is a master only of the rush job. Nevertheless, you know as well as I, Master, this rule of nature: even the most indifferent of artists may be granted a moment of grace. Have you seen his portrait of Lorenzo the Magnificent? It is quite stunningly original for a painter of so little character. Just as the greatest artist might sometimes create a failure, so – occasionally, almost inevitably – the poorest artist can be struck by a flash of genius and suddenly produce an immaculate painting, rich with inspiration drawn from the depths of his soul, animated by the breath of the divine, bursting with harmonious colours, inhabited by figures of perfect proportions who seem more alive than the living, and all of this can suddenly raise him, for one painting and one painting only, into the ranks of the great masters of his age.

Personally, I believe that Vasari was sent by the duke to destroy Jacopo's fresco, since, despite its extraordinary beauty, it no longer conforms to the spirit of the times, now that Rome has banned nudes. Who knows how far the Council of Trent would be prepared to go in their one-eyed fanaticism? You and I share the same opinion of this vile Pope Paul IV. But we both know that the duke would be willing to please the devil himself if it could bring him his title of King of Tuscany, which is in the gift of only one person in this world: that pig who currently occupies the Apostolic Palace. Did the duke order Vasari to kill Pontormo, or was it an accident? Did Pontormo discover him inside the chapel? Did the verger wake up? Perhaps Vasari's mission was not to kill Pontormo, but his death was an excuse to stop work on the frescoes. The duke and the duchess, having no choice but to ask me to complete the work, since Vasari is too busy redecorating the palace, assumed that I would be more docile than my former master, but they could not be more wrong. I will defend Jacopo's work with my dying breath. God willing, it will outlive anything created by Vasari.

84. Cosimo de' Medici, Duke of Florence, to Giorgio Vasari

Florence, 8 March 1557

Master Giorgio, I still do not see the two nuns hanging from the palace windows. And yet you are usually so prompt to execute my orders. Kindly explain the delay, if you will.

85. Vincenzo Borghini to Giorgio Vasari

Florence, 9 March 1557

A plague upon the drunkard! Giorgio, I let you down. I betrayed your trust, and I pray that my serious failings do not have irreversible consequences. When I was recovering from our drinking session the other day, you asked me to examine Sister Catherine de' Ricci's correspondence. Instead of which, like the halfwit that I am, I decided to waste your time with my pointless list of painters capable of imitating Jacopo. Concentrated upon that task, I did not notice, amid the pile of letters that I seized in Prato, the one that exonerates Sister Plautilla, written in her own hand. Read this: 'Such matters are immaterial to me now, however, because I am devoting almost all my time to a painting: a *Deposition* in a new style that I hope you will like at least as much, if not more, than my previous pictures.' In my defence, this paragraph was at the very end of the letter in question, and I missed it because I was reading too quickly. But the letter is dated 11 February, and that date corresponds with the reply from Sister Catherine de' Ricci, who received the painting that she hated so much on 1 March.

I beg you to do what is necessary, Master Giorgio, to save that innocent woman.

86. Giorgio Vasari to Vincenzo Borghini

Florence, 9 March 1557

My dear Vincenzo, calm down. Let he who has never drunk too much cast the first stone at you, but I will certainly not.

Your discovery is of the utmost importance, to be sure, but it does not exonerate the nun. Indeed, the paragraph that you cite attests that the *Deposition* painted by Sister Plautilla truly did exist, while Sister Catherine's outraged reaction indicates that Plautilla's style must have radically changed, which makes it plausible that she was capable of imitating Pontormo – and, therefore, of painting both the Noah on the fresco and the Venus with the head of the duke's daughter. In any case, the value of this information is sufficient to delay the nuns' execution, if not to free them.

Above all, though, if it really was this *Deposition* that ended up as ashes in Sister Catherine's fireplace, that means something else: the painting of Venus was not destroyed; it is hidden somewhere, and we must find it.

87. Benvenuto Cellini to Piero Strozzi, Marshal of France

Florence, 9 March 1557

For the most complex problems, Master Piero, one must always find the simplest solutions. Since everyone was in Santa Croce yesterday to watch the calcio match against the Santo Spirito team (which has markedly improved since your departure and is now even better than that of Santa Maria Novella), the palace was practically deserted. There remained the obstacle of the guards, however, who were under orders to check every object taken through the doors, and who have become extra-vigilant since the painting's disappearance, having been severely admonished for that crushing humiliation even though they actually bear no blame for my magnificent conjuring trick. So . . . what should I do? Once again, I fell back on the only tactic of which I have ever been capable, and which has served me so well: audacity, mother of surprise. To avoid the door guards, all I had to do was . . . not go through the door.

After everyone had fled the palace – leaving, as was the case last time, nobody except myself and old Bacchiacca, who seems to have taken root in the wardrobe – I took apart the bedframe, removed the painting, wrapped it in my cape, and went up to the palace ramparts, where I had taken care to leave a rope, at the furthest spot from the Piazza (although this proved an unnecessary precaution since the square was emptier than on a day of the Black Death). I tied the rope around the painting and lowered it down the wall. Now all I had to do was exit through the main door, empty-handed, whistling innocently as I passed all the watching guards, and walk around the palace to recover my prize.

Unfortunately, as life has taught me – and as it has taught you too, Master Piero – nothing ever goes as planned. This adventure did not prove an exception to that rule. As I descended from the ramparts, I heard some guards climbing the stairs. Since I had no business being up there, I would have had no excuse to justify my presence if they had seen me. So I hurried back to the roof. But you know the palace better than I, so you know that there are no hiding places up there. I ran to the wall; a leap from that height could be fatal, even to me. But God rewards the brave: at the foot of the wall was a cart loaded with hay, left there by some groom. It all happened in a flash: the decision, then the execution. I climbed onto the parapet, arms outspread like Christ on the cross, I closed my eyes and I dived. During my fall I heard the cry of an eagle. My landing was as soft as on a feather bed, and in a second I was up on my feet again, completely unscathed.

Now I just had to grab the painting, hide it in the hay, then single-handedly drag the cart away.

But I still had to find a safe place to keep it. Even though I had escaped the guards and nobody had witnessed my leap of faith, my reputation is such that I did not think it a good idea to conceal the object in my own home. It was then that I had a brilliant idea: I could hide it in the home of someone I knew to be absent – and for good cause. So I went to Bacchiacca's house, where I left our painting at the back of his studio, hidden among some dusty old sketches. And, as I write this letter, the painting is still there. Please salute Queen Catherine on my behalf, and do not be sparing with tales of my exploits – the French court deserves to hear them.

88. Marco Moro to Giambattista Naldini

Florence, 9 March 1557

Battista, listen to this story of the son of a wool carder who went by the name of Donatello. When the great sculptor was old and close to death, he was visited by some relatives who were hoping to inherit a property he owned in Prato. And this is what the brilliant Donatello replied when he heard their request: 'I cannot help you, for it seems reasonable to me to leave that property to the farmer who has spent his life working there rather than to you, who have done nothing but expect to inherit it just because you paid me a visit. Go now, and God bless you.'

Do you know which distant cousin will soon come into possession of your master's studio, Battista, a place where he has never even set foot before? And who will defend your interests then?

89. Giambattista Naldini to Marco Moro

Florence, 15 March 1557

In four days' time I will eat supper with Allori at Bronzino's house. The coast will be clear until morning because he is not the type of painter who likes to work in the middle of the night.

90. Giambattista Naldini to Giorgio Vasari

Florence, 15 March 1557

You know, Master Giorgio, how attached I was to my master, good Jacopo, who – despite his occasional bad temper – always treated me like a son. So, since you are working to avenge his death, I would like to help you. In four days' time, a secret meeting will take place at San Lorenzo. I cannot tell you much more, because that is all I know, but it is possible that the people you will find there are connected in some way to the crime. They will gather in the main chapel at dinner time.

91. Giorgio Vasari to the Duke of Florence, Cosimo de' Medici

Florence, 20 March 1557

To inform His Magnificent Lordship on the operation with which he entrusted your humble servant, regarding a secret meeting in the church of San Lorenzo, based on information given by Naldini, please find enclosed the detailed report on last night's events, followed by a transcription of exchanges heard during said meeting.

After ordering the Bargello guards to surround the building, having first verified that a number of rarely seen visitors had entered the chapel by night, your devoted servant slipped inside via the new sacristy and silently approached the chancel, where, hidden in the shadows under the great Donatello's Passion Pulpit, he saw and heard the following.

About sixty individuals, all of a visibly mediocre condition, were listening to an orator who, having climbed up the scaffolding left there by Pontormo, was haranguing them with a seditious speech.

At first I thought it was a meeting of heretics and I was expecting the vicious words of a Juan de Valdés or a Reginald Pole seeking to instil in Florence – in a house of God, in the very church where His Lordship's ancestors once worshipped – the sacrilegious venom of the German monk.

Soon, however, my eyes having adjusted to the darkness, I recognised the colour-grinder Marco Moro (whom Your Excellency so wisely ordered me to watch closely) and, when I paid attention to his words, I realised that he was exhorting his audience to revolt against the city's nobles, as Friar Savonarola once did (although Marco Moro at least spared us repeated invocations of divine wrath). In truth, the speech given by the colour-grinder – even if in some ways he resembled a preacher, with his position high up on the scaffolding and the passionate tone he employed to rally the assembled men to his subversive ideas – concerned purely earthly, political subjects, as His Excellency will remark when he reads the transcription enclosed with the present report.

Once I had heard enough to conclude without any doubt that this was an illegal meeting with seditious aims, I silently withdrew the way I had come and went outside to order the captain of the guards to arrest the individuals assembled inside the chapel without further delay.

Unfortunately, despite my recommendations, the guards did not bother to ensure that their weapons and armour would not knock noisily against each other as they entered the church, resulting in a tumult that proved harmful to the successful completion of their mission, because they made so much noise that it was as if the arrival of the pope or the emperor were being announced amid great fanfare. Alerted by this uproar, the seditionists immediately scattered like a flock of birds, some to Brunelleschi's chapel, some to the cloister gardens, some through the aisles of the nave. One of them was even found trying to hide inside the sarcophagus of Lords Piero and Giovanni, Your Excellency's glorious ancestors.

Nevertheless, most of the rebels were arrested – fifty-four, to be precise – the majority of whom are employed in various artists' studios, although some also work in printing presses or weaving mills. There was, in addition, a cobbler, a locksmith and a wool carder. Among the few who managed to escape, I must regretfully inform His Excellency, was the colour-grinder Marco Moro.

According to the testimony of the first prisoners to be interrogated, the meetings had been taking place secretly in the chapel for several months, at the instigation of said colour-grinder. The conspirators were alerted a few days in advance, or sometimes the day before or on the day itself, by messages passed discreetly from studio to studio. The purpose of these meetings, they said, was the improvement of their condition.

To conclude without abusing Your Serene Excellency's precious time, I feel obliged to mention an accident that occurred after the Bargello guards' intervention and the chaos that ensued. His Lordship no doubt remembers the beautiful stucco tondi in the old sacristy that Master Donatello dedicated to the evangelists. One of them was damaged – I do not know how or by whom – but thankfully it is not irreparable, and if Your Excellency would put his trust in me once again, I will personally oversee its restoration at the hands of Ammannati or Bandinelli, both of whom I believe to be fully capable of carrying out this task.

91b. Marco Moro to the workers of the Arte dei Medici e Speziali

Transcription of his speech at San Lorenzo,
19 March 1557

Comrades, remember the ancient motto of the Medici family: 'The time is coming.' Make this your motto, too, and prepare. Spread the news: the time is coming. The more workers we rally to our cause, the more strength we will have to demand that the duke gives us the rights we seek. The fishermen and the fishmongers, who have no guild, are our brothers. The alum miners of Volterra who work themselves to death for wealthy drapers are our brothers. The peasant farmers who cultivate land in Tuscany on behalf of landowners from the cities are our brothers, as were the peasants massacred thirty years ago by German princes because they had the temerity to revolt against their iniquity. If we do not want to meet the same fate, we must present ourselves to the duke in a position of such strength that we can demand his protection from the greed of the merchants who employ us. And so, once the *popolo minuto* are united in an army so great that it will be impossible to deny us, we can force the passing of laws that forbid the avarice of the few to keep the many in poverty. To those who think these are pipe dreams rather than perfectly reasonable demands, remember this: there is nowhere more suited to such laws than Florence. In this city, there is a law stating the amount of steel that must be used to make a helmet. In this city, a shopkeeper is forbidden to sell certain objects, so as not to encroach on his neighbour's speciality.

Nothing would be easier for the duke, in a city where there are already so many laws about everything, than to enact one that would guarantee a minimum wage.

92. Cosimo de' Medici, Duke of Florence, to Giorgio Vasari

Livorno, 20 March 1557

So, if I understand correctly, Florence, the city that God entrusted to my care, is now infested not only with conspiracies of murderous nuns but with seditious plebs too? Enough. I must put an end to all this. Find me this Marco Moro, arrest him and throw him in a damp cell. I regret getting rid of those lions that were stinking up the palace. But damn it all! If that colour-grinder wants to play Spartacus, I will grant his wish by crucifying him, along with his comrades, by the side of Via Larga.

What a fitting spectacle that will make for our New Year celebration.

93. Giorgio Vasari to Vincenzo Borghini

Florence, 20 March 1557

To hell with the nuns of San Marco, Prato, Arezzo and anywhere else! Leave your orphans and come and meet me at the palace the moment you receive this letter. The duke has given us five days to find the colour-grinder. The men guarding the city's gates are already all on high alert, which means he can't have left Florence. He must be hiding, but where? Or rather, let us ask: who is hiding him?

94. Marco Moro to Giambattista Naldini

21 March 1557

Fear has never enabled great feats, Battista. On the contrary, it is often the source of the vilest actions. I know it was you who alerted the duke's men, you son of a whore. Did you think you'd be left in peace once you'd delivered me to the Bargello? Ah, but I know San Lorenzo better than your father ever knew your mother when he put a bastard in her belly. When Vasari let slip the duke's dogs inside the church, I was on the scaffolding: taking advantage of the sudden chaos, I climbed up to the hole in the roof made last year by drawing students who wanted to peek at the frescoes hidden behind the screens. All I had to do was remove the few tiles that I myself had put there, and I was able to escape via the roof. So I am still at liberty. And Pontormo's madness finally proved useful, because that was what saved me.

As for you, you have chosen your side: you are with the *popolo grosso*, even though you are not one of them. Not a rational choice, but at least you can console yourself with the courage of treachery. But no hard feelings, my friend. I pray that God protects you and gives you good health. Take care, and don't forget to keep looking over your shoulder whenever you're out in the street. Don't step too close to the banks of the Arno, and whenever you go to the tavern, make sure that nobody poisons your wine. Tell your new friends that Marco says hello. Go ahead and be those men's pet dog, Battista, since that is your ambition. I hope they toss you lots of bones. But be careful, and remember this: Pontormo's death showed that they are wolves with one another. Are you really sure you want to sit at their table? Let me give you one last piece of advice: stay a dog, don't try to be a wolf. Nobody should wear a suit that doesn't fit him.

95. Benvenuto Cellini to Piero Strozzi, Marshal of France

Florence, 22 March 1557

May this missive find its intended recipient in the person of the brave, magnificent Lord Strozzi, who – rumour has it – is about to take the Kingdom of Naples as Jupiter took Leda. I hope, Master Piero, that the example of your courage will give those French wastrels a little dash of the martial spirit that their ancestors once demonstrated. Although, it's true, they have always struck me as being more gifted in the art of retreat. In any case, I have no doubt that under your command this campaign will have more success than that of the late King Charles VIII.

As for your servant, only his remarkable foresight has kept him out of the duke's dungeons. You cannot possibly imagine the frenzy that has gripped Florence in recent days, and believe me, it has nothing to do with the Carnival. The Bargello guards are scouring the city for a seditious colour-grinder who, it is said, was plotting a plebeian uprising against the duke. No artist's studio has escaped their inquisitorial fury, and now they have turned up at my house. They didn't find anything, of course, and for good reason: because, in the case that concerns us, I am the thief but not the fence. Presumably they will remember old Bacchiacca in the end. But if you want to get hold of your painting before they do, you will have to find someone else for this task, because the duke's spies are watching us all closely, and this time, your devoted Benvenuto is unable to carry out the mission himself. Believe me, nobody is safe: they have even arrested Bronzino's little catamite, Allori.

96. Agnolo Bronzino to Michelangelo Buonarroti

Florence, 22 March 1557

How wise you were to flee to Rome, and how stupid we all were not to follow your example! Never come back to Florence: justice has deserted this city. I am sure you are justified in your complaints about Carafa, who hates artists, but at least he doesn't throw them in his dungeons. See how the duke repays his most devoted servants: my best apprentice, my son, my friend, young Allori has been arrested. I do not know what paintings of Sandro's you were able to see while he was visiting Rome, but I am certain that you, whose eye is so attuned to grace and inspiration, will have recognised those qualities in that young man's work.

Some sketches of Princess Maria were found in his room that bear a resemblance to the face of your Venus. That is the sum of their evidence! And since he is friends with Naldini, and thus had access to Jacopo's studio, he is suspected of having taken that cursed painting. As for playing a role in our friend's death . . . well, why not! What does it matter that Sandro always showed him the greatest filial devotion? What does it matter that his sister Alessandra always cooked splendid suppers for us, which Jacopo loved? What does it matter that the Allori family always treated him with the greatest respect? Nowadays, this is all it takes to be accused of murder. Sandro, smashing a hammer over Jacopo's head! Sandro, driving a chisel into the heart of a man he loved like a father! Poor Sandro . . . Poor Florence. All those years working to serve the duke, never letting him down, painting portraits of Medicis living or dead, decorating the duchess's chapel, honouring all their commissions, seeing my paintings given away to every passing prince, and this is my reward. For a long time, I believed that I was under the protection of the duke when news of the Council of Trent made us fear that we would end up on a pyre. But is there anything he would not be prepared to do to be crowned King of Tuscany? Oh vile submission! To reign, he must punish, and if he judges that my Sandro's head is the price of his authority, he will shamelessly sacrifice the life of that innocent boy. A plague upon the Medici family! A plague upon their house, and that of Toledo too. Pontormo was right. Our time is coming to an end. The world has turned away from us, he used to say. We no longer belong here, and the nobles make that clear to us.

97. Giorgio Vasari to Vincenzo Borghini

Florence, 23 March 1557

Master Vincenzo, I hope that you will find this letter when you return. I have gone to the tavern to wait for you for fear that, had I stayed at the palace, I, too, would have ended up killing someone. Since those imbeciles from the Bargello did not find Marco Moro despite turning the whole city upside down, they decided to arrest Allori, on the evidence of a few sketches that they found in his room. Which is plainly ridiculous because, if he had painted the *Venus*, then why was it found at Pontormo's house? It's not that complicated: if a painting was found at Pontormo's house, it's because it was painted by Pontormo. It was the frescoes that were repainted by another artist! But how am I supposed to explain all this to those bumbling ruffians? From now on, they are forbidden from visiting any painters or sculptors unless accompanied by you or me. I feel bad, my dear friend, at asking you to assist me in this thankless task, but experience proves that we cannot leave those mercenary morons unsupervised. As for them searching for Marco Moro in his comrades' houses, let them continue as they like. If they find him, good. But the colour-grinder seems much more cunning than them and – if I am honest – more cunning than us too, for the moment. God only knows where that devil is hiding.

Allori will be held for a few days before being released, so the duke can't accuse us of neglecting any lead. The boy will tell us what we already know: that he was practising copying his master Bronzino's portraits of Princess Maria. You know my suspicions about Bronzino. It is true that the mystery of the painting has not yet been solved, but if anyone is involved in this, it is him and not his apprentice. As for the business with Marco Moro, I sincerely doubt that a painter firmly established at the duke's court would have anything to do with that plebeian rabble.

98. Agnolo Bronzino to Michelangelo Buonarroti

Florence, 24 March 1557

I am writing to you again, divine Master, because this time I need help. And not just anyone's, but yours.

I hid the colour-grinder from San Lorenzo at my house. Hunted by the duke's guards, the poor man had nowhere else to go, all his friends having been arrested. According to what he told me, their crime is nothing more than organising secret meetings for workers in the arts. At the palace, all the talk is of an attempted revolt in the manner of the Ciompi. Not that it matters to me. I have never had cause to complain about him since he began working for me, and – having spent time with him – I am certain that he did not kill Jacopo. Consequently, I refuse to hand him over to Vasari. Or anyone else, for that matter. My colour-grinder will not join my apprentice in the dungeons of the Bargello. For now, he is staying in Sandro's room, where nobody will think to look for him.

But the duke is searching for him everywhere: the Bargello guards have already been to my house once, and they will come again. I must smuggle him out of the city, but time is running short and all the gates are vigilantly guarded. And that is why, divine Master, I am asking for your aid, because it was you, was it not, who built the walls of Florence, back in the days of the Republic, when we were besieged by the Spanish? So surely you must know some secret passage or tunnel out of the city. Perhaps you even built one with your own hands. Please help this poor wretch, Master, in memory of the Republic that you once defended.

99. Malatesta to Maria

Florence, 24 March 1557

As soon as the Mass is over, you will say that you don't feel well and ask for permission to rest in your apartments. You will pretend to head towards the palace, but in reality you will go to the San Gallo Gate, accompanied only by your maid-servant. I will be waiting for you there, with a safe conduct that your father signed without reading. Remember to wear a cloak with a hood so that you can hide your face. Amid all the celebrations, you should have no trouble melting into the crowd, but even so, try not to attract attention. It is imperative that news of the duke's daughter leaving the city breaks as late as possible. I have chosen two good Spanish horses, and I will have them harnessed to our carriage in the morning. Before noon, I will load your belongings onto the carriage, while you are still at Santa Maria. Meet me at the gate, and then we shall set off for France! Until tomorrow, my beloved. I am yours now and forever.

100. Eleanor of Toledo to Cosimo de' Medici

Florence, 25 March 1557

I have given orders to the bearer of this letter to find you, come what may, and to hand it to you immediately, even if you are in the company of the emperor himself. Your daughter has vanished! Nobody has seen her since she left Santa Maria. I have already had the matter investigated: a carriage is missing, along with two of our best horses and your page Malatesti. How can you pay so little mind to the people in your entourage, my friend? That corrupter must have taken her during the New Year festivities, and all the evidence suggests that the little whore followed him of her own free will. And to think I was worried about her! But this is your fault too: the reputation of that half-brute half-eunuch Alfonso can hardly have encouraged her to think calmly and serenely about her forthcoming marriage. Whatever happens, if you persist in your project of selling her to the Duke of Este so he can send her to Ferrara, then you must find her first. Find my daughter!

101. Cosimo de' Medici to Eleanor of Toledo

Florence, 25 March 1557

Pressing business once again calls me to Pisa, obliging me to leave immediately so I can be there tomorrow morning, but do not doubt this: your daughter will be returned without delay, you have my word upon it. As for that sack of shit Malatesti, I'll have his cock cut off with a billhook; that way, Maria will have no cause for regret, will she? And I will swear this to you too: before summer, she will be married to Prince Alfonso. You claim he is incapable of procreation, but who knows – perhaps our daughter will give him an heir in no time. Such miracles have happened before. You know as well as I do that the courts of Italy are filled with bastards born prematurely. In any case, entreaties have already lost us enough time. See how your daughter thanks you for having pleaded so eloquently on her behalf! Maria has defied her father's authority, and consequently, as soon as she is back in Florence, we will send her on her way to Ferrara, even if she has to be escorted by a regiment.

102. Cosimo de' Medici, Duke of Florence, to Giorgio Vasari

Pisa, 26 March 1557

Take as many men as you need. Your mission is to find, arrest and bring back to Florence Malatesta de' Malatesti and Princess Maria. I want my daughter unharmed, and Malatesti alive.

103. Maria de' Medici to Catherine de' Medici, Queen of France

26 March 1557

Dearest aunt, do not scold me. My heart is pounding, but whether with terror or exhilaration I know not. I committed the folly of eloping with my Malatesta. I followed him because we are now united before God, if not yet before men, and because he swore to me that the painting had been destroyed by some possessed nun.

So I am leaving behind my cruel parents and my beloved homeland. But you knew exile before I was born, and it is your example that lends me the necessary strength to carry out such an undertaking. I am a fugitive, whereas you were sold like a slave. I do not know which fate is less enviable. Please, tell me about France – it will give me courage for the ordeals to come. Is it true that we will be welcomed at King Henri's court? Oh, but how stupid I am! You can't possibly reply to this missive since you will not know where to find me. I do not know myself where I am. Some dark forest . . . How will I ever get through this without your support?

We left Florence on the first day of the New Year, and we are travelling cautiously, far from the beaten path, so that the men my father has undoubtedly sent to hunt us down will not be able to find us. I tremble for my Malatesta, because even if the duke is not an unfeeling man, those feelings are unlikely to help us: he is incapable of pity, but he is certainly capable of anger. Here in Tuscany, and even beyond its borders, my father's wrath is the equal of God's. You know how he had Lorenzino assassinated in Venice, eleven years after he slew their cousin Alessandro. It is said that his body was thrown in the lagoon. I wonder if those same assassins are now after us.

104. Giorgio Vasari to Vincenzo Borghini

Pistoia, 27 March 1557

The duke knows that my devotion to him is limitless, which is why he abuses it. I would have thought myself more useful to him in Florence than running after a lost princess, even if she is his daughter. I am a painter and an architect, not a nanny or a chaperone. All the same, I am hopeful I will be back in the city soon, for I doubt whether the young lady can have got very far with her foppish beau. A young couple out on the road without an escort will quickly attract notice, and possibly even a ransom. The boy will be lucky if he is not left for dead in some ditch. As for the girl, I am led to believe that the treasure of her virginity is no longer intact, which lifts a weight from her shoulders in one sense, even if it also reduces her value. Happy are those for whom the sword of Damocles has already fallen, particularly when they cut the thread themselves.

105. Piero Strozzi, Marshal of France, to Benvenuto Cellini

Rome, 27 March 1557

In all honesty, my dear Benvenuto, it seems unlikely that Naples will be ours, since your letter still finds me in Rome. Montluc, who is the only remotely reasonable Frenchman, has managed to thwart the Duke of Guise's fanciful plans for now. Charles VIII at least entered Naples before being chased out of Italy. As for us, we are struggling to make it out of Lazio. I liberated Ostia and Tivoli, but the Duke of Alba's troops are still prowling around. If we don't stop them, that cursed Toledo family, having already taken Florence and Naples, will soon help themselves to the entire peninsula. You have told me of your problems with the duchess, but believe me, her uncle is no pushover either, and even less so since he became viceroy of Naples. Maybe he doesn't spend all morning on the shitter, but he has an army – and he knows how to use it.

As for our business, have no fear. In less than three days you will have a man on the spot to take care of Bacchiacca.

106. Catherine de' Medici, Queen of France, to Piero Strozzi, Marshal of France

Fontainebleau, 30 March 1557

Read this letter from Maria, which I am having copied for you. Isn't it sweet? Isn't it just delicious? Isn't it every bit as gothic as you could wish? Help them reach France. There will be plenty of time, afterwards, to send them into exile somewhere. But we still don't have the painting. The ideal thing would be for it to join the handsome couple in Venice, so that the Venetians can judge for themselves how closely the model resembles her portrait. Truly, I would like to see them side by side myself.

107. Maria de' Medici to Catherine de' Medici

28 March 1557

Oh aunt, if you only knew! I wish you could know. The knight of Malatesti, when he takes me in his arms and kisses me . . . I feel like a woman. I no longer regret what struck me at first as an act of folly. On the contrary, I am now certain before God that I made the right choice because I feel God's breath every God-given night. God made men free, did he not? And women are God's creatures too, are we not? I am no longer the same, in my body or in my mind. I have run away from my father and that is a sin, I know, but in doing so I have moved closer to God, I am certain of that. And the proof of it is that I have not bled this month. Our Lord redeemed my sins on the cross, did He not?

108. Michelangelo Buonarroti to Agnolo Bronzino

Rome, 28 March 1557

Master Agnolo, I am sending you the map of the fortifications, which I finally managed to find among all my papers; you cannot imagine how many drawings, maps, contracts, bills and ledgers I have accumulated during my working life. I have marked the location of the passage through which your man will be able to escape without being seen.

109. Giorgio Vasari to Vincenzo Borghini

Bologna, 29 March 1557

I am like a poacher, travelling from inn to inn, following a trail of rabbit droppings. But our two lovebirds are more like hares, constantly changing direction to shake off the hounds. I do not know when I will return to Florence, which is why I am depending on you, my friend, to visit all the painters and artists who are, for one reason or another, on our list. (In fact, I think anyone who can paint at all is on our list.)

Anyway, I was planning to ask you to see Cellini because he can't stand me. You should visit Bronzino too. Who knows – you may find something that those boors from the Bargello missed when they were arresting Allori. Knock on Ammannati's and Bandinelli's doors. And if I am not back within a week, go to see old Bacchiacca, just so we can say we have left no stone unturned. After all, the colour-grinder must be hiding somewhere. And perhaps, when we find him, we will find the painting with him, along with an accomplice, if not the killer himself.

110. Agnolo Bronzino to the prior of the Charterhouse of Galluzzo

Florence, 31 March 1557

In the next few days, God willing, a man claiming to be me will knock at the door of your monastery. For the love you bear me, father, please show your generosity by welcoming this friend of mine as you once welcomed me, without asking any questions of him – or of me – in memory of the frescoes that Jacopo painted in your house, in which labour God gave me the honour of lending Him my hand.

III. Giorgio Vasari to Vincenzo Borghini

Parma, 31 March 1557

My friend, have you done what I asked?

My two starlings were seen in Modena and in Parma, but appear to have headed towards Mantua. I fear that they do not know where to go, which makes their movements more erratic and my mission all the more difficult. It is impossible to predict how someone will act next when his own intentions are obscure, constantly shifting and hidden even from himself. The minds of young people are like sand. Try to enter them and you find yourself sinking. All this to say that there is a risk I will be detained far from Florence for God knows how many more days. I am sorry I won't be able to accompany you, but you must make those visits we spoke about on your own. The time for discretion is over. Search everywhere, and forget people's feelings. You must bear the weight of the entire investigation on your shoulders now, my friend, and you must find the colour-grinder too. Tell me the fruits of the visits you have made up to now. And, above all, what you found at Bronzino's house.

112. Vincenzo Borghini to Giorgio Vasari

Ferrara, 2 April 1557

You know, Master Giorgio, that you can always count on your faithful Vincenzo to accomplish the tasks you set him, even when exceptional circumstances force him into unforeseen delays. So I went to the court of the Duke of Este, as you asked me, and I will now give you my thoughts on the matter.

First of all, I must acknowledge that the Duke Ercole is an excellent host. Every night, he offered his guests a feast worthy of the court of France. To be perfectly honest, my belly has been so full for the past four days that I must move my bowels every hour if I don't wish to burst like an overfilled wineskin. I feel like Rabelais's giant Gargantua, and here in Ferrara even my ears and eyes are constantly stuffed, for the duke loves musicians and jugglers so dearly that there is barely a single moment in the day that is not accompanied by a tune played on a lute and some kind of play or dance.

A friend of the arts the duke most certainly is, as his collection of Flemish tapestries attests, along with the abundance of paintings created by those artists with whom he has always loved to surround himself: the Dossi brothers in former times; Girolamo da Carpi, whose death last summer I have the sad honour of reporting to you; young Bastianino, who is following in their footsteps and is, to my mind, the best of them all; and Garofalo, who – though not the equal of our Florentine masters, nor entirely worthy of the nickname 'the Raphael of Ferrara' which this city has somewhat prematurely bestowed upon him – would not be out of place in our *Lives*. I must admit that, along with the Dossi brothers, he has painted some altarpieces that caught my eye and that, if you ever happen to be in these parts, I believe will prove pleasing to you.

I would not wish you to think, however, that this Duke of Este is simply an arts lover with a taste for fine food. This prince governs his city with an iron fist, and pity is a sentiment wholly unknown to him. He himself told me, in front of his wife, how he had her locked in the castle dungeons because she joined the Lutherans, and abandoned her to the tender mercies of the Inquisition until she agreed to start attending Mass again. In those same cells, he also keeps an uncle who once conspired against his father; the man is seventy-nine years old and has spent fifty-one of those years behind bars, but the duke – who seems to have inherited his father's old grudges – obstinately refuses to pardon him.

If his son takes after him, then I am not surprised that Princess Maria is less than thrilled at the idea of marrying him. I do not know if the rumours about him are true, but I did meet the prince and he did not seem to me to possess the qualities one expects of a gentleman. His baleful expression, his arrogance, and the way he treats his people with a harshness that borders on cruelty lead me to conclude that Alfonso II d'Este is another name that we should add to our list. I swear that man has a murderer's disposition. And wasn't he in Florence precisely at the moment that Jacopo was killed? Imagine if he found the painting, so offensive to his future wife . . . Who knows how he would have reacted, given his bilious temperament, his natural inclination to anger.

If our list is lengthening, however, I am hopeful that we will soon be able to permanently remove from it the names of the two nuns. Before leaving, I went to see poor Plautilla, who is recovering from her interrogation. I took her some paints and brushes and asked her to paint me a *Deposition* like the one that she claims to have given Sister Catherine de' Ricci. So we will see what she is capable of, particularly as regards her imitation of male figures.

One last thing: to avoid work on the palace being delayed even further by our absence from Florence, I hired young Naldini to work on it. I think he will make you an excellent assistant.

113. Giorgio Vasari to Vincenzo Borghini

Mantua, 7 April 1557

Vincenzo, you buffoon, who cares about Ferrara or its duke! Why do you bother me with all this nonsense about banquets and flute players, about old men in dungeons or reformed wives? The husband can eat his wife in a stew for all I care! A plague upon that family! So the Duke of Este and his son strike you as degenerates? So what! Are you really the only person in Italy who doesn't know that the duke's mother was Lucrezia Borgia, the pope's whorish daughter? How long exactly do you intend to stay in that city, studying its mores and local customs? The murderer is a painter. Can the duke's son paint? Didn't I tell you to visit Bronzino? That is where we will find our killer, I can sense it. But I am still stuck running all over Italy in pursuit of my prey. I cannot work out whether our two hare-brained lovers are trying to reach France or Venice. I was already on my way to Piacenza when I realised they were headed north. I am in a rage at all the time they are costing me. And your letter, which took almost a week to find me! I beg you, my friend, to waste no more time telling me about the feasts and lutes of Ferrara. Leave the enchanted castle that has tormented your bowels and turned your brain to dust.

114. Maria de' Medici to Catherine de' Medici, Queen of France

Verona, 7 April 1557

If all the men in his service are as cunning and intelligent as my Malatesta, my father is a lucky man. But I have to say, I doubt that is true. You should hear him inventing all manner of tales to explain why a young couple are travelling the roads of Italy. This time, he told the innkeeper that we were newly married and he was taking me to visit his lands in Lombardy. In fact, he always introduces me to people now as his wife, which fills me with pleasure. I love him so much! I hope you will love him as much as I do. Wait, no, what am I saying? Not as much as I do! How silly I am . . . I feel as if I am a character in a Boccaccio story: some mysterious woman keeping a secret while travelling incognito on horseback, sometimes disguised as a man, who finds love on her journey. What an adventure!

Sometimes I am so frightened that it makes me vomit, but never mind. I have no regrets, and my decision is irreversible. He that hath the steerage of my course, direct my sail! And to think I wasn't sure I wanted to go with him . . . Now, I would rather die than return to Florence. God willing, we will soon be in Milan, and from there we will enter Switzerland, and then France. May God protect us! I will bid you farewell now, dear aunt, because I can hear my Malatesta calling me from the balcony, where he has gone to scan the sky to foretell the weather tomorrow (because he can decipher the secrets of nature too – he knows so many things!), but I am sure we will see each other soon.

115. Vincenzo Borghini to Giorgio Vasari

Florence, 15 April 1557

I am sorry that my trip to Ferrara seemed to annoy you, particularly since I thought that, in visiting the Duke of Este, I was fulfilling a request that you had expressly made of me. No doubt I am a fool, but a docile and faithful fool, always eager to please you. I confess, your letter made me feel ashamed and embarrassed, and I truly regret having vexed you. But, as you know, you do not have to tell me anything twice. I had barely finished reading your letter before I set forth for Florence, without even taking my leave of the duke.

Escorted by a small army, I then went to Agnolo's house. Unfortunately, that visit did not enable me to confirm your suspicions. The guards searched every inch of his home and studio but we found nothing. True, there were some sketches and unfinished portraits of the princess – among dozens, if not hundreds, of others – but that hardly seems remarkable given that Agnolo is the official portraitist of the Duke of Florence, his family, his children, and even his ancestors. The only sure result of our intrusion was to have deeply upset Agnolo, whom I left in a state of furious indignation. I would not be surprised if he complained to the duke about it.

Having executed the task that you assigned me, I took it upon myself to free Plautilla from her cell, the duke having given me his permission without much haggling. As you know better than anyone, he has other fish to fry. I have welcomed the poor woman into the Innocents, where she can paint to her heart's content. For now, my observation is that her paintings, while not bereft of a certain grace, are a long way from the *terribilità* of the frescoes at San Lorenzo or the horrific power that Catherine de' Ricci attributed to her mysterious *Deposition*.

As for the colour-grinder, Marco Moro, he remains at large, although – if I am correctly following your reasoning – it doesn't really matter if he is hiding somewhere in Florence or on his way to New Spain, since he too was not capable of repainting the fresco in the style of Pontormo.

With Giambattista Naldini having been struck from our list for the same reason, I can confirm that he has been hired to work on the palace renovation. As I told you before, I knew him as a child: he was a good boy then, and I am sure he still is now. As for his painting, even if you consider it markedly inferior to that of his master (which is, in a way, good news for him since it exonerates him in your eyes), there is no reason to doubt that, under your influence and your instruction, he will approach, if not equal, that level of artistry. In the meantime, I am sure you will be glad to have an additional assistant, so this is one of those situations where everybody wins.

116. Giovanni Battista Schizzi, member of the Senate and regent of the Duchy of Milan, to Cosimo de' Medici, Duke of Florence

Milan, 15 April 1557

Milan, which has always been a friend to the Medici family, is proud of the excellent relations that it enjoys with the Duke of Florence, Cosimo I. That is why we are eager to ensure no misunderstanding regarding our actions or the object of this letter. I will not attempt to hide from Your Excellency that said object has put us in a difficult situation.

We recently apprehended in our territory a young couple who were travelling from Florence with the intention of reaching France. Unfortunately, the man escaped our clutches, but the woman claims to be your eldest daughter. It is true that they were in possession of a safe conduct signed by your hand, but the fact that they were alone, without any guards and only one female servant, the fact that they had taken rooms at an inn rather than announcing themselves to the city's authorities, the fact that their only luggage was a trunk filled with fashionable

Spanish dresses and expensive jewellery . . . all of this aroused our suspicions and we felt justified in detaining them until we could learn more about their true intentions.

If this young lady really is Your Excellency's daughter, and if we had been forewarned of her visit, we would of course have received her with all the honours due to her rank. However, after repeated questioning, this is what the supposed princess finally deigned to reply: she was sent on a secret diplomatic mission to the Queen of France. As for the young man, he was her bodyguard. But in that case, we asked, why did he flee? To this, she could provide us with no satisfactory answer. All in all, this affair seems somewhat murky to us. Would you, dear Duke, please help untangle this mystery, and let us know what you wish us to do with the young lady?

117. Giambattista Naldini to Agnolo Bronzino

Florence, 15 April 1557

A quick note, Master Agnolo, to ask you to hand this letter to Marco Moro should you happen to know where he is hiding. Do not take fright: you need not fear any indiscretion on my part. Sandro, whom you think of like a son but who is a brother to me, told me everything. I do not claim to know which of us was more joyous when he was released, but I will say that his arrest plunged me into the blackest despair. So you may be certain that I will never do anything dishonest that might cause harm to him, or to you.

118. Giambattista Naldini to Marco Moro

Florence, 15 April 1557

I am not Michelangelo and I never will be. Do you really think I don't know that? But if I, Giambattista Naldini, an orphan from the Innocents, can succeed in making a living from my art, then that is at least something, isn't it? Do you believe that one must be devoid of the slightest ambition because one is the son of nobody? Can you blame me, who came from nothing, for trying to make a place for myself, even a very small place – a little nook under some altarpiece in the chapel of an obscure church – among all the grand masters of Florence? And if I succeed in this, would that not be proof of a certain merit? Each of us must seek out our fate as best we can.

It is true that I gave you up to Vasari. Yes, it was I who sent him to San Lorenzo on the night of your secret meeting. That wasn't too difficult to guess, was it? After all, who else had the motive to do it? Allori? Allori is under Bronzino's protection and already being given commissions. Allori does not need to denounce anyone. But I have lost my master and I am all alone. It seems that God, who provided me with a little talent, did not give me enough of it to enable me to elevate myself without recourse to deceit. But the Lord, in His infinite mercy, did not want the Bargello guards to capture you. Evidently, though, He did want me to draw some advantage from my treachery, because I will soon join the growing ranks of Vasari's assistants on the renovation of the Palazzo della Signoria. Thus was I able to help myself, by getting in the good books of the best-connected painter in Florence, without causing you irreparable harm. As you can see, it would be wrong to judge me too harshly. Each of us must withstand the blows of fortune with the weapons he has at his disposal. What else could I do after my master's death? What would you have done in my place? Oh, I am well aware of the path you have chosen. You incite other workers to refuse their fate. You proclaim yourself their leader and urge them to revolt. But where do you expect that to lead, exactly? Do you plan to overthrow the duke? And who is to say that the next one will not be worse? Do you want a new Savonarola to champion the rights of the poor? Do you know what punishment people like him would inflict on people like me? At least the duke closes his eyes to such acts, condemned as they are by the Church and the world. Perhaps the duke would have had you hanged had he managed to catch you. But I would be burned alive if I ever fell into the pope's hands. Not everybody is capable of surviving an accusation of sodomy, like Cellini.

I don't know if you killed old Pontormo. It seems possible to me because I remember how vile he could be, with you as he was with me – there were days when he made me so enraged I could have strangled him with my bare hands. But if you did kill him, you only have yourself to blame, because everything that has happened to you since then was caused by that first act. Were it not for Pontormo's murder, I would never have denounced you. But, whether you killed him or not, your true crime lay in wishing to have your meetings again while the Bargello guards were still combing the city in search of the murderer. One day you will be caught, and when you are being tortured in the dungeons of the Bargello, and they ask you who informed you of the old man's comings and goings, are you certain that my name will not emerge from between your lips? In that case, think of it this way: my denunciation of you was a pre-emptive act, to prevent you from denouncing me. So, in a way, by forcing you to flee, I saved both of us. Naturally, I do not expect you to thank me, but I hope that, after reading my point of view on the matter, you can now see things from another perspective.

119. Marco Moro to Agnolo Bronzino

Galluzzo, 15 April 1557

Before leaving the refuge that you found for me, I want to write this short note, which the prior will deliver to you. I have no idea why a courtier like you has helped a common worker like me, but I do not wish to be ungrateful. You saved me. So, I thank you. I will go to Switzerland, and from there to Germany, or maybe Flanders. In our line of work, the reputation of Italians is so high that I will not have trouble finding employment wherever I go. I will do everything I can to bring the Kingdom of God to this Earth, not just some immortal afterlife, and to ensure that everyone can enjoy it, not just a lucky few.

But what about you? What will you do? Has your apprentice been freed? I hope so, but I can tell that your masters are no longer exactly to your satisfaction. Helping me was an act of courage and rebellion. Perhaps, in the future, if you decide you no longer want to wear the golden collar and leash that they have put around your neck, then maybe you too will decide you want to fight certain things in this world that do not strike you as entirely fair. Until then, farewell. I have no doubt that you will finish the work of your late master, paying him the tribute he deserves. True, he wasn't the easiest of men, and he and I did not always see eye to eye, but even if I'm only a colour-grinder, I could respect the love and devotion that he showed to his art, and his frescoes were truly beautiful.

120. Catherine de' Medici, Queen of France, to Piero Strozzi, Marshal of France

Chenonceaux, 21 April 1557

You will remember, I trust, that I did not place excessive hope in my niece's little escapade? Well, dear cousin, I'm afraid I was right: the idiot got herself arrested in Milan. By the time you receive this letter, she will probably have been taken back to Florence. So, the crown jewel has escaped us, but we are now in possession of the young page, since he prudently decided to abandon his beloved and strike out for Paris on his own. I don't know what I will do with him. Perhaps I will welcome him into my entourage? After all, who better than this page to inform me about his master?

I console myself for this disappointment by thinking of Cosimo, whose daughter is pregnant and who must now strive desperately to save what remains of her reputation. I know what I would do in his place: marry her to the Duke of Este without delay to legitimise the future little bastard. Cosimo is not an imbecile, so he has undoubtedly already reached this conclusion. But will the Duke of Este agree to it? That is another question altogether.

For the rest, we can still follow through with our original plan, can't we? What news of the painting? Can we hope to see it before the end of time, or will this story drag on as long as the construction of the Duomo?

121. Cosimo de' Medici, Duke of Florence, to Ercole d'Este, Duke of Ferrara

Florence, 21 April 1557

I hope you will forgive the excess of scruples – or, let's be honest, the pusillanimity – that drove me to wish to delay the marriage. I now believe that Maria is ready to become the wife of your son Alfonso. And even if she isn't, who cares. The best way to teach a child to swim is to throw her in the river – am I right? So, I am delighted to inform you that her mother and I are disposed to fix a date for the wedding. What would you say to next month? Let's say, the first of May? Actually, let's make it the eighth, so that my people have time to prepare festivities worthy of such an important event! I can hardly express to you, Duke, the joy and pride that I feel at the prospect of the union of our two houses.

122. Benvenuto Cellini to Piero Strozzi, Marshal of France

Florence, 21 April 1557

I have met with the man Your Excellency sent me, and I can already tell that this Scoronconcolo is a brute after my own heart. Those coal-black eyes, that luxuriant beard, his supple hock and imposing stature, and that way he has of speaking always in a whisper . . . However, I fear I will have to accompany him in his mission, for I can sense that he has only a moderate love of the arts, probably insufficient to identify Pontormo's painting from among all the others in Bacchiacca's studio. We will go soon – tomorrow or the day after, God willing. Acting in broad daylight renders all enterprises riskier than they ought to be, but on the other hand it is the only way of ensuring that Bacchiacca will not be home, because he will be at the palace, as he is every day that God makes, working on the duke's bed, which must surely be worthy of Michelangelo's *David* or my *Perseus*, if the value of an artwork can be reckoned by the amount of time spent upon its creation.

123. Giorgio Vasari to Vincenzo Borghini

Bologna, 21 April 1557

So it's not the colour-grinder or the nun or the assistant . . . but there is still one possible culprit remaining to us, is there not? The fact that you did not find anything does not change my opinion. We waited too long, held back by excessive feelings of fellowship towards a colleague, but there is no point dwelling on that now: what's done is done. Let us never speak of it again. But how can we find the evidence we need? Go through all the Bargello reports. Question Bronzino's neighbours. I'll be in Florence tomorrow, before noon, but since I must deliver the princess to her father and make my report to him, I probably won't be available that day. Forgive me if the tone of my last letter was a little severe, but I just think we've wasted enough time. Forget Ferrara. I am counting on you, my friend, to foil Bronzino. As for me, I will take two guards with me and pay a visit to Bacchiacca, even if I doubt the poor old man has any connection to this case, because I would not like you to think that I am leaving all the drudgery to you.

124. Ercole d'Este, Duke of Ferrara, to Cosimo de' Medici, Duke of Florence

Ferrara, 29 April 1557

We are flattered, dear Duke, by your sudden haste to unite our two families, and of course I too am eager to be able to call you my brother. However, you will not have forgotten your previous letter. Your request deeply moved me. How could I not yield to the wishes of a father who desires only to protect his daughter? So I am writing to you today to grant you satisfaction, in perfect agreement with Alfonso, for whom the thought of rushing his bride is anathema. Your charming child is frightened by the thought of being torn from her loving parents' arms; perhaps she fears the cold austerity of the Este castle; she imagines herself being thrown into a court where, although she would of course be warmly welcomed, she would not know a soul. She trembles; she isn't ready for all of this. I understand. After all, there is no hurry, is there? Isn't it enough that the Este and the Medici should publicly state their shared desire – firm and unshakeable on both sides – to unite their houses, by one marriage or another, to seal the friendship of our two families and the alliance of our two cities? Since I would be devastated at the thought that you might doubt my determination to please you in this, my dear Duke, I would like to prove that these are not mere words. So let us say that the wedding is postponed until the autumn. That way, the passing of time will disprove the ugly rumours that are currently being spread by the vile slanderers who always swarm around such events. By the by, I heard that your dear Maria went to Milan earlier this year. I hope she is not too exhausted after her journey; travel is always wearying for ladies, especially for young maids. Please help your daughter to recover from her exertions and assure her that nothing is more important, to my son and to myself, than her good health.

125. Sister Catherine de' Ricci to Sister Plautilla Nelli

Florence, 29 April 1557

God wished for your release, offering us further proof of His mercy. As for myself, I was transferred to the Bargello, and I will continue to suffer for as long as it pleases Him, because I am married to Our Lord, His son: I defy anyone to claim otherwise, now, after seeing my body tortured by the rope as His was upon the Cross. As a matter of fact, the stigmata have returned. Thank you, my God, for having shut the mouths of Sister Marie-Séraphine, Sister Marie-Perpétue and Sister Marie-Modeste, those impious prostitutes, who were never able to bear my divine election. I would not be surprised if, in the future, the convent in Prato was named after me.

I regret only one thing: burning your painting, whose value I was unable to recognise. In hindsight, I can see that I was simply disconcerted by your new style. I now believe that it was perhaps your best work yet. Forgive me, my sister. Is it really true that the prior of the Innocents has taken you in and is encouraging you to continue along that path? I think so, because it was he who allowed me to write to you. He at least is a good man. The next time you see him, would you please say a word, for the love you bear me, about my miserable condition? My soul will soon join that of brother Girolamo, but since I will probably not be given the honour of being burned alive atop a pyre as he was, I would like to be able to pass away in a cell reserved for us by God at the convent, and not in the Bargello.

126. Vincenzo Borghini to Giorgio Vasari

Florence, 29 April 1557

I have spent so many hours within the walls of the Bargello that there are times I feel as if I have been imprisoned there, like all those poor wretches whose moans I can still hear echoing inside the vault of my skull. As a man of God, I cannot complain about the task of assisting you, which is my calling, but I do hope that after an entire day and night spent going through the archives of the current year and six months of the previous year, you will grant me absolution for my trip to Ferrara! Having said that, and as painful and painstaking as the work has been, I cannot deny that it has borne fruit, as you will be able to see for yourself in the letter that I am enclosing with this one, entrusted to the diligence of a guard who has orders to deliver only to you personally. In fact, after searching in vain through the guards' reports for any trace of an incident, of any kind whatsoever, involving Bronzino, I had the idea of tackling the mountain of denunciation letters that arrive at the Bargello on a daily basis, where they are scrupulously conserved. And look what I found! I should point out that this letter was not the only one of its kind – on the contrary, there are half a dozen others – but look at the date: that is what matters.

I trust you will forgive me for not joining you at the palace, nor at the tavern later: exhausted as I am, what I need is the stuff that conserves all beings – sleep. Therefore it is imperative that I go to bed as soon as humanly possible.

127. X to the Bargello

Florence, 1 January 1557

Last night, at one o'clock (I know this because the Duomo bell rang at that very moment), I distinctly heard Angelo di Cosimo di Mariano, otherwise known as Bronzino, a painter, in his lodgings located on Corso degli Adimari, screwing his apprentice, young Sandro Allori. I know this because it is not the first time I have heard them, and because they do not even bother to hide their relations in broad daylight: Bronzino is not shy about teasing him, pinching his cheek or patting him on the bottom, as if he were a young maid. Anyway, everyone in the neighbourhood knows about them. And I can't be mistaken about the identity of the moaners, because those two live alone, in a lodging separate from the house where the Allori family live, behind the armoury of the late Tofano Allori, God rest his soul.

Like our good duke, I believe that those who indulge in sodomy should be punished. That is why I am doing my duty and informing you of these unspeakable acts that offend Our Lord's morals and His Excellency's laws. I don't wish anyone dead, but what good are laws if the guilty aren't punished for breaking them? I should add that they fornicated for a considerable length of time, and that they started at it again just before dawn. Despite that, I saw Bronzino leaving his apartment at matins, showing no signs of fatigue from his nocturnal exertions and even, I would say, looking rather spry. Isn't it peculiar that a man of his age should display such vigour? I suspect some devilry lies behind all this debauchery.

For my own part, I am simply a faithful and obedient subject who would like to be able to sleep at night without being disturbed by the sounds of bestial, unnatural copulation, and I can assure you that all the respectable people on this street think the same.

128. Giorgio Vasari to Vincenzo Borghini

Florence, 30 April 1557

Well, well, Master Vincenzo, it is something of an understatement to say that your zeal has been amply rewarded, and I do not hesitate to send you my congratulations. Isn't it wonderful? You have exonerated our principal suspect with a denunciation letter accusing him of another crime. What a talent you have for paradox and comedy! You should write plays. It is true that Bronzino's alibi is original, to say the least. Although we still need to verify that it is true.

Your letter disrupted my schedule again, and I had to postpone my visit to Bacchiacca so that I could knock on Bronzino's door. I will let you know what he said in more detail once you have finished hibernating, but I will just say that when I informed him about the accusations concerning him, he protested most forcefully, which I found somewhat surprising because surely he cannot be unaware of the rumours about him that have circulated since he was a boy living with Pontormo. As for the duke, despite his recent laws promising death to sodomites, he has never shown much interest in these issues. Do you remember the altercation between Cellini and Bandinelli? The latter called our intrepid ruffian a 'foul sodomite' in front of His Lordship, in the presence of the entire court, preventing him from closing his eyes to the accusation, as he had always done. The priceless Benvenuto riposted with a witticism – 'If only God had allowed me to be initiated in such a noble art!' – followed by a learned speech about a practice supposedly reserved for the gods of ancient Rome, for emperors and kings, while he, the poor little runt, was not worthy of 'such an admirable thing'. His hyperbole reached such ludicrous excesses that the only possible reaction was laughter. That was all it took for the duke to conclude that he did not need to crack down on the practice, and that was not as long ago as one might think. So why would Bronzino refuse to accept a minor stain upon his honour that would clear him of all suspicion in the murder of his master? There is something here that I can't explain.

In any case, I must admit that this unexpected turn of events, which we owe to your admirable stubbornness, has left our investigation in an awkward position. Bronzino brought together the three elements necessary for a guilty verdict: motive, means and opportunity. If it is truthful, your anonymous informer's letter would appear to deprive him of the opportunity, because repainting that section of wall would have taken several hours – all night, in truth, since one must first apply the primer before painting over it. And so, in seeking proof of his guilt, you have found a way to exonerate him. I understand your need to take refuge in dreams, because I myself feel rather overwhelmed by a sudden feeling of weariness. What are we to do if no one person meets all three of our criteria? Must we content ourselves with two? But if we dispense with the need for opportunity, then our list lengthens considerably: among those capable of repainting the fresco as well as Pontormo, we must add Salviati in France (particularly since, if memory serves, he was initially considered for the job of painting the frescoes at San Lorenzo!), Titian in Venice, Michelangelo in Rome . . . Now my head is spinning. How could anyone commit a crime when they are not there? None of this makes any sense, and I think that I too am going to lie in bed. Bacchiacca can wait a while for the honour of my visit.

129. Benvenuto Cellini to Piero Strozzi, Marshal of France

Florence, 1 May 1557

I can't teach an old soldier new tricks, least of all the greatest condottiere in all of Italy and Europe, but here is a truth we would both do well to remember: Fortune is a woman. She gives or refuses her favours as she will, and we will never understand why.

Old Bacchiacca has fallen ill. Consequently, he is bedridden at home. I had a great deal of trouble convincing your assassin to delay our visit to his studio. A strapping lad he may be, but he did not seem to understand the need to recover the painting *in Bacchiacca's absence*.

I hope Fate is smiling upon you at least, and that if we cannot get our hands on that damned painting, you will have the considerable consolation of retaking Naples. In the meantime, be patient. You have put your trust in me and you should keep it there: I can think of no better place for it.

130. Agnolo Bronzino to Giorgio Vasari

Florence, 1 May 1557

You too, Master Giorgio, must decide who you are. The lover of the arts or the servile courtier? The author of the *Lives of the Painters* or the man who does the duke's dirty work? Have you still not understood why Jacopo made that painting, for which you are so desperately searching? You whose eye is so practised in the art of analysing art, are you truly so blind when it comes to things of this century? This pope, this Council, these Catholic kings, and this Inquisition: all authorities to whom our dear duke must pledge his allegiance if he wants to be King of Tuscany – a title he will never be granted, if you want my opinion. Our duke is so liberal, so generous to the artists whom he loves so much, isn't that so? It is true that he could not care less about sodomites or witches or Jews or even Lutherans, as long as they pose no threat to the security of his position. He is not one of those fanatics eager to prove to Germany and to the world that the Catholic faith is not the den of iniquity people think it, full of lustful monks and depraved

Borgias. But deep down, it is even worse. The duke loves us, perhaps, but to find favour with those who hate us and hate our art, he must pretend that he hates us too, and if he had to put us to death or hand us over to Rome in cages like animals, he would do so without hesitation, because nothing and nobody can get in the way of his quest for the Tuscan crown. It is against this formidable hypocrisy, this disgusting duplicity, that Jacopo wished to protest with that painting of Venus that was so offensive to the Medici family. He was angry because he felt abandoned and betrayed. And he was right to feel that way, don't you think? How far do you think the duke would be prepared to go to appease those on whom he depends for his crown?

So you suspect me of having killed Jacopo and I am supposed to feel flattered? Because you believe that I alone was capable of repainting my master's fresco so authentically? And yet, if I had repainted the chancel at San Lorenzo after beating Jacopo to death, I would certainly not have done so in an identical fashion, believe me! I would have shown Noah drunk and naked, the way Michelangelo painted him once on the ceiling of the Sistine Chapel, back when such an image was still tolerated, and I would have enlarged his balls and his member to rub them in the faces of all the Paul IVs and the Philip IIs and the disciples of Savonarola who still infest our city, and all the Spanish duchesses whose prudishness and arrogance and airs and graces sicken me and foment murderous desires within me.

But I am not guilty of the crime of killing my master. As for the other crime of which you accuse me, we are all God's creatures, and I will let your conscience judge whether it merits the punishment that the law provides for in such a case. Whatever you decide, I hope you will be generous enough to spare Sandro, who is still so young and has his whole life ahead of him to return to the straight and narrow.

131. Benvenuto Cellini to Piero Strozzi, Marshal of France

Florence, 2 May 1557

A plague upon your moronic mercenary! He refused to wait until Bacchiacca had recovered from his illness, so I was forced to accompany him, at dawn (since the curfew made any nocturnal outing far too risky), to the old painter's abode, armed with nothing but a hooded cloak and my courage, lacking any conviction that such a hazardous enterprise would succeed. What did he expect to happen? True, entering the house was easy enough since no lock can resist a goldsmith of my calibre. I knew where I had hidden the painting, and we could hear the old man moaning in his bed. But guess what happened next . . . Bacchiacca may have been sick but he was not deaf. He heard us pacing around his studio, and he was not so weakened by his illness that he was incapable of dragging himself out of bed. He appeared before us in the doorway, looking feverish and dumbfounded, his mouth gaping, a nightcap on his head. 'Benvenuto?' he said, because I had pulled back the hood of my cloak since I found it hard to breathe inside it. I was about to ensure his silence by reeling off a speech similar to the one I gave during my incredible feat of audacity in the palace; already, those words – a carefully crafted mixture of reassurances and threats – were on the tip of my tongue, when suddenly your Scoronconcolo (I call him that because he refused to give me his real name, but in point of fact Lorenzino's henchman was infinitely more inspired when it came to helping him kill Alessandro!) took out his dagger and threw it at Bacchiacca, who collapsed with a groan. The imbecile! Yes, another corpse – that was just what we needed.

To crown our misfortune, and as if God wanted to pay us back for your man's stupidity, Bacchiacca's body had not yet hit the floor when we heard footsteps on the stairs. Palace guards! How the devil could they already be upon us? And that is not all: amid the jangling of swords and armour that accompanied their lumbering, I recognised the voice of that little whore Vasari!

With Bacchiacca dying on the floor and Scoronconcolo looking as obviously guilty as a man with 'murderer' engraved on his forehead, it was too late to confound the duke's little dog by telling him one of my tall tales. So I took in the situation in the blink of an eye and settled upon a course of action: hit hard, run fast. In such circumstances, the secret of success is always resolution. Barely had the guards begun to lean over poor Francesco's body than, leaving them no time to react, I leapt upon them like a mastiff. I slit the throats of two of them with my dagger, then attacked the third, who was guarding the door. The door guard, terrified by my ferocity and the gleam of my blood-covered blade, took a step backward and fell to the floor. I jumped over him and rushed down the stairs, leaving your man to be captured by the other guards (I don't know how many of them there were in all, Vasari seemed to have come with an entire battalion). No sooner had I reached the street than I began to yell 'Murderer!' to create the necessary confusion for my escape. Then I disappeared into the dawn crowds before darting through alleys like a ghost.

So it was, miraculously, that I was able to avoid imprisonment in the Bargello. A series of unfortunate events conspired to prevent me from recovering the painting, and you must believe that failure represents a formidable blow to my honour, since I had sworn a vow to you and to the Queen of France, but as you can see, it was hardly my fault. There is no way your man could possibly have escaped with the painting, short of killing everyone in the building, but Vasari cannot be dead because, if he were, the news would already have reached me. We can only hope that your Scoronconcolo has either escaped or shuffled off this mortal coil, or – if he has been arrested – that he will hold his tongue, because otherwise I am done for. Just in case, I am in a state of constant readiness to leave the city. I know from experience, however, that fear is never a good counsellor, so I have decided to wait and keep a low profile, for I am almost certain that Vasari did not recognise me in the heat of the action, my movements being too quick for the human eye.

132. Giorgio Vasari to Michelangelo Buonarroti

Florence, 2 May 1557

I have already told this story to Borghini a dozen times, but I can still barely comprehend what happened to me. As for

Vincenzo, he is utterly incredulous, listening to me open-mouthed while holding me in his arms. Though a very dear friend, he is not a painter. And, even though my hands are still shaking and my shoulder aches and my cheek is burning, I feel compelled to recount to you – God's envoy upon this Earth, adorned with every virtue including that of listening or, in other words, seeing at a distance – this morning's incredible events. The duke will have to wait for his report. I must tell you what happened if I am to see it clearly for myself, by retracing my extraordinary adventure as if I were drawing it.

One sees celestial influence raining the most precious gifts upon certain men such as you, oh my divine Master, genius of a kind that occurs only twice a century. (And even the magnificent Leonardo is your inferior, because he lacks your tremendous piety and because he is no sculptor.) But the benevolent Master of the Heavens who sent you to Earth to enable us to see the beauty of the world through your eyes and your hands, and to offer – in the emotion produced by contemplation of your works – a perceptible sense of the depth of our souls, did not forget, in His infinite mercy, to grant His grace, occasionally but in a similarly supernatural manner, upon men such as me. I give you as proof of this the events of this morning when, without divine intervention, I would have joined the three men (four, in all probability) who are now lying dead, their lives snuffed out forever.

So . . . it was dawn when I went to the house of Francesco Ubertini, known as Bacchiacca, a man whom I doubt you even remember: a disciple of Pietro Perugino, skilled at painting small figures, with a penchant for the grotesque, which is no doubt why the Duke Cosimo so often called upon him to decorate his furniture. His inclinations are visible at San Lorenzo, in the rows of martyrs, and on another section in the chapel of the Crucifixion, but in my eyes that did not make him a suspect in Pontormo's murder. Far from it, in fact, because, while in another century and another place Bacchiacca might have been a first-rate artist, in our days he was just one among many, lost in the crowd. And, besides, he did not possess the capacities to have repainted the fresco at San Lorenzo so perfectly. At least that is what I thought. So I was visiting him purely to satisfy the duke's demands, and to reassure him of our diligence. Since I felt sure that Bacchiacca had nothing to do with this case, I took only two men with me, which should have been sufficient to search his studio, because our priority was to discover the vanished painting.

Arriving at his house, however, we heard some strange noises (like that of a crate being dropped on the floor) and found the door open. Following the sound of his groans, we found Francesco close to death, lying with a dagger in his chest. But as I was leaning down to help him, I heard a second knife whistle through the air; its blade penetrated the back of one of the guards, and he collapsed before my eyes, stone dead. I barely had time to raise my head to see where the attack had come from before a third blade skimmed my cheek before piercing a painting of a young lute player, in the background of which one can see a snowy mountain painted in *sfumato* and some horses pulling a statue of Cupid. If only you could have handed me your bow, little Cupid! Realising that we were exposed and in mortal peril, the second guard and I simultaneously threw ourselves behind a stack of paintings. From another corner of the studio, we suddenly heard the footsteps of a man running towards the door. The guard stood up to stop him, aiming his crossbow at him, but a dagger came flying from the same spot as the others and stabbed the poor guard in the throat. In that moment I understood that the killer's sidekick – probably some little snitch, a small-time crook terrified by the turn of events – was fleeing, because I could hear him hurtling downstairs. And I also understood that the man who had just murdered three men was still lurking inside the studio, and that I would be his next victim.

My final hour was upon me; what I heard then, from my makeshift hiding place, confirmed all my worst fears: heavy footsteps moving slowly, menacingly, across the studio. The dead guard beside me still had his crossbow gripped in his hand. I tried to grab it from him, but his fist remained tightly shut. I had to prise his fingers apart, one after another, but the thumb wouldn't budge. So I tore off his glove and at last the weapon was in my hands. Without thinking, I jumped to my feet and tried to fire a shot, but the thing weighed a ton, and since I had never used a crossbow before, the bolt fell from its rail and I stood there in a daze, facing this giant of a man whose face – gaunt cheeks, short beard, a scar under one eye, the flattened nose betraying an old break – was completely unknown to me. I barely had time to glimpse the glimmer of a flame and to hear the crackle of a burning fuse before a detonation blasted my senses. The next thing I knew, my shoulder felt as if it was on fire, my legs gave way, and I found myself behind the stack of paintings that had served as my shield moments before. As I fell, however, I must have knocked this fragile pyramid, and the corner of one of the paintings now appeared to me, and I saw – yes, I saw! – the face of Princess Maria above the naked body of our Venus. So it was old Bacchiacca (whom I could still hear moaning softly) who had stolen the painting from the wardrobe. But how could he possibly have smuggled it out of the palace?

I did not have time to contemplate this question, however, because I could already hear the killer stuffing powder into the barrel of his miniature arquebus. He knew I had seen him now, of course, so he had abandoned all attempts at discretion. He also knew I was there alone, but armed with a crossbow, and while he had no doubt taken note of my pathetic clumsiness with the weapon, he had evidently decided to eliminate any risk of being shot by shooting me first with his pistol. Once again, I heard the crackle of the fuse. From which side would he appear? Or would he jump over the pile of paintings to attack me head-on? I couldn't wait for an answer – not unless I wanted to die. My shoulder was burning, my head spinning, but I managed to pick up the bolt and slide it into the rail. Luckily, I remembered a sketch by Leonardo that I had seen many years ago: I knew I had to tighten the cord until the mechanism clicked into place, and with a superhuman effort I succeeded. What followed took place in a flash, although to me it seemed to last a century, or even two. From a crawling position, I dived out from behind my hiding place, the weapon in my arms. I saw the man, who turned his pistol towards me. I saw the black eye of the barrel, and the fuse that had almost burnt down. And at that moment something supernatural occurred: the killer aiming a gun at me, the room all around him, the sketches, the furniture, the paintings on the walls, the canvases, the empty frames, the easels, the paint stains on the floor, the dead guard in the foreground, the other dead guard in the background, the dying Bacchiacca (I could no longer hear his moans, nor any other sound) . . . all of it appeared to me like a perfectly composed painting. But that is not all: I saw the lines being drawn through space, forming a geometric grid, and I recognised Alberti's diagram, his pyramid of spokes converging on a single point. It was the laws of perspective taking shape before me, as clearly as if I had traced them myself with a ruler; I touched the surface of things, because it was no longer the real world that I could see in all its depth. Or rather, it was the real world, but I saw it as if through the camera obscura devised by Master Brunelleschi – may his name be honoured until the end of time! – and in the space of a second the world appeared to me as a flat surface, adroitly squared, in all the dazzling clarity of the theory that was revealed to us by those supreme geniuses: Brunelleschi, Alberti, Masaccio . . . may you all be crowned in glory, you eternal Tuscan heroes! And so, as the killer was about to fire at me, because the fuse, as I told you, had almost completely burnt down (this, too, I could perceive with perfect lucidity), I saw – yes, I saw! – the vanishing point drawn on his forehead as if by Alberti himself and (recalling those words of the great master that gave me heart: 'It is in vain that you bend your bow, if you do not yet know where to aim your arrow!' – and *I* knew; in that instant, I knew exactly!) I pulled the trigger, and the bolt shot from my crossbow, following the perfect trajectory that my mind had *calculated* and that an invisible hand had traced through the air, embedding itself *exactly* midway between his eyes. He fell backwards, his shot missed, and – hearing the detonation – I felt as if I had been woken from a long dream that had lasted no more than a second.

But I hadn't dreamed it. I had *remembered* perspective. And this is what I want to tell you, Master Michelangelo, my dear Master. In our thirst to find a new style of painting so that we can surpass (or, rather, circumvent) the perfection achieved by our forefathers – yours, Raphael's and Leonardo's, the three of you having reduced the geniuses of past centuries to the ranks of mere precursors to your reign: that line of Tuscan prophets, from Giotto to Botticelli, that preceded the dawn of the Holy Trinity – have we not forgotten what underlay the very essence of that perfection? It is not that we are unaware of it; we all studied Alberti's theory. But, little by little, all of us – Sarto, Rosso, Beccafumi, Salviati, Pontormo, Bronzino, you yourself, and your Roman friends – we have attempted to free ourselves from it, we have left it behind, we have disdained it. And we have begun to elongate our bodies, to make them float through space, to stretch out where we should foreshorten, to turn our landscapes into dreamscapes, and rather than cutting them up in accordance with mathematical principles that we consider too severe, to twist reality. Order and symmetry have become anathema to us. We have never disowned our great ancestors – Brunelleschi, Masaccio, Uccello – but, while continuing to pay tribute to them, we have abandoned them in our wake, like deaf old men who have lost their minds, the ones we seat at the end of the table during banquets and whom the other guests no longer address except with a few polite, empty greetings when we first see them, before forgetting all about them for the rest of the meal, never thinking about the fact that, were it not for them, there would be no food, no wine, no banquet at all. Without them, there would be nobody at the table. Don't you agree?

Now that I owe it my life, I feel like a terrible ingrate to remember how I once wrote that Paolo Uccello, say, had wasted his talent and ruined his health in his studies of perspective. And how cruel Donatello seems to me, who mocked his friend and, laughing, called out: 'Hey, Paolo! Your perspective makes you abandon the certain for the uncertain. That stuff is only good for marquetry!' I now believe the exact opposite to be true. There is nothing more certain than perspective, nothing more essential, nothing more eternal. It is perspective, and perspective alone, more than all the battles and all the poems and all the treatises by Machiavelli or Castiglione, that gave our Tuscany its immortality, that means people will talk about us for centuries and centuries, from China to the Americas. 'Oh, what a sweet thing is this perspective!' Master Uccello murmured ecstatically when his wife called him in the middle of the night. And truly, if it was sweet to him, it was no less useful, thanks to him, to those who practised it after him. This is what my misadventure brought to mind this morning, and that I wished to share with you. Forgive your friend, my dear Master, for these feverish flights of fancy.

133. Vincenzo Borghini to Giorgio Vasari

Florence, 5 May 1557

After the terrible peril from which you miraculously escaped, and notwithstanding the corpses that are piling up around us – or, rather, because of the murderous epidemic that is striking the members of your guild – I could give you no better advice than to forget about your renovations of the Signoria, the Pitti and all the other palaces, and to go home to Arezzo and get some rest.

Unfortunately, you have been given the responsibility of untangling this bloody imbroglio, and I fear, my friend, that I am about to add yet another element to its confusion: a letter that Bronzino sent to Rome, intercepted by the duke's spies and handed to me in your absence. I will let you read it when you return to the palace because, for now, your nerves need rest, after coming so close to death, and I would not wish for all the world to disturb your rehabilitation with evidence that shines a new – and deeply troubling – light on our investigation. In a word, we have learned that Bronzino hid the colour-grinder Moro before helping him escape. But, as surprising as this may seem, I think that is the least of our concerns. This letter is highly instructive, to say the least, and I must confess that reading it made my head spin a little. Tell me if you interpret it the same way I do.

134. Agnolo Bronzino to Michelangelo Buonarroti

Florence, 4 May 1557

By the time you receive this note, dear Master, my Sandrino will already be on his way to Rome where, you can be sure, he will be safer than he is here. I know how oppressive is the weight of this pope's yoke, and the endless harassment to which he subjects you, but at least you are not yet at risk of the noose or the pyre.

Thanks to you, Sandro was able to leave the city by the same secret passage that you were generous enough to reveal to us previously for the colour-grinder's flight. And although my heart grieves over his departure, it rejoices equally, for every league that takes Sandro away from Florence distances him from the madness that seems to have gripped this cursed city. The day before yesterday, Bacchiacca was found dead in his home. The rumour is that it was Vasari who killed him.

Sandro escaped in the night, with nothing but a purse that I gave him and a few paintbrushes, not even a horse. It is not to God that I entrust this boy who is dearer to me than a son, but to you, Master, because I know your good heart, and I know how touched you were during his previous visit to Rome by the nobility of his sentiments. I would also like to believe that you were impressed by the promise of his art. Furthermore, there is nobody in the world whom he admires more than you, not even me. So I dare to hope that you will not refuse him your friendship or – even more importantly – your protection. I am begging you, as a man on the brink of despair: take care of him. Save my student, Master. He is the heir to all I taught him and, consequently, all you taught me.

135. Giorgio Vasari to Vincenzo Borghini

Florence, 6 May 1557

Where are you, my friend? I was so hoping to find you at the palace, but instead all I found was your message. I read Bronzino's letter, and I think I understand what is agitating your mind, which has grown even more feverish than my own: 'After all, the man we thought in Rome perhaps had the opportunity to kill Pontormo, since he had the means to enter Florence without going through the city gates, and therefore without anyone knowing about his presence.' But, Vincenzo, that is quite simply impossible. The great Michelangelo could not have disappeared for more than a day without people worrying about his absence. And it would have taken him at least two days to cover the two hundred miles that separate him from Florence and then return to Rome. And even that hypothesis would only be valid for a man in the prime of life, enjoying robust good health, not a venerable old man of eighty-two who has not set foot in his home city for twenty-five years and who, moreover, has complained of his decrepitude in every single letter he has written for years and years. It would take him a whole week to make that return journey!

I am going to have this note delivered to the Innocents in the hope that, whatever business is detaining you, you will find a way to drop it and join me.

136. Vincenzo Borghini to Giorgio Vasari

Florence, 6 May 1557

In fact, it is your Arezzo nuns who are currently causing me a headache: would you believe that they are complaining that their cells are too cramped? (We only have a limited amount of space available, so they are each having to share with several of their sisters.) But did they think they were being invited to an inn? They even have the nerve to moan about the quantity of wine that is graciously allocated to them at the refectory, considering it insufficient. And now they are demanding a wall so that they can play real tennis – as they were at liberty to do, or so they claim, in Siena! I want to nip this rebellion in the bud before it spreads through the rest of the hospital, and that is why I cannot meet you at the palace straight away. But the subject that occupies us is too important to leave you without a response until tonight (because I will see you at the tavern, won't I?), so I am taking a moment to write you this message.

In response to your note: you credit me with thoughts, Master Giorgio, that I am utterly incapable of having. Who could imagine our universal genius – to whom the heavenly Creator granted, in addition to all his other gifts, a true sense of moral philosophy, sprinkled with a sweet poetry that compels the world to consider and admire him as its unique mirror – capable of such a terrible crime?

However – and since, according to your own advice, we must consider all possible theories in the light of a cold, abstract logic – it does occur to me to mention a story I heard at the tavern: when the great Lorenzo the Magnificent became so ill that he was at death's door, his friends naturally rushed to his bedside, along with a crowd of courtiers, among them a certain Aldobrandino, who boasted of having ridden from Rome to Florence in less than eight hours. At the time, nobody believed him and they put his claim down as a courtier's typical empty bragging. But apparently the man always insisted he was telling the truth. And while I know very little about the equestrian arts, since I can barely ride twenty leagues on my ass, it does not strike me as mathematically inconceivable, with a good charger, to cover the distance separating the two cities in such a short time.

And so, if we assume for the purposes of our investigation that Aldobrandino was telling the truth, then the impossible becomes *theoretically* possible: eight hours to ride from Rome to Florence. Eight hours to enter San Lorenzo, kill Pontormo, and repaint the fresco (including time for the primer to dry). And eight hours to return to Rome. But I'm sure you're right! All of this is merely sterile speculation, because it would require the entire odyssey to be carried out without a single minute's rest, which seems highly improbable even for a young man like Aldobrandino (and even he didn't mention returning at the same speed), never mind for a venerable old man like Master Buonarroti, even if he is (as you always maintain) God's envoy upon this Earth.

137. Giorgio Vasari to Cosimo de' Medici, Duke of Florence

Florence, 8 May 1557

I will say nothing to His Excellency beyond what I know and what I can, but – devoted solely to obeying the truth – I will share with him what I am certain about and, sometimes, what I believe to be true without being entirely sure of it, since it is almost impossible to avoid any kind of mistake in such a tangled affair.

First, the painting was destroyed, in accordance with His Lordship's wishes.

Second, Francesco Ubertini, known as Bacchiacca, in whose home the painting was found, is still hovering between life and death, and cannot be questioned. However, it is known that Bacchiacca spent almost every day working in His Lordship's wardrobe, where I encountered him several times, and where several witnesses state that they left him alone on numerous occasions, from whence we can legitimately conclude that he must have stolen the painting, using a stratagem that we have not yet discovered.

Third, the identity of the assailant who killed the two sergeants remains unknown, but his accoutrement and his skill with arms suggest that he was a mercenary, a soldier or a deserter, and perhaps a professional assassin. His sidekick left no trace, but the fact that he fled, abandoning his accomplice when they might reasonably have been expected to have the upper hand – given the balance of power – supposes that they were not partners and did not know each other well.

Fourth, the painting is undoubtedly the work of Pontormo and nobody else. His motivations remain obscure but appear to be connected to a form of resentment that he developed towards His Excellency, demonstrating a distinct lack of gratitude to his patron and benefactor. It is also true that the old painter was no longer in his right mind, and those around him have unanimously remarked upon the deterioration in his character, manifested as a growing acrimony towards everyone and everything. It does appear, however, that Pontormo did not intend to damage His Lordship by showing the painting to anyone, but preferred to keep his insolence a secret, hiding the painting in his studio. The same is probably not true for Bacchiacca. For what reason, or for whom, did Bacchiacca go to the trouble of stealing it? The most likely trail leads towards your republican enemies, whether they were sent from outside by the *fuorusciti* or whether they were secretly conspiring within the city's walls. (This last hypothesis seems the least likely, since the proverbial magnanimity of His Excellency long ago won the hearts and minds of all Florentines, but I feel I must mention it out of a scrupulous determination to be methodical.)

Were they the same people who killed Pontormo? There is nothing to suggest this, since the theory of the republican conspiracy would not explain why the fresco at San

Lorenzo was repainted. Regarding this part of the puzzle, I can at least assure you that Bronzino is cleared of all suspicion, along with his apprentice Allori. We must hope that Bacchiacca recovers from his wounds, so that we can interrogate him, because for now he is more dead than alive. In the meantime, I must investigate a new theory that Master Borghini, with his customary self-sacrifice, has enabled us to formulate.

138. Cosimo de' Medici, Duke of Florence, to Giorgio Vasari

Florence, 9 May 1557

You have more than earned some rest, my good Giorgio, and I order you to spend a few days at your home in Arezzo. I know how ardently you work to embellish it with paintings and frescoes. For once, you may take care of yourself, and not of Florence. Let your wife nurse you back to health. Paint some pretty lunettes and tondi above your doors, then return once you are fully recovered.

Soon enough we will be able to sweep away the last shadows of this affair. For now, know that I am quite satisfied, and receive my gratitude: you brought back my daughter, you found the painting that was so offensive to my family, you identified its thief, you uncovered several plots against the Duchy of Tuscany, interrogated the Savonarolist nuns, stifled a new Ciompi rebellion, and even slew an assassin sent by my enemies among the *fuorusciti* (for I am certain that if you were to scratch the surface of that plot a little, you would soon find the trail of that dog Strozzi). Thanks to you, everybody knows that defying my authority carries a high price. All you need do now is discover Pontormo's murderer, although personally I have little doubt: I believe it was old Bacchiacca, since all the evidence points to him.

139. Agnolo Bronzino to Sandro Allori

Florence, 10 May 1557

Sandrino, it was not Vasari's generosity of spirit that I was counting upon, but his self-interest. What did he have to gain by giving credence to slanderous accusations from an anonymous source? He is no fool, and the duke ordered him to find the killer of a painter, not to persecute sodomites. So I made a deliberate calculation when I pretended to place my fate and yours in his hands. His discretion cost him nothing, and probably gave him a feeling of nobility that coddled his vanity (because, beneath his humble airs, he does not lack in that regard), and that is why he at first appeared to go along with it.

Unfortunately, the situation has changed. Vasari is now in possession of a letter in which I rather imprudently confessed to having helped the colour-grinder escape, and that is a very different story. Because while the duke, for all his desire to conform to the new spirit of the times and despite the laws that he himself decreed, has no interest in exposing all the sodomites in his court, the barest whisper of a plebeian revolt is enough to plunge him into the dark depths of dread and anger. Sodomites? Fine. But the Ciompi? Absolutely not. Any prince who has read his Machiavelli will always know whom he can tolerate and whom he must fear.

Vasari has not denounced me to the duke, but in exchange for his silence he is demanding certain information about Michelangelo that you alone can obtain for me. You must tell me if the Master was in Rome between 30 December and 3 January, what he was doing, and who he was with, or I will soon be locked in a dungeon of the Bargello. You can imagine how mortified I am at having to ask you to do such a vile thing, but Vasari showed me the letter, and it is damning for me.

140. Sandro Allori to Agnolo Bronzino

Rome, 17 May 1557

You know that for you I would repaint the Sistine Chapel while hanging upside down, and what you ask of me really isn't much at all. Here, Michelangelo is a little like our Jacopo was in Florence: irascible, solitary, but forever meeting with his many friends. And his prestige remains so great, despite his age and the fact that the pope is ill-disposed towards him, that anyone who has the honour of encountering him remembers the day and the circumstances of their meeting with the Master perfectly. So it was not too difficult to reconstruct his schedule. All it took was a little patience.

During the first two weeks of December, our divine Buonarroti spent several days in the hills of Spoleto, where he likes to walk through the woods and enjoy the company of hermits, far from the crowds in Rome. He came back around the 15th or the 16th, then did not budge until the end of the month. Every day, he went to the basilica to work on his dome, a monumental task that any other man would long ago have given up in despair. On the 30th, he was summoned by the papal chamberlain, Master Pietro Giovanni Aliotti, the Bishop of Forli, who caused him great distress once again by talking about His Holiness's plan to paint over all his frescoes in the Sistine, about which he complained bitterly to his good friends, Masters Sebastiano del Piombo and Daniele da Volterra. Back at home that evening, he received some cheese from Casteldurante, sent by the widow of his dear Urbino, whose children are his godchildren and for whose needs he provides almost entirely, as well as a letter that appears to have plunged him into a state of unusual agitation, even considering his naturally bilious character. I have this information from the two Antonios who have looked after him since Urbino's death, and with whom, on the morning of the 31st, he generously shared that cheese that he adored. He was seen again at terce, on horseback, riding the splendid destrier that Paul III gave him some time ago, which he now takes out only rarely. That day, he was not seen at St Peter's, but this surprised nobody since he often doesn't set foot in the basilica for several days at a time, occupied as he is with other work. He returned there the next day at vespers, when Master Sebastiano Malenotti from San Gimignano, who supervises his work at St Peter's, recalls an altercation with Master Sallustio Peruzzi, the pope's architect, who had come to check on his progress. Master Sebastiano assured me that such disputes are commonplace. However, Master Antonio, the stonemason, believed that this argument was what led Michelangelo to spend the next week sick in bed, doing nothing but composing sonnets and loudly lamenting his fate.

As you can see, I have not been idle. And to respond more precisely to your question: nobody seems to have seen him on 31st December after the middle of the morning. But the next day, at nightfall, he was there.

141. Eleanor of Toledo to Cosimo de' Medici

Pisa, 18 May 1557

My friend, your daughter's health is not improving. She hardly eats – which, given her condition, is a danger for her and for the child – and spends all day in bed crying her eyes out, in the state of languishment that you have seen for yourself. I can barely manage to get three words out of her. The news of the painting's destruction has had no effect on her. Why didn't you listen to me? You should have burned that painting the day you discovered it! It was the painting that allowed that Malatesta boy to seduce Maria, under the pretext of informing her about and comforting her against the outrageous insult of which she was the victim. My poor daughter, the innocent expiatory victim of a madman, an ingrate whom you coddled for years. This is the result of all those cases of florins that you squandered on the countless commissions that Florence and the whole of Tuscany granted your Pontormo! While he was profaning Heaven with his vile frescoes, he was also ridiculing our family and insulting our daughter by painting that obscene picture. My only consolation is knowing that he will burn eternally in Hell with all those naked bodies he was so fond of.

142. Benvenuto Cellini to Piero Strozzi, Marshal of France

Florence, 20 May 1557

If I am to believe the news that reaches us here, the road to Naples did not open up to the prince of Lorraine's army, and the Duke of Alba's Spanish soldiers gave you a hard time. But you are alive, and that is reason for rejoicing. Your Benvenuto is alive too – another reason for rejoicing. I regret not being able to help you triumph on the field of battle. Who knows – if I had been beside you, perhaps I would have rid you of Alba with an arquebus shot, as I once did with Bourbon.

For my part, after Vasari burst into Bacchiacca's house and the fiasco that followed, thanks to the idiocy of your man, the words of our good King François when he was taken prisoner in Pavia are apt: '*Tout est perdu fors* *l'honneur.'** (A misfortune and a glory that is not likely to happen to the Duke of Florence, since Cosimo, more prudent than our knightly king, wisely avoids battlefields.) In truth, however, all is perhaps not lost. Your man died before he could tell anyone my name, and the dying Bacchiacca is in no fit state to say a word; so I remain free in my movements. If God is with me, as He usually is, I still think I will be able to obtain what you desire.

I will send this letter to Rome, where it will await your return, because I have no doubt that you will go through there, with or without Guise, whom, I have heard, remains in a rage against the pope.

143. Piero Strozzi to Catherine de' Medici, Queen of France

Rome, 21 May 1557

To hell with the pope and his filthy, scheming nephews! We are too harsh on Fortune, whom we too often blame for our failures, when the causes can almost always be found in treachery. Not only did that old bastard Carafa not send us the promised reinforcements, fatally compromising our chances of taking Civitella, which would have opened up

* In French in the text. An English translation: 'All is lost but my honour.'

the road to Naples, but Guise is sure that that shit-eater is in secret negotiations with the Spanish, without success for now, so that His Holiness – who fears another sacking like the one that ravaged Rome thirty years ago – shamelessly begs us to stay here with the French army to protect his city, after he let us down so badly when we needed him. Add to that the fact that Suleiman's fleet, which was supposed to raid the Naples coastline, has not left the Bosphorus, and you will see how impossible was the mission to which Guise committed us. But I told him that from the beginning. He would have been better off marching on Florence.

As for me, I am on my way home. I am bringing your husband the king a few hostages, which I hope will make him happy. God willing, dear cousin, I will see you very soon. Sadly, I regret I will not be able to bring you the painting I promised, since events there have not turned out as we hoped. However, there remains a slender hope; I set no great store by it, but hope costs us nothing. We must simply wait, and we will soon find out if that devil Cellini is truly a miracle worker, as he claims, or if he is, as you thought all along, a loud-mouthed wastrel.

144. Cosimo de' Medici to Eleanor of Toledo

Florence, 27 May 1557

How is Maria? Make her eat, whether through persuasion or force, because she must recover as quickly as possible, before her condition becomes too visible. Actually, I am coming around to your point of view. If the Duke of Este no longer wants her for his degenerate son, so be it! We will find her another husband, and a better one, because the situation is already looking much more favourable. The news that reaches us from the Kingdom of Naples is excellent, and the credit for that belongs to your uncle and his glorious feats. The Duke of Alba is leading the French army into a pitiful retreat. Guise has taken refuge in Rome, and Strozzi is already on his way back to France. The pope is in secret negotiations with your uncle, which is to say with the Spanish Crown. Once the French have left Italy for good, then His Holiness – abandoned by his allies, isolated and defenceless – will have no choice but to submit to King Philip. You have always insisted that I should flatter the pope, despite his hostility towards us, and I congratulate myself for having listened to you. I will show him that Florence tolerates no breach in morality, and that I am his most faithful servant in his battle against heresy and depravity. Thus, thanks to your wise counsel, shall I obtain his blessing to be crowned King of Tuscany by the emperor. And then, fortunate indeed will be he who marries my daughter!

I send you kisses, my queen, and commend you to God.

145. Giorgio Vasari to Vincenzo Borghini

Florence, 30 May 1557

Vincenzo, see below the calculations that I made after our discussion:

- Departure from Rome at dawn.
- Arrival in Florence at 11 o'clock at night.
- Meeting with Pontormo, argument, fight, murder. Primer. Painting.
- Departure from Florence before dawn, at 4 or 5 in the morning.
- Arrival in Rome around 5 in the evening, 6 at the latest, since he was seen arguing with the chamberlain at vespers.

No horse in the world could cover such a distance at that speed. I blush at the thought that I ever imagined the Master guilty of such a terrible deed – so contrary to his good nature and to the God who sent him to live among us here on Earth. In any case, the divine Buonarroti could not be in Florence that night, and in Rome the next day. It is impossible, unless he was riding Pegasus.

146. Vincenzo Borghini to Giorgio Vasari

Florence, 30 May 1557

I cannot join you now because I am detained once again at the Innocents, where I must continue negotiations with your nuns, whose list of demands grows longer every day, like the order book of a Flemish decorator. Now they want to eat in the same refectory as us. God in Heaven, Master Giorgio, why did you have to send me those cursed sisters?

I will see you tonight at the tavern, if God allows me to survive this endless bickering!

P.S. You are right: with only one horse, it would be impossible.

147. Sandro Allori to Agnolo Bronzino

Rome, 6 June 1557

It wasn't easy this time, but I think I have the information that Master Vasari asked you to obtain.

On 31 December last year, Master Michelangelo went to Orvieto, apparently stirred once again by the sudden desire to see the astounding frescoes by Signorelli that decorate the cathedral there. This is what he told the stonemason Antonio, who was concerned by his absence that evening and even more so the next morning. Master Antonio (as Master Michelangelo calls him, because the two men are good friends) remembers this because the Master asked him not to tell anyone about that trip, to prevent the pope reproaching him for deserting his work at St Peter's without permission. The stonemason divulged this secret to me (after a great deal of patience, caresses and wine) but did not consider that he was betraying his friend in doing so, since I had neither the intention nor the possibility of reporting it to the pope or one of his cardinals. However, he was deeply regretful afterwards and made me swear not to speak of it to anyone. I promised him that I would never do anything that might harm the divine Michelangelo. Was I wrong, Agnolo?

148. Giorgio Vasari to Michelangelo Buonarroti

Florence, 13 June 1557

Oh magnificent Michelangelo, my quill is made of lead, but the duke is my master and I do what I do in search of the truth. I beg you to forgive me for the impertinence of this question, but I must ask it of you: were you in Florence on the night of 31 December last year?

149. Michelangelo Buonarroti to Giorgio Vasari

Rome, 21 June 1557

Master Giorgio, my dear friend, you cannot imagine how little it pains me to write this letter that, God willing, you now hold in your hands, or, on the contrary, how relieved I am to set down the truth.

You must understand – you who do not shirk the weightiest commissions and who, consequently, know with what suffering and anguish we are rewarded for our ambitions – the state of exhaustion that has been mine for the ten years since I took on this task at St Peter's. The more I devote myself to this dome that has given me so many worries, the more I feel you were right regarding the revelation you were granted during your misadventure at poor Bacchiacca's house: Brunelleschi is the greatest genius that Italy has ever produced, that Europe has ever known. My double-shelled dome has sixteen interior sections and sixteen exterior sections! A monumental undertaking, I'm sure you will agree. No doubt it is more solid than his was, but without his, mine would never have existed, not even in my dreams.

Believe me, there was only one thing I desired: to finish my work at St Peter's, then to return to Florence with the intention of taking my rest in the company of Death, with whose presence I have been seeking to familiarise myself, night and day, in the hope that he will not treat me more harshly than he does other old people. Alas, I now know that this wish will never be granted.

Brunelleschi's discovery of the laws of perspective was like Prometheus stealing fire and giving it to mankind. Thanks to him, we have been able not only to illuminate our walls as Giotto once did with his golden fingers, but to reproduce the world as it is, identical in every detail. And so it was that the painter could imagine himself God's equal: because now, we too could create reality. And that was how we came to try, poor fishermen that we are, to surpass Our Lord. We could copy the world as faithfully as if we had made it ourselves, but that was not enough to quench our thirst for creation, because our ambition as artists, intoxicated by this new power, now knew no limits. We wanted to paint the world in our own style. We didn't merely wish to rival God, but to alter His work by redrawing it to suit our desires. We distorted perspective, we abandoned it. We erased the chequerboard floors of our predecessors and let our figures float in the ether. We played with perspective the way a dog plays with a ball, or a cat with the corpse of a sparrow it has killed. We turned away from it. We scorned it. But we never forgot it.

How could we? Perspective gave us depth. And depth opened the gates of infinity to us. A terrible spectacle. I can never recall without shivering the first time I saw Masaccio's frescoes at the Brancacci Chapel. The wonder of his foreshortened figures! There stood man, life-sized at last, having found his place in space, his substance given weight, cast out of paradise but standing on his own two feet, in all his mortal truth. Far from constricting the imagination of artists, perspective gave us the image of infinity on Earth. The image only . . . yes, of course. In reality, we could not claim to equal the Creator of all things, but we could, better than any priest, proclaim His word through mute images or stone statues. Painters, sculptors, architects: the artist is a prophet because, more than any other man, his mind contains the idea of God, which is infinity itself, that unthinkable, inconceivable thing. And yet . . . Even if we could not conceive it, we could represent it. It was perspective that enabled us to see infinity, to understand it, to feel it. Depth on a plane perpendicular to the axis of the visual cone is infinity – infinity that we can touch with a fingertip. Perspective is infinity brought within reach of all who have eyes to see. Our mortal perception did not and could not grasp the notion of infinity, so we thought. But, by grace of the painters who mastered optical effects, this miracle was made possible: we can *see beyond*. Our eyes can see through walls. That half-arched vault at Santa Maria Novella, traced in perspective, divided into coffers decorated with ceiling roses, each smaller than the one before so that the vault appears to sink into the wall: a *trompe l'œil*, an illusion, but what a marvel! Let no one ignorant of geometry enter here? Plato was more right than he knew! A painting is not only, as Alberti thought, a window through which we can see a fragment of the visible world. Or perhaps it is only that, but even so, isn't that already miracle enough to attest to its divine essence? We are God's windows. Yes, that is what we are. It is true that he who exceeds the role given to him on this Earth commits a sin, but he who shirks his task and leaves it to another or who does not take it seriously is also a sinner, and that is why we must not underestimate our works, but must, on the contrary, respect them and take care of them and defend them against anyone who seeks to harm them. Our own and those of others, when they are worthy.

You ask if I was in Florence on 31 December last year, and I know that if you are asking me that question, you already know the answer.

So, it was the beginning of winter. I returned from Spoleto, where I had been living as a recluse, purging myself of Roman corruption, and that brief stay had given me enough strength to start work again on my thankless task, in the service of God. I was already prey to the pettiest chicaneries, preoccupied as never before by the oppressive burden of carrying forward the construction work at St Peter's to the point where it could no longer be ruined or altered against my wishes, when I received a letter from poor Jacopo. And what a letter! You remember your own, asking for my help in clearing up the mystery of his death? He, too, was asking for my help, but his missive was so utterly desperate. I didn't know him well, and he had written to me only rarely during the twenty-five years since I had left Florence, but no sooner had I read his opening lines than I knew him to be a brother suffering the same tribulations that I must endure here. The entire letter was one long lament, the cry of a creature abandoned by his protectors, the inarticulate moaning of a dying beast, the words of a madman who believes the entire world is conspiring against him. And despite these rambling lines, behind the apparent exorbitance of his distress and the litany of his imprecations, that howl of pain and despair – unintelligible to the mass of men – was only too comprehensible for me. I know how mistaken is the fickle passion that leads us to make Art our idol and monarch, and how surely our desires conspire to hurt us. Pontormo had thought he was pleasing his benefactors by painting for the glory of God, but Earth's clock does not tick in unison with Heaven's. He had become convinced that his masters were no longer satisfied with him, and that in fact the work to which he had devoted more than a decade of his life was repugnant to them; and that it would be repugnant, too, to the people of Florence, who had lost their desire to enjoy true beauty. So he had made the decision to bring an end to his life, and to take his work with him into the tomb. Before killing himself, since his frescoes were no longer beautiful in the eyes of the duke and the duchess, he swore he would destroy them, would reduce the chapel at San Lorenzo to rubble, to render it immaculate, erase all trace of his presence within, all trace of his labours, from the eyes of the princes who had entrusted him with its decoration.

To me, that idea was unbearable. When I thought of those frescoes despoiled, it was my Sistine that I saw in ruins, or – worse – repainted, lost beneath the daubings of some soulless drudge. I had to prevent that crime. And I wanted to see those frescoes. Jacopo's letter had been written three days earlier, so I knew I didn't have a second to lose. Terrified of arriving too late, I made the decision to leave for Florence that very moment. But I couldn't tell anyone I was going, because I knew that the pope, who holds me prisoner in Rome, would never permit it, and also that the duke, if he learned of my presence in Florence, would never let me leave again. You know how these princes fight over your poor Michelangelo, each believing he has the right to dispose of me like some precious merchandise, a trophy coveted by all, a slave with no will of his own, sworn to obey their every command. So I left in the morning, without warning anyone, pretending – in the event that the pope enquired about my whereabouts – that I was going to visit Signorelli's frescoes in Orvieto. I straddled my Arabian steed, who had lost none of his speed or grace, and rode so hard that I reached Orvieto in only five hours. There, I left my horse in the tender care of the verger and, without even setting foot in the basilica, continued the rest of the way on post horses. Where did a poor old wretch like me find the strength to ride for twelve hours straight, never leaving the saddle except to mount a fresh steed? Evidently, God was on my side. I arrived that same evening in Florence completely shattered, my arse red and aching from its leather pounding. I used the secret passage that I myself once dug, without marking it on any map, when the Republic entrusted me with the task of building the fortifications for the siege of 1529, and – without being seen – I crept towards San Lorenzo like a thief, hugging the walls.

There, I found poor Jacopo painting a leg, which seemed like a good sign: perhaps he was ready to move forward again, his fit of melancholy having dissipated? Sadly, it was nothing of the kind. As soon as he saw me, he fell into my arms weeping and began to thank God. As he was shedding his tears on my shoulder, as he was moaning and embracing me, I had time to contemplate his frescoes in the candle-light. And I, too, thanked Our Lord. Tuscany, mother of beauty! I knew it at first sight: Florence had its own Sistine. How could you have been so wrong about those frescoes, Master Giorgio? Does the duke have such influence over you that he has clouded your very eyes? Those frescoes are a miracle of art, of the kind seen only three times a century, and if the mob does not understand them, it is because they would call the sun darkness if it was beyond their comprehension. Poor Florence. Heaven must be sleeping for one man to take for himself what was given to all.

The more I told Jacopo how much I loved and admired his work, the more bitterly he wept. 'Master! You came! You came!' he cried, trembling with emotion. He thanked me repeatedly and knelt to kiss my feet. Now that I had seen his frescoes, he could die, he told me. I tried to reason with him, to comfort him, saying that he had to remain alive so that he could finish his work. But at those words, he went into a rage. He crawled away from me, grabbed a burin, and – yelling 'I bring a flood of waters upon the Earth!' – started smashing it against his Noah. He struck the wall again and again, damaging the fresco with each blow. I tried to stop him but, in an uncontrollable rage, he shoved me to the ground and continued his work of destruction. Speechless and terrified, I watched as fragments of paint went flying. 'Why was I born, if only for such misery, for such a wretched life?' he bellowed. 'How glad I would be to see and feel nothing!' And as he roared this, he was animated – by what miracle, I do not know, this man who had done nothing but paint his whole life – with the fury of a sculptor, carving ever deeper into the stone.

Suddenly he stopped for an instant, then stared up at his Last Judgement and declaimed: 'Oh, shadow of death, you heal our sick flesh, wipe away our tears, soothe our weariness, and lift the weight of rage and troubles from the righteous.' Just then, I thought he was going to end this madness, that his nerves had finally been overcome by fatigue. How wrong I was! I saw a fire in his eyes, burning with an infernal resolution. He moved towards the central panel and raised his damned burin like a dagger. The next blow would have been all the more powerful, coming from above like that, and I foresaw the irreversible damage it would cause. So my hand groped for a hammer that had been left beside some other tools on the floor and, possessed by the same fury as he, all thoughts fled my mind and in a flash I was upon him, bringing the hammer down upon his head, so strongly that he collapsed unconscious at my feet.

How long did I stand there before that desolate sight? I do not know. But time was a luxury I no longer possessed. You know I am not a bad painter and that I have some experience with the art of frescoes. What I had seen was emblazoned in my memory; it had taken only a single glance to remember it perfectly. I prepared the primer, slathering it over the damaged parts of the wall, sealing the cracks. I had to grind the colours myself since my dear Urbino was not with me, and that was the most difficult part because I did not know the method Jacopo used to obtain those pastel tints of his. Then I repainted Noah. My hand has always been quick and decisive in execution. A mediocre painter could not copy a master, and a master would have great difficulty copying a mediocre painter. But Jacopo was not mediocre; he excelled in his art, so I was able to imitate him easily. I had finished my work when I heard him waking up. I leaned over him to make sure he was all right – or as all right as he could be, given the circumstances and the hammer blow I had inflicted upon him. I was supporting the back of his head when I noticed that he was looking at me. And in his glassy eyes I saw the same infernal gleam that had burned in them before. I knew then. It was nearly dawn, and I had to leave Florence before my presence there was discovered, but after I departed, in a day, or a week, he would start again. Nothing could prevent him from destroying his own work. So God whispered that terrible resolution to me. I picked up a chisel, and before he had completely recovered his wits, with a precise gesture determined by my perfect knowledge of human anatomy, I stabbed him in the chest, the blade penetrating his heart and granting him the release that he had so ardently desired. His death was instantaneous. But his work had been saved.

It was almost dawn. I had to hurry. I left the city the same way I had entered it. Feverish and shaken by what I had done, I flew through Tuscany like a ghost, riding post horse after post horse, chasing the endless horizon. I found my Arabian waiting for me in Orvieto, and from there I rode back to Rome in even less time than it had taken me in the opposite direction. That evening, I was at St Peter's. Less than a week later, I received your letter asking me to help you identify Pontormo's murderer.

I can think of nothing else to tell you. Make whatever use you wish of this confession.

150. Giorgio Vasari to Michelangelo Buonarroti

Florence, 27 June 1557

Dear Master, divine Michelangelo, forgive my delay in replying to you, but it was St John's Eve, and as usual I was in charge of preparations for the festivities. You know Florence: not a week goes by without a feast day, and it is almost always I who must organise things. This makes it extremely difficult for me to find time to take care of the many other tasks with which the duke has honoured me, not to mention the interminable work on the Palazzo della Signoria, which has become for me what St Peter's is for you – not, of course, that I would ever compare my modest abilities as an architect with yours, which are beyond all human measurement. This year's Palio was especially dramatic, with the Santa Croce team beating Santa Maria Novella to the finishing line.

His Excellency the Duke has asked me to reiterate his invitation: you are always welcome in Florence, and our city would love nothing more than to see you return. He promises that you would be greeted with every honour due to your genius, and vows that Pontormo's fresco will be completed according to your wishes: the duke himself will ensure that Bronzino respects the spirit in which Pontormo originally conceived it.

Regarding the latter, the duke guarantees that nobody will hold you responsible for the unfortunate circumstances that cost Pontormo his life, for the simple reason that they will remain secret, known only to three people other than yourself: the duke, your servant, and Don Vincenzo Borghini, upon whose honour I would stake my life. Officially, Pontormo committed suicide. For the small inner circle who are privy to certain details of the affair, we will offer this second version, leaving the winds of gossip to carry it through the rest of the city: it was Bacchiacca who killed Pontormo, over some obscure rivalry. If Bacchiacca ever recovers (because he is still gravely wounded and his fevered mind seems perpetually in limbo), the duke, in his magnanimity, will offer him exile as an alternative to hanging, in exchange for his discretion. (Besides, the old man knows nothing and can do nothing to harm us.) I would add that the duchess herself has been kept out of these negotiations, and that the duke has chosen not to inform her of any details that you provided me in your last letter. As far as His Lordship is concerned, he does not reproach you for anything other than travelling to Florence without notifying him, before returning immediately to Rome. But you never came to Florence.

So, from the point of view of His Excellency (which is the only point of view that counts), everything has been resolved. The painting that Pontormo created in a moment of madness – demonstrating an unjustified ingratitude towards the family that had showered him with honours and commissions – has been destroyed. The assassin hired by republican exiles has been killed. Likewise, the seditious activities of the conspirator Marco Moro have been brought to an end, since he was forced to flee the city, ridding Florence of his presence. The young Princess Maria will be married soon and will provide the duke with a grandson. The nuns Plautilla Nelli and Catherine de' Ricci, having been cleared of any involvement in Pontormo's death, will be pardoned for their sympathies towards the Dominican friar Girolamo Savonarola on the condition that they publicly renounce his teachings and recognise their errors, and that they promise never to get mixed up in painting again. Bronzino alone will finish the frescoes in the San Lorenzo chapel, for which he will be granted a salary of two thousand ducats. If his disciple Sandro Allori wishes to return to Florence, he will be pardoned. Both will be cleared of the accusations of sodomy that were hanging over them.

Therefore, by order of His Excellency, this case is closed. Everything will return to normal. It is a calmer, more peaceful Florence that awaits you.

151. Agnolo Bronzino to Sandro Allori

Florence, 10 July 1557

Remember, Sandro, that you must not trust anyone. Above all, stay in Rome, because Florence is a cesspit full of mangy dogs. The court delivered its verdict yesterday: the hosier gets everything. The house and the drawings. And yet the duke himself had promised me that, since Jacopo died without an heir and he considered me like a son, it was I and I alone who would inherit his belongings. Now you see what a prince's word is worth! All it took was for this sock-maker to suddenly appear out of nowhere, this supposed fifth cousin that nobody had even heard of before, and the judges ruled in his favour. They are called custodians of the law, but a better name would be murderers of justice. I was lucky they even agreed to let me keep the sketches of San Lorenzo so I can finish the frescoes – and even then I must hand them back to the Tax Chamber once my work is done!

You must not believe that that is all, for the chalice was not yet full. Among the corrupt witnesses who declared under oath having seen this Schiazzella in Jacopo's company, or heard my old master talking affectionately about him, was that piece of shit Naldini. I have no doubt that the prodigal cousin will give him a few drawings in return for his false testimony.

Florence is nothing more than a rotten apple that deserves to be picked by France or Spain. Look at this poor duke, willing to lower himself to the basest villainy to win the favour of the pope and the emperor, in the hope that they will toss him a crown the way guests at banquets toss bones to the dogs that prowl around the tables. Who will take pity on him and strip him of his illusions? A king ought to be just, and appreciative of his most devoted subjects. In the past twenty years I have painted every member of the Medici family: mother, wife, children. Not to mention the portrait I painted of the duke himself, in that ridiculous armour! Not anyone can be King François. True, Cosimo would never have been taken prisoner in Pavia, but for the very good reason that he has never been seen on a battlefield! He dreams of being Alexander the Great, but he is no better than Giovanni the Commoner . . . Jacopo was right to use his paintbrush to mock the vanity of this parvenu. An insult is no longer an insult when it is aimed at iniquity – it is simply the truth. Isn't that the definition of satire? A weapon of the weak to ridicule the mighty. And since this duke is no better than a pander, he deserved to have his daughter depicted as a whore.

152. Maria de' Medici to Catherine de' Medici, Queen of France

Florence, 12 July 1557

I am not dead, aunt, but I suspect that death will come for me soon. Either that or I will go mad, which will be just as good because I will no longer remember who I am, and if my body continues to move – however weakly, and for reasons independent of my will! – at least my soul will have dissolved into thin air. If a lake's water is transformed into a cloud, is it still a lake, or something else?

My parents keep me under guard. I live alone in the Palazzo Pitti, where the endless construction work deafens me daily, and the only pleasure I am allowed is to go out into the gardens where I may contemplate the Tuscan countryside. How I envy the cypress trees that I can glimpse on those distant hills!

The major-domo of a gentleman who is being sent to France on a diplomatic mission has taken pity on me and agreed to deliver this letter to you, by some convoluted means. I write in haste because he is waiting in the entrance hall for me to hand it to him. I beg you, madame, to give the enclosed letter to the knight Malatesta. I wrote it as soon as I returned from Milan, and I have been rewriting it every day while waiting for an opportunity like this to allow it to reach its intended recipient.

153. Maria de' Medici to Malatesta de' Malatesti

Florence, 12 July 1557

Where are you, my knight? Did you arrive safely in France? That is the only thought that keeps me alive. Oh, how cruel your silence is to me, even though I know it is not your fault. Why didn't you save me from the clutches of that vicious Vasari? But I do not blame you. Your life is more precious to me than my own, and I would already have died quite happily, if my life still belonged to me, but I am carrying your son now, and even if he will not bear your name, I feel as if it is you that I can feel growing inside me. The poor innocent creature! I have heard that the Duke of Este has refused to accept a bastard in his family. I am glad of that at least. But no doubt my father will find some other prince to whom he can sell me. Not that I care! I would be lying if I said that escaping marriage to the sinister Alfonso was not a relief. But whoever I end up with, it will not be my Malatesta.

Tell me, now that you are at the French court, surrounded by pleasures, do you still remember your Maria or have those beautiful Frenchwomen already eclipsed me in your memory and your heart? Oh, how jealous I am of them and of anyone who can enjoy being in your presence! Has Queen Catherine given you a warm welcome? You must not, at least, court her, out of respect for me, since she is my aunt, and also out of respect for King Henri, her husband. Although, now I think about it, those considerations didn't stop you, you naughty boy, when it came to seducing the daughter of your master, the duke! How I wish I could relive that moment when, trembling at your own audacity, you declared your love for me . . .

Come and rescue me, my knight! Abduct me again! What a man does once, he may do again, don't you think? Be a man, my handsome lover, and come rescue your wife. We are married before God, aren't we, if not before men? Come and rescue your son. Come and rescue the two of us. Don't let the wicked men call your son a bastard and your wife a whore.

No, don't come! If anything were to happen to you, I would never forgive myself. Watch out for traitors and assassins. The forces of evil are waiting here in the shadows. Florence is a deadly trap, and you must never set foot in this city again – do you hear me? Oh, how I suffer! What will become of me? To whom will I be sold? Oh, but what do I care? I must live for our son. (How I hope it won't be a girl! That would just be one more misfortune for the poor child.) Fate couldn't be so cruel, and you will find a way. Who knows? My aunt Catherine has already done so much for me. I sense she is capable of performing miracles. She is so good, and so strong. If only I had her strength and her wisdom . . .

I am finding it hard to stop writing, but I must. Farewell, my love. I pray that this letter will find its way to your hands, even if I can't. Alas! However deranged I might be, I do understand that isn't possible. Farewell, and forget me not. Who knows? Life is long, and the future unwritten.

154. Benvenuto Cellini to Piero Strozzi

Florence, 19 July 1557

My word is my bond, Lord Marshal. I live by that motto, and – in consequence – I have your painting. No doubt you are wondering how I could have achieved the impossible for a second time . . . I am going to reveal to you a secret that you may already know, since it also applies to the art of war: never play the same hand twice.

This time, the challenge was not to steal the painting from the most heavily guarded fortress in Tuscany, particularly since it had almost certainly been destroyed on the duke's orders. So I simply paid a visit to Bronzino and asked him to paint another copy. I persuaded him that a *Venus* painted by him, with a Medici head atop its naked body, would be a perfect tribute to his master, whose last act on this Earth was precisely that gesture of insolence. In truth, he did not take much convincing, because he was, it seems, already extremely angry and resentful towards the duke.

So he repainted the image from memory, identical but for one detail, which I am quite sure will please you. Since rumour has it that young Maria was impregnated by her page, he drew Venus with a hugely swollen belly. The result is highly gratifying. This Bronzino is a talent, and a character too: your cousin the queen should invite him to France.

Now that Vasari has got his hands on Pontormo's *Venus*, there is no reason why I can't keep this one in my house. I have no fear that they will come looking for it since nobody suspects its existence. All you need do is send someone to pick it up. It will be waiting patiently here for you, and this time I can guarantee that the operation will be free of the complications that hobbled it before. As for me, I have already begun writing the pamphlet that will accompany it, which is a great source of amusement to me. I can give a copy to whomever you like or send it to you directly.

155. Giambattista Naldini to Giorgio Vasari

Florence, 21 July 1557

Master Giorgio, I could never express the gratitude I feel to both you and Master Vincenzo for favouring me to work on the renovation of the palace. Nor could I articulate how proud I am to be counted among the assistants of the illustrious Vasari. I hesitated for a long time before writing you this note, because I did not want to disturb your rest, particularly since I have been told how rare it is that you take a holiday from your numerous obligations and responsibilities, and I am also aware that it is not considered correct to incriminate a colleague, particularly one with such a prestigious reputation, but I would feel even more ashamed, knowing what I know (which I discovered by chance), if I did not inform you of it.

If you go to Master Benvenuto Cellini's studio, you will find a certain painting that gravely insults the duke's daughter and stains the honour of the glorious Medici family.

I am sorry that I cannot tell you how I came by this information, but I would not wish to put anyone in an awkward situation if it can be avoided. In any case, I hope you will consider this indiscretion as a further token of my devotion.

156. Piero Strozzi to Benvenuto Cellini

Fontainebleau, 24 July 1557

Bravo, Master Benvenuto! How I wish I had more men like you in my army, capable of such audacity and inventiveness! A word from you, and I will make you a captain. Wait, what am I saying? A general! It is true that, had you been by my side, we would be in Naples now. Instead of which, the French army must march to Champagne to defend that land from attacks by the Spanish troops based in Brussels. But now, of course, we are saved, because Paul IV has excommunicated King Philip! As if the King of Spain is going to care about that . . . I say what we need is more Cellinis and fewer Carafas. As for me, I am on my way back to Rome with trunkfuls of écus to fund the next war in Italy.

Since, from what you tell me, leaving Florence with a painting whose existence is unknown to anyone in the city should not pose a problem, why don't you bring it to Bologna? One of our men will be waiting for you there, and he can take it directly to Venice, where our people will give it the fanfare it merits and let it be seen by as many eyes as possible. But don't bother with the pamphlet. We would like to spare you the trouble of writing it, and I know someone who can do an equally good job. You might know him, actually: his name is Lodovico Dolce, a prolific writer who was a close friend of Aretino, and who has just brought out a slim treatise on painting written in the form of a dialogue. I'll have it sent to you – you should receive it shortly.

157. Giorgio Vasari to Vincenzo Borghini

Arezzo, 25 July 1557

Vincenzo, I have just received this letter from Naldini, which I am having copied for you. I am uncertain whether we ought to consider it, and if we do I am not sure what measures we should take. Should I even reply to him? Do you think it possible that the young man is so eager to secure our good graces that he might invent such a plot?

And even if what he says is true, we can't send the Bargello guards to search painters' studios – that would make us the target for so many protests that they would end up in league against us. Do this, please: tell Naldini to keep his eyes open and to find one or two sergeants to watch Cellini – but discreetly. I'll let you know when I'm returning, but it will not be for a while, God willing, because I intend to make the most of my well-earned rest, without having to constantly come and go between Arezzo and Florence.

If I happen to receive a letter from Michelangelo in my absence, have it sent here.

158. Vincenzo Borghini to Giorgio Vasari

Florence, 2 August 1557

Master Giorgio, my friend, I would not want to disturb your peace for anything in the world, but I cannot leave you in ignorance of the latest events here. Sadly, God did not want Sister Plautilla to remain sunken any longer in the melancholic state in which she emerged from the Bargello dungeons, for she is now leading the rebellion of your cursed Siena nuns, and I would not be surprised if they soon start calling for my head, with the aim of installing the Nelli woman in my place. Thus am I rewarded for my hospitality. I wish with all my heart that you could summon your nuns back to Arezzo, and if you could arrange it so that they take Sister Plautilla with them, I would be delighted. Promise them a convent, an abbey, a monastery, or the Holy See itself if you must, but please, please rid me of these turbulent harpies!

As for Master Michelangelo, he has not replied to your letter, nor has he written to anyone here in Florence except for his dear nephew Leonardo, in a missive devoted purely to family matters. We have no other news of him, and – if you want my opinion – that is how things will remain.

As far as Cellini is concerned, he is under surveillance as you asked, but our spies' reports have not indicated any unusual activity on his part, at least nothing that departs from his ordinary routine: he gets drunk, fights, fornicates, and does very little work.

159. Benvenuto Cellini to Piero Strozzi

Florence, 15 August 1557

I received the little treatise on painting that you sent me and, unluckily for me – or for you – I read it. Lodovico Dolce is an idiot, and you will not have my painting. Tell the queen that I am sorry, but I feel so deeply offended by your lack of confidence in me that I would rather destroy it than entrust it to the commentaries of a brainless Venetian who prefers Raphael to Michelangelo, and who even places his Titian above our divine Buonarroti. Besides, his prose is execrable, and if he writes a pamphlet against the Medici, it will have no more power than a heron's fart.

160. Piero Strozzi to Benvenuto Cellini

Rome, 1 September 1557

Have you gone mad, my friend? Why do you speak of destroying that painting whose very existence – nay, whose resurrection! – is due solely to your tireless genius? Do nothing. I am coming. Yes, you read that right. In the name of the queen, in the most perfect disguise, the Marshal of France – who, God willing, will succeed the present Duke of Florence as *primus inter pares* – is coming to pay you a visit so that we may calmly discuss, like two soldiers, whatever it is we said that caused you such offence. Please believe that, if there was any offence, it was entirely involuntary and came about through no fault of our own. In fact, I am certain that it must be a misunderstanding that we will easily be able to dispel once we are facing each other in person.

You said I showed no confidence in you. Well, here I am now, placing my life in your hands. I still have sufficient resources to be able to secretly enter Florence, but if anyone were to inform Cosimo of my plan, my death would be certain.

161. Vincenzo Borghini to Giorgio Vasari

Florence, 10 September 1557

Master Giorgio, this time you must return immediately, and for a reason so extraordinary, so incredible, so contrary to all logic that you would not believe me until you had witnessed it with your own eyes. Piero Strozzi is in Florence. Yes, you read that correctly: the Strozzi son himself! No, I have not lost my mind. I do not have a fever, and I have not drunk a drop of wine since yesterday. He was seen entering Cellini's house by the spies who are watching the sculptor, and those same spies assure us that, barring some form of magic, he is still there now. Since I want my letter to reach you as quickly as possible, I will say no more on the subject.

I am sorry to have to bring your holiday to such an abrupt end, and even sorrier that you must travel in such terrible weather, but your presence here is absolutely essential, because the Bargello guards are awaiting my instructions (since you delegated your authority to me), but I – whose only real qualities are being able to read a little Latin, Greek and Hebrew – am awaiting yours.

162. Maria de' Medici to Malatesta de' Malatesti

Florence, 11 September 1557

I am taking advantage of another opportunity to write to you, despite my imprisonment and the strict surveillance to which I am constantly subjected by my father's orders. But don't worry, my knight: this letter, if it reaches you, will be the last you receive from me. Maria – if you care to remember for an instant the name of the poor girl who, having believed the oaths of love you swore to her, is carrying your child – will bother you no more.

What I have heard about your behaviour at the French court justifies the anxieties I was weak enough to share with you in my previous letter. It seems, indeed, that you have gone to great lengths to prove me right. I would have forgiven you your mistresses had I been able to believe that they were nothing more to you than bottles of cheap wine in which you desperately sought to forget the golden nectar you had tasted and lost. I would have let it pass had I thought that you were simply drowning your sorrows at being separated from me. But several accounts, all of which agree, have swept away my illusions: you are, I am told, wonderfully cheerful, a friendly and outgoing young man always in the mood to celebrate, to the point that every man and woman in the court seeks out your company. I am so pleased, sir, to find that you have managed to console yourself over the loss of she to whom you once, if I remember correctly, swore eternal fidelity.

How could you be so cruel? By what miracle are men able to forget so quickly what they once adored? Because you loved me, I know you did, and if you were to tell me the contrary I would not believe you, even now that I have tasted bitter disillusion. I was young, I was naïve, I had never heard the words you spoke so boldly to me, and I sacrificed everything for you: my honour, my reputation, my parents' love. You can be satisfied with your work. It is true that loving you gave me some surprising pleasures, but it also cost me some strange pains, and overall you have taken me from one extreme to another. And you . . . what have you sacrificed for me? Where were you in Milan when I needed to be rescued? What qualities did you demonstrate in winning my love? Fancy words; an audacity that might be mistaken for courage; and a youthful vigour and ardour that a young, inexperienced girl might confuse with passion. Not much, at the end of the day, and all of it quite common, I believe, to people of your kind. I despise myself for the ache of loss I still feel.

The officer who is supposed to carry my letter is urging me to hurry because it has been raining steadily for several days here, and he says that if his departure is postponed any longer the roads will be impassable. But I haven't finished, so he can wait a little longer. Haven't I waited months for you to come and rescue me? If I am writing to you for the very last time, I do not want to forget anything.

The Duke of Este has not changed his mind. He refuses to let his son marry me, and since, in the end, that marriage will have been prevented because of you, I suppose I ought to thank you. However, he has not given up on his plan to unite with the Medici family, for he has now suggested to my father that he could let Alfonso have Lucrezia in my place. The poor girl does not have the good fortune to have become damaged goods, like me. But it must be said that she is only twelve: very young to be impregnated by a servant. So, in addition to what you have done to me, you have also ruined my sister's life.

As for me, I will not be marrying anyone any time soon. Who would want to expose themselves to the ridicule of marrying a girl who is seven months pregnant? The convent awaits. Or perhaps, once I have given birth to our child and she has been stolen from me and handed over to a nursemaid, I will be offered to some prince in a country so distant that the rumour of my dishonour has not yet reached there. Hungary? Poland? Somewhere even more remote? Who knows, perhaps my father will send me to the Americas! If I am captured by pirates and end up a slave in Algiers, then one thing is sure: the duke will not pay my ransom. If it were up to him, I would already have been sent to Suleiman's harem. And you wouldn't rescue me from there either.

The rain is pouring down now. I must bring this to an end. Farewell, sir. I leave you to your pleasures. I will try to forget you the way that you forgot me. Sadly, though, I am not as shallow as you.

163. Giorgio Vasari to Vincenzo Borghini

Arezzo, 12 September 1557

I love and cherish your prudence as much as your loyalty and your confidence in me. You were right to contact me before attempting anything. Do nothing, Master Vincenzo, and tell the Bargello guards not to move under any circumstances. The news you have brought me is so outlandish that I want to make certain it is true, for if we must break down Cellini's door, it will be my responsibility. Until further notice, be wary. We do not know what Strozzi is capable of. If it really is him, which I still doubt.

I am entrusting this letter to a messenger who should arrive a few hours ahead of me, if he doesn't drown in the torrential rain falling on Tuscany.

164. Vincenzo Borghini to Giorgio Vasari

Florence, 13 September 1557

Our men have been in position around Cellini's house for more than twelve hours now, and I still haven't heard from you. The Arno has burst its banks and the streets are flooded. We can wait no longer. I must order the assault while it is still possible, because if the water continues to rise at this rate, it will soon be up to our waists. I am sending this note to the San Niccolò Gate in the hope that it will find you safe and sound. I dare not imagine the state of the roads and I pray that this deluge has not swept you and your horse away.

165. Benvenuto Cellini to the Duke of Florence, Cosimo I

Florence, 14 September 1557

Benvenuto Cellini, goldsmith, sculptor, creator of the *Perseus* that has pride of place at the palace beside Master Buonarotti's *David*, and – above all – His Excellency's devoted servant, wishes to lodge a complaint with His Excellency concerning the unspeakable actions of Vincenzo Borghini, prior of the Innocents – or so he claims – but without any doubt an unparalleled reprobate.

While I was battling the flood that had entered my home, busy raising my floor to save the art that I labour over night and day for the greater glory of Your Majesty, armed men burst into my house, knocking down my door without any announcement other than a great deal of yelling and panting. Thinking myself under attack by some vile scoundrels desirous of profiting from the disorder created by the flood to lay their hands upon the treasures of my studio, and little inclined to facilitate their task by graciously handing over pieces that cost me so much work and so many sleepless nights, but rather determined to defend these priceless works with my life, I welcomed them with my sabre. Of course it was hardly a fair fight since, from the noise they were making, I could tell that there was quite a gang of them, but they should have brought the entire battalion. Seeing myself outnumbered one to fifty, I knew I wasn't going to have an easy time of it. Even so, without a second thought, and with the water already up to my knees, I repelled the invaders, aided by the configuration of the battlefield. Since the enemy was obliged to come through my doorway to take possession of my house, and since only one man at a time could pass through said doorway, I engaged in a series of duels in which I confronted them one after another. No sooner did one enemy fall than another took his place, but at least they could not attack me en masse. And so we crossed swords for several hours, until the assailants opened another breach by coming through a window. Attacked from both front and flank, I had no choice but to surrender, though not without some final flourishes that left my mark in the flesh of those dishonourable rogues.

How astonished I was when I saw the prior of the Innocents appear! And my stupefaction increased when he informed me that he was acting in the name of the Duke of Florence. My confusion grew even further when I saw his band of sword-wielding shirkers start ransacking my studio, supposedly because they were searching for a fugitive whom I had hidden there, as well as a certain painting, which the prior assured me concerned Your Serene Lordship. I honestly have no idea what they thought they were looking for, but in any case they didn't find it. Having reduced my home to rubble, they left without a word of explanation, never mind an apology. I implore Your Lordship to answer me: have you ever heard anything so scandalous?

I am, therefore, addressing His Magnificent Excellency to claim compensation for my door and for all the damage they caused in my home, which included some objects of great value, as well as a trapdoor granting access to the roof via the upper floors, for which I had lost the key and which they were absolutely determined to open. I am happy to provide Your Lordship with a full list of the damages caused by those corrupt ruffians. If those men really were from the Bargello, as they claimed, that venerable institution must be purged of its rotten branches for the good of the city and of Your Majesty.

166. Giambattista Naldini to Vincenzo Borghini

Florence, 13 September 1557

I am entrusting this letter to my assistant Bastiano del Gestra, because he is a better swimmer than me, with the order to find Master Vasari or Master Borghini, wherever they may be, and hand it to him in person.

Having taken refuge at the Innocents to escape the waters of the Arno, which are presently flooding Pontormo's house, I have once again witnessed something that I think will interest you. While I was observing the desolate spectacle of our drowned Piazza della Santissima Annunziata, I spotted a man carrying something above his head that, from its size and shape, appeared to be a painting wrapped up in blankets.

Since he was struggling to move forward, being submerged up to the chest in water, Sister Plautilla, who had also seen him, went down to open the doors and offer him asylum. I was therefore able to observe the man more closely: he was in his forties but well built, with a red beard and a haughty expression, and although he was dressed quite simply, I could tell that his clothes were made from expensive fabrics, particularly his boots, which were of the highest-quality leather. He wore a sword at his belt like the ones I used to see at the armoury of Master Cristofano Allori, Sandro's father, and I could see that it had been forged from an excellent Toledo steel.

As for the painting, he didn't unwrap it from the blankets, but from the one tiny corner that I could see sticking out, I could have sworn it was the very painting I told you about before, the one you were supposed to seize from Master Cellini's house.

167. Vincenzo Borghini to Giorgio Vasari

Florence, 14 September 1557

Treason! I have been overthrown in a *coup d'état*! Where are you, my friend? Apparently that hellish Sister Plautilla has finally decided to take my place because, in my absence, she is acting as if the hospital is hers to govern!

Having found nothing at Cellini's house, after a long and difficult search (I will spare you the details), I ran to the Innocents, as quickly as the city's catastrophic weather would allow me, because – having been alerted by Naldini – I hoped to find the man and the painting there.

Plautilla did not even deny that she had taken it upon herself to open the doors to what she described as a poor wretch in an onerous situation, invoking our duty to provide asylum and other insolences of that kind. But by the time I arrived, whether because he had seen the troop of guards accompanying me or for some other reason, he had already departed. Naldini says he saw the man swimming towards Santa Maria del Fiore, where people are crowded outside the entrance in the hope of finding refuge. The painting cannot be found anywhere, and Plautilla refuses to tell me where she has hidden it. (I have no doubt whatsoever that it was this demon in the form of a nun who secreted it somewhere. To what end? I have no idea. But the pleasure of defying my authority would be motive enough, I suspect.) While I wait for your response, I intend to pull apart my hospital stone by stone, if need be, in search of that cursed painting.

168. Giorgio Vasari to Vincenzo Borghini

Florence, 14 September 1557

Vincenzo, I was almost swept away a dozen times by the flood, but finally I made it here, alive and more or less unscathed. I found the two messages that you judiciously left for me at the San Niccolò Gate. Stay at the Innocents and find the painting. I will go to Santa Maria with a company of sergeants as soon as we have assembled the necessary fleet of boats, because it won't be long before even horses are swallowed up by this torrent.

169. Sister Plautilla Nelli to the Duke of Florence, Cosimo I

Florence, 15 September 1557

I beg His Excellency not to give credence to anything that might be said about me in this latest affair, and I swear before God that these accusations are false, and that I am just as innocent of these new crimes as I was of the previous ones.

Yes, I offered help to a man in difficulty, and what harm is there in that? If I had let him drown, surely I would have been guilty. I knew nothing of his identity, and how could I possibly have guessed that he was His Lordship's greatest enemy? Wasn't this Piero Strozzi, whom I have never seen in my life, supposed to be in France? What was he doing in Florence? And, above all, how was I supposed to know who he was? God says we should help our neighbours, and that rule has always guided my conduct. Yes, I opened the doors of our refuge to the stranger.

He was carrying a painting wrapped up in blankets, which he left in the cell that I had made available to him so that he could get some rest, because he looked very tired. When he rushed off, leaving his painting behind, young Naldini begged me to let him see it. His insistence, I confess, awoke in me the sin of curiosity that is so common in those of my sex. After the stranger's departure, I went to his cell to uncover the painting. This is my sole confession: I have had only one love in life, apart from God, and that is my love of painting.

But what I saw, after removing the blankets, left me in a state of shock. It was a demoniacal vision that must have been the product of a mind possessed, and I myself was bewitched by this sight. I was torn from my stupefaction by the return of the prior accompanied by a troop of guards. I thought they had come to arrest me again. In a panic at the idea that I was responsible for the presence of that obscene and sacrilegious picture in a place hallowed for its sheltering of innocence, not lust, I decided I had to get rid of it. So I threw the painting out of the window. Thus, when Prior Borghini appeared before me, or rather when I went down to greet him, the object that he was looking for was no longer in the hospital, but had been damaged in the floodwater. Terrified that I might again be accused of some misdeed, I preferred to deny all knowledge of anything relating to that painting. Perhaps, once the water level has receded, you will find pieces of broken wood from which the painting has been washed clean by the waters of the Arno. In fact, I believe that this Flood sent to us by Heaven was nothing other than the expression of God's wrath and the solution to the problem of this impious painting. If that is the case, then justice has been done, and while I would not go so far as to claim that I was God's instrument, I think I can congratulate myself for having modestly played my part.

I swear before God that this is the whole truth, and I beg His Excellency's great mercy: may he grant me the right to continue painting and allow me to return to my convent in San Marco, where I promise to honour Catherine of Siena, our Lord Jesus, our blessed city and our beloved duke, and not to stir up any more trouble.

170. Giorgio Vasari to Cosimo de' Medici, Duke of Florence

Florence, 16 September 1557

Everything that follows really did happen. I can confidently assure Your Excellency of that because I was there, in your service. I saw what I saw, and not only that, but I think I can say without exaggerating that I also played an active part (however modest) in the events that I must now report to Your Lordship.

After leaving the Hospital of the Innocents in a great hurry, Piero Strozzi was spotted at the cathedral of Santa Maria del Fiore, so I went there with an entire company of soldiers. Inside the cathedral, the doors having been draughtproofed, the water level was no higher than our knees, which is why – in addition to seeking the aid and protection of Our Lord – hundreds of Florentines had taken refuge there, which meant that it was no easy matter to enter the building and extremely difficult to find a man concealed among all those dazed and confused people. After several hours spent searching every nook in the naves, the transept and all the chapels, however, we felt certain that Strozzi was not there. And yet he had to be. I deduced that there remained only one possible hiding place: the dome. I ordered six men to climb up there with me. We were ascending the steps when, just before we reached the first circular walkway, we glimpsed a figure that could be nobody but our man. I yelled: 'Strozzi, surrender, in the name of the duke!' The only response we received was a volley of stones thrown at our faces and certain imprecations that I do not think it useful to transcribe, but which I will say revealed republican opinions hostile to Spain, the emperor, the Duchy of Tuscany, and Your Excellency's family. We had come in search of Strozzi, and here he was. But no sooner had we guarded all the exits to ensure that he could not escape than he disappeared as if by magic from the stairway leading to the lantern. However, the magician who enabled this vanishing act has a name, and that name is Brunelleschi. Your Excellency is well aware of the ingenious device that the architect used to build the marvel that towers over Florence, Tuscany and the world: the dome of Santa Maria consists of two calottes, like an eggshell within an eggshell, the interior shell having been built to support and enable the construction of the exterior, without recourse to any ribs, and the consequence of this brilliant idea is that there is a passage between the two structures, into which Strozzi had crawled like a rat. Realising that he was attempting to shake us off by climbing up to the summit of the dome, I went after him, armed with a crossbow, for my recent misadventures have not only taught me how to use said weapon, but also how efficient it is compared to a musket, which is inaccurate, slow to fire, and useless when wet, something that – in the situation as it was – was obviously an important consideration. At the same time, the men who had accompanied me stationed themselves around the walkway to cut off all possibility of escape for our fugitive. Or so we thought. But we had not factored into our calculations the ingenuity of the divine Brunelleschi. To build the interior dome without scaffolding, he invented a fishbone arrangement of bricks, a brilliant device that only a genius could have conceived, in such a way that the bricks form an arch that supports itself. But it was this very arrangement that gave Strozzi the possibility of escaping us, by climbing up the inner dome and supporting himself on the bricks, which are sometimes horizontal and sometimes vertical, as if he were climbing a bas-relief staircase. So it was that I saw Strozzi rising above me, scaling the calotte like a salamander on a wall. I fired at him, but my bolt missed its target, and he, having reached a height of about twenty-five fathoms, leapt towards one of the orifices that pierce the outer dome, into which, with surprising agility, he dived, his whole body disappearing in a flash. Since I couldn't pursue him with my crossbow, I left the weapon behind and climbed up after him, my feet stepping on the great Brunelleschi's celestial bricks. When I too reached the height of the oculus, I crawled out of the dome. Balanced at my waist, my legs still inside, my head lashed by the driving rain, my eyes half-blinded by the lightning that zig-zagged the sky, my ears deafened by the thunder, and my whole being shocked by the sudden icy blast of that deluge, I saw Strozzi slide down the tiled roof, taking advantage of its convex incline, almost breaking his neck when the slope grew vertical, then grab hold of God-knows-what since there is no cornice around the drum at the base of the dome, bounce miraculously back onto the roof of the north transept, slide once again along one of the flying buttresses, and finally dive downward into the void.

Ordinarily, nobody could have survived such a fall, and we would have found his body splattered on the cobblestones below, but since the water had risen so high in the street, reaching close to the houses' first floor, I wanted to make sure that he was dead. So, pulling my head back inside the dome, I shouted to the guards to go out and find his corpse.

But the situation made my order difficult to obey. We couldn't open the cathedral's sealed doors without letting the Arno pour inside. So the guards who had stayed in the naves were forced to break the panes of a window that was high enough to still be above the floodtide. And while I descended from the dome, I heard them suddenly yell: 'There he is! I see him! Seize him!' They had indeed spotted Strozzi, who was swimming between the cathedral and the baptistery, clinging for a moment to the Ghiberti door as if to the gates of paradise, then continuing on his way southward.

The guards were dumbstruck at the sight of this man defying the elements, seemingly protected by the gods, but as soon as I joined them, I decided upon the next stage of our operation. I began by asking the guards who among them could swim. I told those men to take off their helmets and their armoured breastplates, to wrap their swords in their capes, and then to jump in the water and pursue the fugitive. After a dozen had done as I ordered, I dived in after them and we all swam towards the palace, because that was the direction they had seen Strozzi take. On the way, I requisitioned a boat that a group of Florentines had filled with their belongings: some furniture and bundles of clothing that I had to toss into the water in order to make space for my men. Five guards were able to get in with me. This action caused us a slight delay, but after that, with the aid of the oars that the unfortunate Florentines had left behind, we were able to make up for lost time.

Strozzi had swum with such vigour that he had reached the Ponte Vecchio. There was little doubt that he was trying to reach the hills of Oltrarno, to escape not only the Bargello but the floodwater. I don't know where he found the strength, but somehow he managed to hoist himself on top of the bridge's shops. When we caught up with him, we could see him, visibly exhausted, catching his breath. He saw us too, and he again took flight. This was easy for him since he had pulled himself out of the water and now no longer needed to swim but could simply run across the rooftops of the buildings that line the Ponte Vecchio, at least until he reached the other bank (with the exception of the part where there are no stalls, which would have required him to dive back into the water). Perhaps his plan was, having reached that bank, to sprint across the roofs of Oltrarno to escape us, but he would have needed a free run over the corridor of rooftops, instead of which a river patrol was arriving from the Oltrarno side, so that Strozzi found himself caught in a pincer movement. However, having abandoned our crossbows and muskets at Santa Maria so that we could swim after him, we had no means of driving him out from a distance. So the guards had to seize him at close quarters, and to do that they first needed to find a way to reach him: no mean feat, since the boats were being tossed about by the current in that part of the river and were extremely difficult to keep still. Not to mention the smell from the tanners' and tripe-mongers' shops, which made us feel ill and distorted our faculties, already severely weakened by the bone-chilling cold. While the guards struggled clumsily to tie up their boat so they could climb onto the rooftops (which were only three or four fathoms above the surface of the water), Strozzi waited for them there, standing sword in hand. As soon as one of the guards dragged himself onto the roof, Strozzi cut him down, before running to the other side of the bridge to do the same to the guards from the river patrol. But he couldn't hope to maintain this position very long, and he must have known that the trap would soon snap shut. So he decided to wait halfway between the two patrols, planted on both feet, his blade lowered but ready to fight. It appeared that he would rather die fighting than surrender. But as the guards cautiously approached him, and as the storm intensified, pounding the city with the violence that you saw for yourself, a vast wave suddenly rose from the bed of the Arno, reaching an unbelievable height. The guards, who were advancing on all fours, fearful of losing their balance, lay flat against the roof tiles, but Strozzi, standing tall, was knocked backward by the wave and swept away by the current. This time, we did not see him reappear above the water's surface. So everything suggests that he did not survive, but perished by drowning. Perhaps the Arno will cough up his body in the spring, or even before then, when the river returns to its bed.

171. Giorgio Vasari to Vincenzo Borghini

Florence, 5 October 1557

Bacchiacca died without ever regaining consciousness. So he will carry his secret to the grave and we will probably never know what role he played in this murky affair, nor how he managed to smuggle the painting out of the palace. It is my understanding that Cellini paid him a visit the day before he died. The duke knows my opinion on this. We can never be too wary of that one.

172. Vincenzo Borghini to Giorgio Vasari

Livorno, 29 November 1557

This letter brings you sad news, and it grieves me to write it. Poor Maria died during labour. The duchess is devastated and has retired to Pisa with her boys. The duke is inconsolable, but not to the point of neglecting affairs of state. His youngest daughter, Lucrezia, will marry Alfonso d'Este, and in that way the alliance between Florence and Ferrara will be consolidated, as planned. Enjoy your time at home in Arezzo. The palace frescoes can wait. Who knows how long any of us will be granted?

173. Catherine de' Medici, Queen of France, to Piero Strozzi, Marshal of France

Paris, 7 January 1558

This is a glorious day for the Kingdom of France, and I am not surprised at all that once again my invincible cousin played his part in it. Two hundred and ten years Calais has been English, and it took us only a week-long siege to snatch it from them! Clearly, Guise is no slouch on the battlefield, but I know how important your role is to him. France can be proud to have a general like you in its service, cousin. And now, down with the Spanish! With God's help and yours, Guise will reconquer his native Lorraine, drive the Spanish out of Luxembourg, and finally break up the Habsburg legacy in Burgundy.

In the meantime, I have some news from France that I think you might find entertaining. Do you remember the knight Malatesti, who took refuge at the French court after impregnating Cosimo's eldest daughter? He was stabbed to death in the middle of Paris, where he was living a life of debauchery amid our compatriots. His corpse was fished out of the Seine where his murderers had thrown it. Rumour has it that he died in a tavern brawl, but I know where I would pin the blame: Cosimo always did hold a grudge. He would have sent his killers after the page, just as he sent some to Venice ten years ago to murder Lorenzino. Who knows, maybe the same ones? His daughter is dead too, which is very sad, but he still has lots of children because his Spanish wife was extremely fertile. It seems that Il Popolano is putting down roots. Well, so are we! Thanks be to God, I have produced boys who will ensure the Valois lineage. You are Marshal of France, cousin, and I am Queen of France. Miraculously, you survived your crazy foray into your native city, where everyone now believes you to be dead, a victim of the flood. Very well, let us accept that as a sign. God did not want you to die, but nor did he want us to succeed in our enterprise. The time has come, perhaps, to forget Florence and Italy. We have bigger fish to fry.

174. Agnolo Bronzino to Michelangelo Buonarroti

Florence, 23 July 1558

Forgive me, dear Master, for breaking these long months of silence by sending you news that you did not ask for from a city where you wish never to return. You rejected Florence, and you were right to do so. I should have done the same as you, or the same as that colour-grinder who set off on an adventure.

Yesterday was the inauguration of the San Lorenzo frescoes, which I completed as faithfully as possible. In the end, the duke gave me free rein to paint them in the style I wanted, and the duchess too, much to her chagrin, left me in peace. I would like to believe that the results are more or less what Jacopo would have wanted. And yet the public to whom the frescoes were revealed did not seem to share my satisfaction. It is something of an understatement to say that their reception was reserved. It was barely even polite, in truth; you know, that cold politeness whose true meaning cannot be doubted, and which is just as bad as the loudest repudiations. No doubt the duke's presence spared me from more obvious manifestations of opprobrium, but I could read the expressions of embarrassment on people's faces. Added to that was another disappointment: everyone had been hoping that you would appear, for it is no secret that the duke renewed his invitation to you and desires nothing more than your return, for which he is ready to move Heaven and Earth. I, too, would have loved to see you there. Who else than you could appreciate the true value of Pontormo's work? At least, I am in no doubt that time will do him justice.

Sandro sends his greetings and kisses your hands. I do the same. Think of us sometimes.

175. Michelangelo Buonarroti to Agnolo Bronzino

Rome, 10 August 1558

Dear Agnolo, I was saddened by what I read in your letter, but I would be lying if I said I was surprised. Our time has passed, Agnolo, even mine. The flatteries that the duke heaps upon me are in reality just eulogies for the dead. Even your melancholy seems unduly optimistic to me. Time will not do justice to anyone. Tomorrow's men will be no better than today's. All will be destroyed. In the end, nothing will remain of us but ashes and ruins. Pontormo understood that. Look at what he wrote to me. I kept his letter and, since I know how much you loved him, I am sending it to you. Farewell, my son.

176. Pontormo to Michelangelo

Florence, 27 December 1556

Oh, my Master! The time has come for me to settle my debts. And that is simple enough: I owe you everything. I would like to tell you that I regret nothing. Now that the hour is approaching for my descent into the tomb, I remember your words: 'If God gives life to this young man, he will elevate our art to the sky.' What a source of pride for the child I was! But also, what a burden. Angel of God, what did you do? From that day on, I devoted my life to justifying your prophecy. What nobler task could be assigned to me? But how dearly I paid for it in suffering. It is true that I rose to the sky, but I fell from such a height. On the upper panels at San Lorenzo, I painted Adam and Eve, and I look up at them now with full knowledge of the truth: the higher the rise, the harder the fall. Where did I go wrong? I know not.

Come, Master Michelangelo! My solitude is driving me mad. Naldini mistreats me, he takes me for a fool and steals my meat. Bronzino is after my inheritance. The Allori family treat me like a senile old man. The duchess hates my frescoes. The duke regrets asking me to paint them. Varchi is pleasant to my face, but he disavows all the subjects for the chapel, despite the fact that he and Master Riccio helped me compose them in the first place. Riccio is locked up with the madmen and soon I will be too, if I do not die first. They are all in league against me and terrified of the pope, while I shit blood. If God wanted to prove that He had deserted me, He could hardly do a better job of it. In truth, though, I believe He has abandoned Tuscany, Rome and all of Italy. God has forsaken all of us! Even my colour-grinder grumbles and quibbles with me constantly.

Curse the Medici! What the duke gives with one hand, he takes away with the other. Is that conduct worthy of a prince? I have spent eleven years of my life decorating his church. He wouldn't think twice before demolishing it all, I swear. And if it wasn't him, his descendants would do it, for this family now considers Florence its private property. Curse that lineage! Well, I won't give them the pleasure! I will not let anyone destroy my work. Farewell, my Flood! Farewell, my Resurrection of Souls. Farewell, my Ascension. Farewell, my Noah, and farewell my St Lawrence, who gave me so much trouble. But what do these people know of a painter's woes? What do they know of our aching bodies and fatigued minds, the sacrifices we make for art? Was I too ambitious in wanting to imitate nature in all its colours so that it appears identical, or even to improve it by rendering it more richly and with more variety, creating flashes of light, nights lit by fire or other similar lights, skies, clouds, landscapes distant and close, dwellings with diverse observations of perspective, animals of all sorts in various colours, and all the things that it is possible to frame within a scene in a way that Nature never has? To improve them, and through art to give them grace, to compose them in such an arrangement that they will be at their best? What do these people know about our different working methods – frescoes, oil, distemper, and so on – all of which require a great deal of practice in handling so many different colours, knowing how to recognise their effects and their various blends, pale, dark, shadow and light, infinite combinations of luminosity?

Oh, how I miss that time at the Charterhouse, where I painted the Olive Garden . . . Agnolo was so young, and as beautiful as an angel he himself had painted . . . Rumours of the plague ravaging Florence barely even reached us. The days passed peacefully, and I was happier than I have ever been since. Perhaps the plague will descend upon Florence once again – and I am not far from thinking, like Savonarola, that this would be poetic justice! – but we will never relive the happy days of Galluzzo. Once it is gone, happiness leaves us with nothing but the bitterness of a paradise lost.

But I will not leave without wreaking my little vengeance. I still have the sketch of your *Venus*, did you know that? The duke and the duchess offend me with their contempt. Isn't it only fair that I should do the same to them? I am preparing an unpleasant surprise for them, and your sketch will be my instrument. So they don't like nudes? Well, they are about to be reminded one last time just what kind of painter I am.

So, like Leonardo, or like you in the Council Room, I will leave my frescoes unfinished, and they will meet the same fate. Painting lasts no longer than cheap cotton tossed in the fires of Hell. But who cares! That's just how it is. I have only one remaining desire before I die: that the divine Michelangelo will look upon my frescoes. You alone, out of all the world, understand absolutely what it's all about: surpassing nature by giving spirit to a figure, and making it appear alive by making it flat.

See my frescoes, just once! Come and see them, and come and see me, I beg you. Do not refuse the last wish of a condemned man who will disappear with his work. Only then will I be able to die in peace, washed clean of all the world's rottenness, and of my own. After all, there is only one noble thing upon this Earth, and that is art. Man is merely a fading stain on a wall.

Acknowledgements

My thanks to Philippe Costamagna for opening the doors to Italian mannerism for me, and to Marcello Simonetta for guiding me through the Florence of the Medici.